SUCKER

WITHDRAWN

by

Mark Lingane

First published in Australia by Insync Holdings Pty Ltd
PO Box 526, The Gap, Queensland, Australia 4061
ABN: 74 087 648 600

Cover design by by Creativindie Covers

Cataloguing-in-Publication (CiP) entry:
A catalogue record for this book is available from the National Library of Australia.

Sucker
Lingane, Mark

ISBN: 978-1508455981 (pbk)
ASIN: B00TJ9D802 (ebk)

To those who believe ...

CHAPTER 1 ...

The phone rang, all innocent and coy. If I finish my drink before it stops I'll answer it.

It was a bad bet. The glass had little more than ice and a bucket load of regret. I knocked back the last drops of the sickly sweet juice that burned as much coming up as it did going down.

Click.

"Yeah?"

"My man's taken off with my money." The woman sounded as bored with life as life was with her.

"You sure?"

"It's money, sugar. You notice that kind of thing."

Mina Camilla was her name. It sounded like a Spanish cabaret act.

"Meet me at the Stylus," Mina said.

I sat back and stared at the shadows of the ceiling fan flicking fast and slow. Mina sounded like lo-fi trouble, but the rent monster sniffed around this time of night looking for its bones, and the Stylus has the band. I liked the band. She could buy me a few drinks, and I could tell her I was too busy.

Wonderboy was playing the double bass. There were stories and rumors about his talent, but he was a natural on it. Always had been.

"Welcome to the Stylus. Stool, table or booth, sir?" The young girl bounced nervously, with her chest half hanging out of her top, selling the view to keep her job. Eyes on the prize.

"Booth."

Ten came and went, as did its neighbor. I was a couple of bottles into the Southern amber when Mina walked in. Her blond curls bounced as she strutted, hardcore, across the checkered dance floor. She was wearing a short red cocktail dress, and was every part the cat's particulars. She sat down on a stool by the deep mahogany bar and looked around. She saw me and beckoned with a curling finger.

She whispered my name like a disgraced angel, but it was her curves that got me over there.

"You always this conspicuous?" I asked.

"Hello, Van. You always so smooth with the ladies?" She swiveled to face me, and leaned back against the bar, putting her assets out for evaluation. "I sit where men can see my legs. It gets me my drinks."

I checked out her outfit. The place was upmarket, but she floated away on a zeppelin with the concept. Her bedroom eyes were framed by curls, half of which were tied up with a hairpin in the shape of a broken heart.

"You dress for cocktails," I said.

"You dress like a hobo. You like cocktails?"

I shrugged. "I like free."

She clicked her fingers at Jackson, the bartender, and ordered a martini.

"You wear red," I said. It wasn't a question or observation, but an exploration.

"It doesn't show the blood."

"Your blood?"

"Depends how I feel at the end of the night."

Jackson gave me a relaxed nod. I reciprocated. The claustrophobia of the night closed in around me as the dancers jumped and twirled precariously close. Moonlight beckoned outside with empty streets, hot and wet. I wasn't one for politics, but this place could bring the wolf out in anyone.

"Two fingers, Jackson."

Jackson nodded as he flipped a glass and poured a double shot. He'd clipped his black curly hair short again, now shaving it on the sides. It offset the bizarre contrast of his bebop glasses, horn-rimmed into a past decade. The girls went crazy for him when he was slick. His dark skin glistened in the overheated air.

I sat on the small round stood and placed my hands on the bar. She grabbed one and turned it over in her own.

"My, what big strong hands you have."

"I'm not your grandma," I replied.

"With hands like that I'm not crawling into bed with anything but the big bad wolf."

I sighed and pulled my fingers from her clutches. "What's the chase?"

She knocked back the martini in one go and shook the empty at Jackson. "My no good, SOB lover emptied my drawers, and took off with some skinny blond thing. I found them together in my bed."

"I take it he wasn't your husband."

"Do I strike you as the marrying type?"

"What does he look like?"

"He looks like a loser. Wears a bad attitude that he tries to sell as rebellion."

"Distinguishing features?"

"Fat, lazy backside. Penchant for excessive beer."

"Babe, that's every man."

"He's not like you." Her voice softened and she played at coy, like a major-league pro.

"What did he take?"

"Some money. Some family heirlooms. My dignity."

'You sure he took it?"

"I didn't give it away."

"You know the blond?"

"You've seen one skinny blond thing, you've seen them all. They could be rotting in hell together for all I care, holed up in Disappointment Motel. Let me tell you, honey, he didn't live up to any of his promises once he peeled out of his clothes."

"Any idea where he is?"

"You do the detecting and I'll pay for good service."

I gave Jackson a nod and slid the empty tumbler across the polished wood. He hit me up again, not worrying too much about the optic's accuracy. He glanced at Mina and slipped me a smile. I looked down into the glass. The vision reflected the mistakes of my past. I swirled the drink and knocked it back. Jackson stayed close.

She had turned around to face the bar. Now she looked over her shoulder at the booth, noting the empty bottles. "You drink a lot, Van," she said.

"I've seen a lot."

She looked into my face. "You're not old enough."

I looked into my glass. "I made a deal."

Those big blue eyes swept over me, holding me, and I knew it was going to go sideways. So I gave Jackson another nod, and told him to tell Shady that tonight his drumming sounded like bombing to the soft ear. He needed to wind back the weed.

I thanked Mina for the drinks and said no thanks to the chase. My stretcher was calling me back to the office. I blew her off before I got too entangled. The drinks were good, the band, as always, was good, but the streets called.

On the way back, some late-night birds came flapping in over the home route, highlighting how quiet the streets were. The slow oscillations filled the silence with an eerie counterpoint.

Night fell on me like a gorilla.

The morning shouted my name, and sleep loosened its grip

on me. I was on the way out the door when I tripped over a pretty little lady lying dead across my doorway, wearing nothing but some upmarket lingerie.

Some skinny blond thing.

CHAPTER 2 ...

Chief Inspector Rami Watcher had wandered a few years back. He up and left his pregnant wife for three months for a lady with legs that could crush a man's will to live but leave him smiling. He crawled back again, but now his wife hunted him by phone incessantly, checking up hour after hour. He didn't blame her. He'd broken her heart so badly he thought he deserved an eternity of damnation. But then he decided to take it out on me.

Just as well our history ran back to the Dark Ages. Occasionally I caught a glimpse of the cross around Watcher's neck when its silver surface caught the light. He had gotten it in the war; the company chaplain gave it to him after a bullet passed through Watcher's shoulder while they were talking. A couple of inches lower could have done us all a favor. I always thought his credence unusual considering how impiously he acted these days.

Watcher kicked my desk absentmindedly as he responded to the domestic inquisition.

"I'm not at the office because I'm at a crime scene ... No, I'm not in a bar... The music? The suspect's spinning an album ... I'll call when I'm back at the office ... Yeah, yeah, you too."

A young slowhand, a uniformed officer, was watching him

closely. Her nameplate read *L. Mallory*. Her uniform was a little too tight, by design, and buttoned up to the collar proud. Her hair was pulled back into a squirrel that hinted at her being something different when the lights went down. Another skinny blond thing.

Watcher hung up the phone, my phone, and shouted at his milling staff like the military man he once was. Several loafers from forensics were crawling over my office, in between the slowhands, looking for clues. I could see in their eyes that they thought I did it. They'd be looking for something to pin on me. Like always.

"You notice anything about her?" Watcher asked me.

"She had good skin." I leaned back in the chair and flicked some bad habits into his face.

"Either you're the worst detective ever, or you're not telling me everything."

"It's a crime scene."

"So?"

"Not my jurisdiction."

"I've often found in the past, my friend, that this small legal distinction has not impeded your interference."

"I've learned," I replied.

They tried to teach me the hard way, at the end of a bunch of brass knuckles requisitioned from the evidence store, but the pain didn't do much anymore. Watcher wasn't buying my denial, but he was right. Normally I wouldn't give two hoots from a half-dead owl over something like the law, but this felt wrong.

"The great metal spike through her chest doesn't pique your interest?"

I shrugged. "Looks like just another piercing."

He should have asked if I'd put it there. What the cops hadn't seen yet were the five tiny burn marks in a ring in the center of her chest. I knew that small detail would get lost in the filing, somewhere between boredom and delegation.

He pulled out a clipboard and sat on the edge of my desk. "Where were you last night?"

"Attaining psychosis at the Stylus."

"All night?"

"Ask the bartender."

"Yeah, we might do that." He licked the end of the pen he pulled out from behind his ear and made a note, scratching noisily across the paper. The questions continued without him lifting his eyes. "What time did you get in?"

"Midnight."

"You were here alone until you found her?" He raised an accusatory eyebrow at me.

It didn't look good. Alibi was a five-letter word that had moved out without leaving a forwarding address.

"Is this the story you want me to write down? This is your only chance to get it right." He gave me a steely stare, although to me it looked rusted.

I nodded.

He sighed, either in exasperation or indifference. He got up and looked around the room, poking into anything of value. I watched him and his light fingers carefully, as did L. Mallory. Notably, he ignored the medals in the little display case the military had handed me after stupidity had triumphed over common sense and preservation. They had called it bravery; I hadn't felt brave at the time.

Watcher stepped out into the corridor, bent down, and wiped his fingers over the dirt on the floorboards. Finally it sank into his skull.

It had rained last night. The streets were muddy. There was only one set of footprints leading up to my floor. Mine. I watched the mental cogs ticking over as he knelt down beside the girl and scraped his hand over the muddy footprints.

He stood up and motioned to a couple of loose leaves standing nearby. "Take him down to the cells. I don't like the smell of this place."

They bundled me up and led me off to the tank. L. Mallory watched Watcher carefully until she could no longer keep a straight eye on him.

The tank walls shared a heritage with the other government buildings of the era. The great downtown factories that had churned out the diesel airships during the war were quiet now, but the tank continued to thrive. The effervescent pre-war ideology had led to an ingrained level of disobedience. It was all part of the social evolution that sold the place to hell in a hand-basket. The amalgamation of assorted rough bricks filled expansive spaces that failed to relent for anything as luxurious as a window. Oddly enough, it was the cells below that had the glass, tiny as they were; the subterranean levels filled up with poisonous diesel fumes that had to escape.

Like most of the buildings in the city, the tank had great diesel-powered monstrosities thundering away, powering the place and making the floors shake. They set up a harmonic wave in the hanging bulbs that cast crazy shadows over the place. Freaky.

L. Mallory sat up straight, just like the ergonomic poster next to her desk illustrated. She placed a set of oversized eyeglasses on her pretty face, using both hands, and then started to read the microfiche. I was surprised to find parts of my body ringing alarm bells.

"You have a record." The youngster flicked through the file, her eyes widening.

This could go either way, I thought. I crossed my fingers.

"You were in the war. You have a war record. It says you were decorated."

"Like a Christmas tree."

"But since you've been back you've been … interesting. You sure are no angel."

"Saint."

"Huh?" She raised her eyes from the information in front of her.

"I'm no *saint*."

"You say tomato, I say tomato, let's call the whole thing stupid."

"There's a difference."

She gave me a look that left no doubt about her indifference to the precision of the debate.

"You've been incarcerated fourteen times, most of the time due to ignoring the law. This town doesn't need a shadowed vigilante flapping around. We have enough trouble in the shape of wannabe rebels."

"Sometimes the chase goes bad."

"You're an interesting dichotomy, Mr. Avram." She hesitated and picked up a pencil. "You got a license?"

"Yeah." I fished out the little piece of paper from my wallet and handed it over. Stained with blood and diesel, it had seen better days.

She made a crack about moths escaping from the concertinaed leather, turned the card over, and diligently took down the details. She looked up at me for a moment, and then continued.

"You're three years older than me." She looked at me with an unsettling, fleeting smile. There was an unbelievable chasm between her youthful appearance and the documented evidence. It looked like she had done her own deal. There was a market for that kind of appearance down on the terrace.

"You still in good shape?" she said. "You look like you're in good shape." Her voice lightened up as she relaxed a little.

"A shape's a shape."

Her face registered ambivalence. "You married?"

"No."

"Then who is Lilly?"

Before I could answer, her attention was snapped away as Watcher strode noisily into the tank. He extended an accusatory finger at the two of us.

"That's enough," he shouted. "Throw him in the overnight."

"Cuffs?" L. Mallory scrambled to her feet. Her hands swept down over her uniform, smoothing out the creases and highlighting her dangerous curves.

Watcher paused and rubbed the small silver cross thoughtfully between his fingers. "No."

"What's the charge?"

"Watcher," shouted the sergeant on the front desk, "your wife's on your office phone."

Watcher's head cracked around to face the desk sergeant, displaying a combination of anger and impotence. He returned his attention to L. Mallory. "Forget it. Doesn't matter."

We both watched him disappear into his corner office and pick up the phone. The transformation from the tall, occasionally eager man he normally was to the cowering, hunched shadow whimpering in the shadows was spectacular. L. Mallory and I exchanged glances. I kind of wished it had been phone numbers.

"Do you live at your office," she asked, "or do you have a home?"

"They're the same thing."

"Your record says your parents are dead. Is there anyone else in your life who can pick you up?"

"No."

"Any friends?"

"No."

"Maid?"

"You've seen my office."

She let out a light, infectious laugh, and then quickly stopped herself. "I guess you could achieve the same outcome if you opened the window on a blustery day. Your records only show from the war onwards. What did you do before?"

I hesitated. The black pit of lousy life decisions fired by an ill-tempered youth opened up before me. The army had been redemption for the mistakes I'd made, but the horrors of war, man against man, sent any recollection of innocence into the wind.

"I don't recall."

"You must remember something." Her face offered an eager inquisition that I couldn't deter.

"I loved and lost."

Watcher appeared at his doorway. "Why is he still here?"

"You said to forget it, that he doesn't matter."

"No, you moron. The *charge* doesn't matter. Get him into the cells, quickly. Make sure it's thirty-eight. And see me after." He glanced at his watch then slammed his door closed.

She looked like she'd been punched. I felt for her. He'd given bad instructions then blamed her for it.

"Could you follow me please, sir."

Her voice had returned to its original brittleness. She didn't look at me but took out her hammer, long and black, and placed it in the small of my back. I twisted around, grabbed it out of her tight clutches, and handed it back to her.

"No need for that." I made toward the steps to the cells, with her pretty face behind me as she hurried to catch up.

The cells officer slammed down the keys in his hand with herculean contempt. "You. What are you doing here?" His jaw was clenched. He hadn't forgotten, and he hadn't forgiven. But he had healed. Except for the missing tooth. He should've been happy; it gave him character.

"It's okay," L. Mallory said. "For some reason Watcher wants him in the cells."

"We don't need no reason for this sucker, not after last time," the man shouted.

"Why, what happen—"

"It's okay," I interjected.

"He can have cell thirty-eight," the officer said.

"Watcher said the same thing. We have a cell thirty-eight?"

"Yeah, it's a stinking, disgusting small hole we keep for people exactly like him."

The officer led me down to the pit of the tank, where the smell was so bad you could have spread it on bread. He unlocked the cell and tried to push me in. He didn't have much luck. I looked back over my shoulder at him and stepped into the cell. He slammed the gate behind me, sending the ringing tones through the entire floor.

"I'm"—L. Mallory paused as her thought processes drifted off to the moon and back—"sorry."

I gave her half a smile, saving the rest for when I needed to bank it, and she took off for civilization. She had a genuine face that had the grace and manners to reflect her words. Maybe she was sorry. Maybe she was even sorry for me.

I took off my shoes. They were their own kind of civilization. I sat on the cot. It returned a level of comfort unmatched by my stretcher. Food would be coming soon. All in all, it wasn't a bad deal.

(HAPTER 3 ...

I watched the night ride in through the diminutive window. This month it was a super moon, fitting perfectly inside the edges of the window. Round peg, square hole. Where had I seen that? Oh yeah.

About eleven they threw some whimpering old hobo into the cell next to me; he was so full of singing juice he couldn't speak straight. Bojangles sang until he collapsed into a cranky pile in the corner, nibbling on his fetid nails. He perked up around midnight and started playing some battered old mouth organ. Odd thing for a hobo to have; he could've traded it in for a week's worth of liquor. But I guess we've all got to find something that gets us through the night.

The bell tolled down at the dock. The port was closed. Midnight.

The lights went out as the building's generators powered down. I felt the hum descend through the octaves until the silence wrapped around me.

Bojangles started up again. The mouth organ followed an ancient sad tune. A tremolo entered the performance. The hobo was visibly being harassed by something; one hand snapped at invisible bugs flapping around his head, causing him to miss the occasional note. He went quiet. Then he jumped up and stared at me through the bars, his filthy hands wrapped around the cold steel. His face freakishly caught the moonlight. His body started to shake. His eyes rolled back into his head, leaving the yellow sclera piercing me. His eyes faded to black.

His mouth opened, exposing gray teeth. He exhaled, and a cloud of insects flew straight at me. I pulled the sheet off the bed and wrapped it around me. I felt the insects bounce off the fabric. They were concentrating on my head. I swept the sheet up, capturing them, then flung it to the floor and stamped on it until the buzzing stopped.

"It's time," Bojangles said. But it wasn't his voice. My head snapped up and I looked at him. "The change is coming."

I wondered if this referred to my shorts.

"You must prepare, Samael."

I looked around. There was no one else he could be talking to. "For what?" I said.

"The change. The old will end. The new will begin. As it is written."

The window at the other end of the corridor exploded and two enormous bird-like creatures flapped their way down to our cells. The lights flickered, powered now by some unseen source.

The birds dived through the bars of Bojangles' cell and started to rip him apart. As well as I could tell in the dim, flashing light, they seemed to be shredding his skin with their claws. He flailed his arms to keep the creatures away, but they were too strong. His face ruptured and he screamed, but there was no sound. One creature slashed his throat, and blood spurted across the floor.

He stopped moving.

The birds crashed against the bars of my cell, but couldn't enter. One flew back down the corridor to the window and was gone. The second paced up and down, testing the bars. Each time it touched the metal it shrieked and fluttered backward. It turned its rat-like face to me and let out a strange whining sound. It sounded sad.

The largest hound I had seen bounded down the corridor, spitting and snarling. It launched at the winged creature, barring its teeth and snapping, opening its jaws wide. The two creatures rolled together on the floor, slashing and clawing at each other. The bird sank its claws into the shoulder of the dog, which yelped, momentarily releasing its captive. The bird took its moment of freedom and crashed out through the window, half ripping itself apart against the jagged glass edges.

The dog turned and stared at me. It let out a low growl, then turned away and ran down the corridor to the window.

In the morning, Bojangles was dead.

They worked hard at it for a few hours, but in the end the slowhands couldn't pin the hobo's death on me, so they had to let me go. Reluctantly, the cell officer recorded "natural causes." You got to laugh. My nerves were still on edge. If L. Mallory had been there it would have helped. But she wasn't.

The afternoon heat rolled up from the gutters. On the way home I stopped at some joints to drink some nerves. But it didn't help. I wandered up the stairs to my office. The keys jangled as I flicked through them. I didn't need them. The door swung open.

The first thing I saw was the chair, over on its side with a broken leg. The trashmen had been and hadn't left one item untouched. It was clear they weren't looking for anything; someone was angry. The damage wasn't bad, but it was going to take a few hours.

I heard hurried footsteps on the staircase behind me, dainty and small. I turned around. L. Mallory smiled at me. She had undone the first two buttons on her uniform, and refreshed her perfume so it set up a perimeter of allure at five feet. Sure made *me* smell better.

"I thought you might need this," she said. She rotated her wrist and revealed my license folded in her delicate fingers. They were hands that had never seen the dirty end of a desperate altercation.

"Yeah. Thanks."

"Um." The confident girl of yesterday dissolved into a flustered teenager. "Would you like to go for a drink some time? Or we could catch a game if you're into that kind of thing. I like games."

"I ain't a temptation."

"But you're not a cop. I only meet cops and, well, you've seen them. I don't get on with them a whole lot."

"You're with internal audit?"

She looked at her feet and nodded. I felt sorry for her. It was hard enough being a woman in the police force. I could see some Neanderthal jerk taking offense to her because she was smart and pretty, lining her up as an undercover IA informer.

"I'd like a friend. I don't have too many. You look like you could be a friend."

I shrugged. She radiated purity through her brookish stone facade, derived, I was guessing, from an upbringing where life was constant competition with numerous Neanderthal cops.

The sight of the upended contents of the office behind me caught her attention, causing the sad bunnies to come back. "You should report this," she said.

"It's okay."

"It's a crime."

"Only with a theft."

She glanced at her watch, and her squirrel danced behind her. "I've got some time before I have to be back at the tank. I'll help you."

She helped a bit, but in the end she asked too many questions and I said I'd meet her for a drink. After she'd gone and I'd locked the door, I uncovered a large star drawn in blood in the center of the office. On the tips of the star were five burned points, like the pattern you'd find on a dead, skinny blond thing.

(HAPTER 4 ...

I was sitting back, flipping decimals into the tumbler on the desk. The place had the pretense of decorum with tidied shelves and a washed floor. A great darkness descended from the heavens, screeching and howling. The rent monster had turned up early. I sighed. There was no escape.

She flung open the door, giving it a hefty kick with her deformed boot. It crashed against the wall and the inset glass shook in a combination of fear and physics. She opened her mouth and the flames of a hellfire spewed out.

I'll translate: "You got till Thursday to pay up or you're out."

I left out the foul language because I've got some standards. She finished up with the usual abuse and stomped away down the stairs, shaking the building to its foundations.

It was going to be hard to find a place cheaper than this with four walls or a roof. I pulled out the pages and started to search for my next abode. In truth I was fine about moving because crimes had increased sharply in the area recently.

A shadow fell across the glass inset in the door. I knew who it was. It's hard to forget curves like that. She stood there, moving slowly, half dancing; performing some kind of seductive shadow-puppet show. Eventually the door opened.

Click.

"Yeah?"

Mina leaned against the doorjamb. My door introduced me: *Van H. Avram.* She stared at it long before casually deflating into my office. She traced her finger around the embossed gold sticker.

"What's the H stand for?"

"Hell knows."

She wore a white leather outfit that clung to her like a lick of paint, and was about as revealing. From mountains to molehill, it covered nothing. Her hair sat longer tonight.

"You're a hard man to find, Van."

"Hiding in plain sight." I gave her half a smile and gestured toward her like a bad magician. "What do you want?"

"I've placed some faith in my ability to change your mind." She sauntered around the room, checking out all the nooks and crannies. "Where do you sleep?"

"Hanging in the wardrobe."

"Feet up or down?"

I ignored her and poured a drink. I sighed as I fished out the decimals before knocking back the liquid.

She looked over the collection of musical artifacts in the corner. "You've got a sax. I like a man with a big, shiny instrument. Perhaps you'll let me blow it." Her finger stroked upward from the bow to the bell, her reflection stretched and golden in the brass.

She paused at the small wooden box with the army's embossed crest, which was holding down the unpaid bills. "You've got medals, why don't you display them?"

"I don't show off."

Her hand hovered over the box. Her thumbnail flicked the small golden latch but she left it closed. "What did you do in the army?"

"Shot things."

"Is that all?"

"And looked at things."

"You must've looked good to get all these medals. You still

look pretty good."

Flattery. It was a pretty lady going soft, so I let it ride. They say I'm a sucker for a pretty face, so when Mina gave me her eyes, three quarts desire and a fist full of desperate hunger, there wasn't much I could do except see where the ride ended up. These things never end up where you *want* to go, but more often than not they end up where you *need* to be.

"What happened? How does a war hero descend to the seventh rung of society?"

"Bad choices. Bad luck."

She let out a sigh. For the first time her face radiated an emotion other than determination. "Sooner or later we all succumb to the vices. You want to see some of mine?"

"How about later?"

She poured herself a drink and knocked it back while sitting down on the edge of my desk. She swung her knees to the side, retaining a small degree of grace, and rested the heels of her boots on my knees. She removed her broken-heart hairpin and her hair fell around her face, highlighting her features like a classic portrait.

"I'll try and fit you in, honey, but there's a queue of good intentions trying to back up outta the way."

She leaned forward and ran her finger down the side of my face. It scraped against the two-day growth. She placed one boot against my chest and gently pushed me back into the beat-up old leather recliner. She reached for my belt and pulled it free, ripping open my trousers. I couldn't deny I stirred to see her, especially what she was showing, and my body reacted accordingly.

"It's good to have your attention," she said.

Without trepidation she ripped aside her secrets and hovered over me. She teased as she steered me tantalizingly close, grazing her skin. "Will you take the case, honey?"

"Yeah, all right," I replied.

She descended and we joined in a holistic moment of endeavor. She rocked with the uncluttered finesse of a seasoned professional. I'm not the best of judges but she seemed to partake massively of the enjoyment.

"You're not a good woman," I said.

"I tried it but the pay was bad," she whispered. She grabbed my head and sank her teeth into my neck.

Mina put the candy on the desk, my standard rate of a century a week. It would keep the rent monster off my back for a month, and possibly some food in my mouth.

"Where'd you meet?" I asked.

She leaned over and whispered in my ear. "Vinyl."

"You got a picture?"

She fished through her small purse and handed over a photograph folded in half. The waxy paper had aged to a shade of yellow. It was him, singing out the front of some band, using some kind of ridiculous totem pole as a mic stand.

"He got a name?"

"It's on the back."

I turned it over. "You're kidding, right?" I flicked the photo with my fingers as I looked up at her.

"Take it how you like. It's easy to remember, if not entirely accurate."

I wrote down *Hugh*, then his ridiculous surname, *Jorgen*, on a fresh piece of paper. "I need one of you too," I said.

"Would you like it with my clothes on or off?"

I pulled out my battered old Leica and took a happy snap of her. She didn't pose too much, just enough to be a sticker on the front of a warplane. She couldn't help blowing a kiss. Then she was gone, leaving only the scent of her domineering pinnacle, and smudged lipstick on the glass. There was an odd expression on her face as she left, somewhere between shock, surprise and disappointment. It would be interesting to find out why.

I took the film down to the local drugstore where they offered quick and dirty processing for a fistful of decimals. I heard some more of those late-night birds flapping around, like the previous night, and I kept close to the buildings.

CHAPTER 5 ...

The morning made its usual commotion through the window. The sun glared like the inordinate thermonuclear explosion it was. Too early. Too bright. The stretcher was close to a bed of nails, comfort-wise, but it was home. A spot between my shoulder blades was itching, right where I couldn't reach, the spot only accessible if you had a short humerus or two. But from what I'd seen, short arms meant you couldn't be a lawman.

The city had its secrets. Most of the time it was loud and proud about them. You could know the metropolis without knowing about the terrace. And you could know a lot about the terrace without knowing about Vinyl. It was a place I'd heard about in uncertain whispers, but I'd never crossed the threshold, and this represented a dark hole in my understanding of the city.

The street Vinyl was on varied between the razzmatazz of the secrets window dancers—quality at the top of the menu—down to the decimal hookers hugging windbreaks in concrete alcoves. The street was brutal and blatant with its architecture reflecting the various levels of available service. But at least they advertised.

Vinyl was different. It was a big old warehouse made of stone and steel, three stories high and windowless. It presented a blank exterior to the street. No signs. No doors. No mailbox. No thank you. Its aggressive pre-industrial architecture repulsed all who strayed near. Most pedestrians crossed over to avoid the place, as though it might suddenly come to life and devour them like some stone-age monster; part tiger, part religious monolith, and part act of war. The occasional group of individuals could be seen milling on the corner wearing strange black shiny clothing.

There was a large gate on one side of the warehouse. Behind it was a narrow alleyway that ran down the length of the building. I rattled the cage and hollered for attention. No response. I looked at the lock. It was old, older than a teenage embarrassment. I'd seen one before, in the war. The recollection poked around in the back of my dusty memory box. It wasn't coming. I knew I'd seen the lock at a distance, where it held back something horrible. I shrugged. I couldn't remember what that something was, but I did remember how to open the lock.

I flipped through my handy utility pack, extracted the old army Remington picklock and rammed it into the rusty lock. I smiled as it clicked open. Made for each other. The gate swung inward with not so much a squeak as a scream of terror that would carry for a few hundred blocks.

The alleyway was clean, swept with military thoroughness. Either someone was OCD or they were leaving no trace of illegal deeds. One thing that wasn't clean was the air. A familiar smell started to percolate, seemingly emanating from two black trashcans sealed with heavy tape. I ripped the tape free and flicked the lid on the first can.

The smell of stale blood rose up and hostaged the air. I clasped a hand over my nose and mouth, trying to prevent the reflex action caused by the bucket of blood. And there was a lot of blood.

I ripped the tape off the second can. Revealing a pair of eyes staring up at me.

The severed head sat atop several blood-soaked bedsheets. I reached in and pulled it out— by one horn. Blood dripped down, draining what remained into the bin. The two eyes were sad and baleful. I was guessing he didn't want his head cut off. The face was drawn, haggard and old. His brown fur was matted.

Poor goat. There was a chance it was killed for a barbecue, but my senses were saying otherwise. I dropped the head back into the can, gave the goat a sorry-pat, and slammed the lid.

The alley cornered around the back of the building, opening up into a small, cobbled area that made the place look centuries old. A metal door was set into the expanse of bricks and steel. There was a tiny metal grate set into the door. That, too, was shut tight.

The lock on the door was also from another time, so ancient that even corrosion had given up. The old army picklock slid in easily. A minute of twitching and pushing had the thing open. The door swung inward, revealing a dark, cavernous chamber.

I stepped in and the door slammed closed behind me. The space was lit by a couple of dozen thick candles about a foot high set up evenly around the vast room. Going by the amount of wax on the floor, it looked like the candles burned down until near-no-more, then new ones were swapped in. Always glowing, always burning, keeping the shadows away.

A couple of utility tables surrounded by chairs were scattered around the large room, facing inward. A large red star was embedded in the floor in the center of the room, surrounded by five candles that had burned down to nothing but a good time. The star looked just like the one in my office.

I bent down and swiped a couple of digits across the star. It was dry. Not fresh blood, but judging by its color it was less than a day old. Probably drawn some time last night, I guessed. During the full moon. In the center of the star was a great—I hesitate to use the word altar—stone slab resting on heavy stone legs, and in the center of the altar was a hollowed-out depression half full of blood. The smell was bad.

The walls were lined with the kind of equipment people usually use on animals, but in the city, well, they generally use it on themselves. Which I prefer as I don't like to see innocent animals used inappropriately. Just in case anyone missed the hint from the sight of the equipment, the walls were decorated with images showing what could be done—exactly—with said equipment. It was enough to make you give up on humanity.

There were footsteps behind me. A shadow was coming up a set of stairs. A basement. Considering the noise I'd made getting in, a soundproof basement. That couldn't be good.

The shadow evolved into a man wearing rubber waders and an undershirt. He was a big guy, two inches or so taller than me. Well muscled. In one hand he carried a bucket that held a mop, and in the other a shovel. His shoulder-length black hair hung around his face, almost obscuring his green eyes.

I could see defined layers of muscles rippling down his stomach through the thin white fabric. They flexed as he moved. A man who could tip any erring housewife into the cauldron of depravity and make her enjoy it.

He dropped the bucket and shovel. I hoped it wasn't a hand I saw fall out of the tipped-over bucket. He clenched his fists, delighting me with a balletic display of pectoral dancing.

"How'd you get in?" he snarled.

"Door was open." I hitched my thumb over my shoulder.

He looked at me suspiciously. "Would that be the door that I double-checked was locked before I came in? Through the gate that I also checked was locked? You know it's impossible to open those locks."

"Is the proprietor in?"

He strolled over to me, taking a snaking path, until he was a few feet away. "Nah."

"Who are you?" I said.

"The guy who'll take your head off if you ask any more questions."

I held up a picture of lover boy between two fingers. "Have you seen this guy?"

He stepped in closer. He stank of sweat, blood, and possibly a near-fatal amount of alcohol. There was barely enough space between us to squeeze in a pretzel. He took a long sniff over my shoulder.

"You don't smell like a cop."

"I'm worse."

I replaced the photograph in my pocket. The spot between my shoulder blades began to itch again. I shook my head. I'd swear to a preacher the man had become two inches taller.

He swung a hammer-like fist, clipping me neatly on the jaw. I tumbled to the ground, taking out a table and a few chairs on the way. I grabbed a chair leg. The chair came with it. I held it up, and his fist smashed through the seat. I twisted the chair, and he turned and kicked into the side of my head. I went sprawling across the floor, collecting blood, wax, and assorted body fluids.

He ran at me. I jumped up. I grabbed a branding iron off the wall and swung it around and into him. He raised his arm and deflected the blow. It should have snapped his arm clean in half, but the bar just bent. I gave it a quizzical look before throwing it aside. Cheap equipment.

I blinked my eyes in disbelief; the guy now appeared to be a *foot* taller than me. I backed into a corner and he reached out for me. He grabbed me, lifted me into the air and staggered into the center of the room, where he smashed me down onto the stone slab. I landed heavily, on the edge, and rolled off, miraculously still on my feet. My ribs burned.

In the base of the bloody depression I spotted a knife handle. I snatched it out of the mess. It was sharp; it had cut off a goat's head. I turned, but he was coming toward me like the wrath of the gods, with both fists clenched. He smashed them into my back and I collapsed to the floor.

He bent over and grabbed me by my jacket. I slipped free of it and took a couple of quick stabs at him. The knife cut through the fabric of his shirt, but the effect seemed to be nothing more than mild irritation.

He pulled an eighteen-inch-long dagger from behind his back. Its red blade flashed in the light, almost as if it was alive. I glanced down at my own pitiful blade. I rolled my eyes and threw it aside.

He made a couple of lightning-fast lunges at me, with the last overreaching. I ploughed in under his swing, tackled him around the waist, lifted him up, and slammed him onto the floor. I pressed a knee into his chest, wrenched the knife out of his hand, and pressed it to his throat. His stunned eyes filled with the kind of terror I'd only seen in the war. He seemed normal sized again.

"Let's start again," I said. He nodded profusely, staring insanely at the knife blade. "Name?"

"Levi."

"You seen her, Levi?" I pulled out the photo of Mina and shoved it in his face. His eyes danced between the picture and the red blade. It felt warm in my hand.

"Yeah, yeah. She comes in all the time. Been coming for years. She knows the owner."

"Him?" I switched photographs and held up lover boy Jorgen.

"He came in a couple of months ago with someone, and the two of them hooked up."

Sweat was pouring off the guy. I felt I was in imminent danger of going all wrinkly with his heat and moisture.

"Who?"

He stammered for a few moments before a name marched out on parade. "Silbi."

"Why?"

"When Mina gets bored with her boyfriends she looks for distraction. Silbi provides the distraction."

"Where is he?"

"Leviticus Street."

I raised the knife up and drove it down, narrowly missing his neck and sinking the point two inches into the beer-and-urine-soaked floorboards.

"You've been warned."

I staggered out and back onto the Terrace. I clutched at my ribs, wincing with each step. I scanned the area and found a concealed spot behind a stack of trashcans. I sat down and waited.

Twenty minutes later, as the pain was starting to subside, Levi appeared and looked around cautiously. He'd replaced the waders with a set of ex-army pants and thrown on an old lumberjack shirt. He had his hair tied back and wore a large set of cheaters in some failed attempt at a disguise.

(HAPTER 6 ...

I have to admit he was a tricky sucker to track. He moved like the wind, dancing around the pedestrians like they were maypoles. Did he head to Leviticus Street? No. I didn't know what waited for me up there, but his lying was as convincing as a grade school nativity play, and it sure wasn't going to be Silbi.

He rounded onto Paradise Drive. I hated this part of town. Nothing but players, dealers, and con artists soaking up the good land with the good views and clean air.

He stopped in front of a sharp-looking brownstone. He tapped the buzzer three times, then twice, then another three. He waited, glancing around. The wind had picked up and was blowing his hair around, giving him the appearance of an unwashed hound. All he lacked was the tongue hanging out.

I took shelter behind a bus stop. In a few minutes the diesel-powered flying bus had come and gone at its regulation thirty-five miles an hour in a cloud of dark fumes. Levi was gone. There was no sign of him up or down the street.

I ran across the road. A jamoke-man was selling thick wakeup juice a couple of buildings down, bouncing around in his pin-striped three-piece. He tipped his fedora as I approached. No, he hadn't seen a man of that description. After a cup of joe, giving no change for a handshake, and a cray greasing his palm, he could remember better, and yeah, the guy went in the door.

We talked, and the minutes crawled by. He liked the game last week. It had been close. My mind began to melt from excessive banality. He began to preach the wonders of java and the benefits of an alert mind.

The door of the brownstone opened. I slipped behind the jamoke-man and watched Levi slouch away. Once he was around the corner I ran to the door and tapped the same three-two-three pattern on the buzzer. The door swung open, revealing a long dark hallway, beckoning me in.

The hallway ended in a wood-paneled anteroom. The floor was cut marble in the shape of a spiral. Looking at it for too long would send your head into the next dimension.

There was a plain door to the right, and a stairway curving up two flights to a large landing. Behind the plain door was a janitor's cupboard. Mops and buckets. The staircase and landing were made of wood. They looked old enough to be imported from the old country, and given a special coating of old-ium.

The first door on the landing had a label: The Beast lives here. Some rich frat kid thinking he was funny. His door handle was dusty. The neighbor's wasn't. It was also gold plated. It turned easily under my grip. Sounds of activity rolled out.

I stepped off the old wooden floor onto a marble surface so shiny my reflection had a life of its own. The expansive room had warehouse windows looking out onto an infinite plane of smog. Hardly seemed worth the trouble. In the center of the room sat a large bar made of oak inlaid with ivory, with crystal chandeliers suspended above it.

The room was dripping in candy; the finest and most illegal of everything was here: exotic rugs, ancient relics and weapons, missing collector's pieces. Drinks. Drugs. Livestock equipment.

Double doors on the left opened onto a large bedroom draped in velvet. A bed that could take ten dominated the room. To the right, culinary noises echoed behind a closed door. I pushed it open and stepped through. The kitchen reiterated the sentiment of excess in the previous rooms. Standing with his back to me was a slender man with long blond hair. He was washing something in the kitchen sink.

"Honestly, you have the memory of a stray cat. Your age is catching up with you. What did you forget this time?" The voice verged on manic frenzy, tickling the notes of insanity in an octave untouched by the normal.

He turned. He was the most beautiful person I had seen. Even looking straight at him, it was difficult to tell if he was a he. His form seemed to be subtly morphing like some top-shelf illusion as I watched. I thought the beating from Levi must have done something to my eyes. I blinked, hoping to shake the blurry image into focus.

"Oh, it's you," Silbi said, drying his or her hands on a dishcloth. "You want a drink? I've got your favorite."

"No, thanks."

"Come out to the bar. It's more inviting." He or she walked past. I was prepared to believe he was a she now.

As she headed into the next room I saw the big-city heels that were designed more for horizontal movement than vertical, yet she moved with a practiced grace and balance that defied fashion and physics. I followed her to a great mahogany bar.

Behind the bar, she flicked a tumbler down off a high shelf, letting it fall into her hand. She poured a long slug of whiskey rye into the large glass and placed in front of me. "Just how you like it."

I stared at her. I felt saliva collecting in my mouth, willing me to accept the drink. I took a deep breath and reached out for the glass. I was surprised to see my hand shaking. The ache in my mind grew as I tried to resist, but there was no point. The gleam in Silbi's eyes sparked as I picked it up. The pain relented as my hand wrapped around the glass.

I opened my mouth and threw the drink over my shoulder.

Silbi's smile snapped into a frown, but a pretty one. "How about we blow?" she said. "I got some fresh lines clean from the south."

The point between my shoulder blades was itching again. I twisted my head in annoyance. "I'm not blowing," I said.

"You're no fun. It'll be wild. You remember the old days?"

"What old days?"

"Doesn't everyone have old days when they were a little crazy, and did stupid things?"

"We leave them behind."

"Not everyone. I'm living proof of that. I've been disappointed in you. No drinks. No blow. What's left? Let me see."

She came out from behind the bar and stepped in close, running her hand up my trouser leg, fly-fishing between the pleats. "Do you have a fantasy? A special lady friend?"

A vision of L. Mallory flickered through my mind. All buttoned up, but she unclipped her uniform inch by inch and slowly peeled away her shell. It wasn't an unwelcome image, but the timing was bad.

"Or are there two? Oh, you naughty boy," she whispered. She had my full attention within her grasp. "Such a dilemma. How to choose?"

Now a vision of Mina was offering itself up for my consideration, sweeping me along in that determined drive of hers.

"I know," Silbi whispered. "Don't choose. Have both."

Her voice sent chills down my neck. A vision of the two women sandwiching me, the three of us tangled in the red silken sheets in the bed in the next room, tormented me.

"I can feel your frustration, but I can fix that," Silbi drawled.

I looked at her. The image drifted as I overlaid my desires on her. Her appearance shifted between Mina and L. Mallory. The itch between my shoulder blades hammered into my conscience. Then it started to crawl down my back.

Silbi steered me toward her velvet boudoir. I took a few steps, and the image of Mina and L. Mallory grew stronger. The burning spread down my back in a thin line, like it was trying to unzip my skin. My feet continued without much involvement from me, until I put a stop to it.

"Enough." The pain in my head was nearly driving me to my knees. The image of Mina and L. Mallory snapped away, replaced by the thin, brittle appearance of Silbi.

"How dare you defy me?"

She swung her palm around, landing it square on my face. It felt like a red-hot poker had struck me. I staggered to the side and collapsed onto one knee, knocking against a silver gas outlet in the wall. It dug deep into my shoulder. The clamping pain vanished from my head, replaced by the ringing pain of the slap. A minor improvement.

"Fine. Be like that," she shouted. She pulled out a red dagger from behind her. It was about eighteen inches long.

"I've seen that before."

"Yeah, we've got a club. You want to be a member, huh, huh? Oh yeah, you can't."

She thrust the dagger toward me, but I ducked out of the way. Maybe the excessive lifestyle had dulled her reflexes. Her trailing hand caught me on the side of the head. I corrected my last thought.

She kicked into my stomach, knocking the wind from me. She brought down the pummel of the dagger onto my back, knocking me flat to the floor. I was up on all fours when she lowered the tip of the dagger and pressed it into my face.

"Sure you don't want that drink?"

I bowed my head. "Stop asking." The clamping pressure was back in my head.

"It'll just be a little one, then we can have a roll in the sack for old time's sake."

I sagged under the pressure. What I did next I'm not proud of.

I sat up and said, "Okay."

"Really?" She eased the pressure on my face.

"No."

I punched up as hard as I could. The blow caught her on the chin, totally by surprise. Her eyes went wide as she flew up into the air. She flung out her arms, and the dagger clattered to the floor. She landed heavily. I scooped up the dagger and had it at her throat before she could recover. Her eyes held the same terror as Levi's when I held his identical dagger to his throat.

I fished out the picture of lover boy Jorgen again. "Tell me about him." I shoved the photo in her face.

She shied away from it like a phobia. Her eyes danced between the picture and the blade. "Yeah, yeah. He wanted to sing. Be a star. We made a deal. I knew some people. I said I could introduce him."

"Mina?"

"No, no. Industry people. Star makers. Get him on record sounding good then tell everyone how great he was. These"—she paused, her eyes flicked around—"people, they'll believe anything you tell them. You sure you don't want a drink? I can see you're a man who likes a drink. You can't live in denial. Come on, have one for old time's sake. It won't hurt. It never hurts."

"Stop offering me drinks." I thrust the dagger toward her. Each time she mentioned a drink I could feel the metal clamp in my head tightening. I knew that all I had to do was say okay and it would go away. But I also knew that something bad would happen.

"Where is he? Where's Jorgen?"

"He's on … Templeton Drive," she said, "667."

"In the Basin?"

"You know the place? You remember?"

I stood back and gave her enough space to stand up. "Remember what?"

"Don't you know? How can you not know?" Her voice was as dry and frustrated as a land-locked deckhand's.

At the edge of my hearing I thought I could make out the steady hiss of air.

"If you're not going to have a drink, I'll have one. And a smoke."

She poured herself half a tumbler of scotch and knocked it back. Her hands shook as she placed a cigarette between her lips and flicked open a silver lighter. She took a couple of deep pulls and blew smoke into the air. She idly snapped the lid of the lighter open and closed. The swish and click was eerie in the sudden calm. She took another puff of her cigarette.

She dropped her arm behind the bar and jerked out a large black hammer. She ran at me, so engulfed by range that she didn't see the dagger sticking out in front of me. The knife slid into her chest. She hung suspended for a moment and a tear rolled down her face. Her eyes closed and she fell backward.

The lighter flamed as it fell to the floor. There was a flash of light and the entire floor erupted in a ball of flame. I was thrown backward as the flames rolled over the top of me, engulfing me in a furnace.

CHAPTER 7 ...

Fire exploded from the room, tearing the door off its hinges and throwing me onto the landing. I rolled to one side and manhandled the ancient door on top of me, clasping the golden handle tightly. The fire intensified, as if a dragon was bearing down. There was a deep creak, followed by sounds of splintering, and the landing gave way, ripping out from the wall, metal grinding, wood cracking, taking down a ton of masonry with it.

As I fell, the walls twisted and tumbled; the whole building seemed to bow down like a cheap pair of chinos. Bricks and tiles rained down as the walls below me crumpled and collapsed into a sloping pile. The rough descent pummeled my back as I slid all the way to the base of the building and out onto the main street.

I landed heavily on top of the rubble and slid to the bottom. Bricks hammered on top of the door, which I still clutched in my hands. The brownstone continued to collapse, forming a dark prison around me. Slowly I crawled out of the debris and emerged into daylight with the golden handle still in my grasp.

I blinked.

The jamoke-man had a not-unexpected look of surprise on his face. His cigarette drooped in the corner of his mouth. He even committed the unspeakable crime of spilling some joe on the pavement.

"Gimme a triple shot," I muttered. I coughed, and a spray of pulverized brick shot out of my mouth. Standing up presented its own challenges.

Jamoke-man offered a stabilizing hand.

I chucked the golden handle to him.

"You're on fire," he said, his deep voice providing some solidity for the situation.

I patted out the embers smoldering on my jacket.

"I ain't gonna ask how you survived that."

"I ain't sure myself," I replied.

"That other guy came back when you were inside. I thought you'd like to know."

"What happened?"

"A big dog came along and chased him away."

"What color?"

Jamoke-man shrugged. "Dog colored."

"You're not much help."

"I am what I am. I'm just saying what I see. You want more joe?"

Hitching onto a thirty-five was the quickest way to get to the Basin, especially as the traffic was picking up. The great rumbling black shiny machine with the government-yellow banding eased down out of the sky, pouring diesel fumes. I jumped on board, flicked a few hexadecimals into the can, and it took off.

A couple of stops later we descended into the Basin, where urban decay had reached new heights—or depths. In the Basin there were riots over water and phone lines, and insufficient ice-cream availability. People were eternally wired and raged at everything. Burned-out vehicles sat out front of burned-out houses. Bricks and mortar crumbled, along with morals. Hookers turned tricks until they succumbed to the relentless beating of their "owners."

Templeton Drive lay at my feet.

A couple of old ex-factory buildings, that had been converted into housing for hundreds, lined the severe street, which offered nothing else but dead vegetation. I looked behind me. The jamoke-man was there.

"You following me?"

"You betcha. Any chance of a building collapsing, I wanna be there." He had a grin so wide it was in danger of stretching past the edges of his face.

I gave him a skeptical look. I checked the address. There was a mountain of bricks where a building had once stood.

"You been here before?" he said.

My shoulders sagged. Silbi had slipped me a fake address, and now she was dead. A better man might have walked away, thought it was too much trouble for a mere century. Mina and her associates were nothing but trouble that had already landed me in jail and in pain. But something was burning deep inside of me. I wanted answers to dark questions, but everyone was lying.

I caught the thirty-five back across town to the Vinyl, thinking about the events of the day. The vehicle was empty, on my level at least, and apart from the engine drone it was peaceful. Buildings flashed past below.

Levi was burning on my mind. He was about the only source I had, and I was going to pour him over all the steak. Then it hit me.

Something big and black smashed into the side of the thirty-five, rocking the vehicle to one side. The engines whined as they kicked into reverse and fought to lower the vehicle safely to the ground. It crashed heavily across the railway tracks, directly into the path of the overnight transcontinental leaving Central Station.

The train screamed as it plowed into the bus, smashing the top level flat, and crushing the level I was on into barely more than breathing space. The sound of tearing metal filled every molecule of my body. An endless rain of sparks and shrieking steel flew around my body.

Eventually the two vehicles shuddered to a halt. The dying light from the setting sun filtered down through the floating dust and debris.

I blinked.

I pushed the seat off me and slid down the side of the vehicle, which was now the floor. I kicked open the emergency window at the end and climbed out. Glass tinkled down around me and scattered over the ground. There was a small crowd gathering. Better judgment told me to hang around for this one.

I wandered around the wreckage looking for clues as to what had brought down the thirty-five.

The transcontinental had made a big mess of it, leaving the black metal twisted around the supertrain's front end. The driver wouldn't take long to get down, after he'd fortified his nerves.

Wrapped in the wreckage was a young lady, blond and thin, wearing nothing but upmarket lingerie. There wasn't a whole lot left of her. Silk, broken bones, smashed organs, and five small burn marks in the center of her chest. I heard the splash of leaking fuel, then metal scraping against metal. I caught the spark out of the corner of my eye, and dived for cover.

The thirty-five erupted in a great fireball, throwing me into a nearby garden. The fire rolled over me, the last of the flames licking at my clothes. My second fireball of the day; I should invest in asbestos underwear.

I staggered up out of the soft mulch and made my way back to the crash zone. The body of the dead blond girl was gone, consumed in the fire.

My ears were ringing and my head was spinning as I sat down on the twisted train tracks. The super moon rose above the cityscape, but was quickly mugged by passing clouds.

Watcher and the forensic monkeys appeared in minutes, or maybe it was hours. It was all a bit of a blur. The medic had placed a blanket around me, thick and coarse. The blanket, that is. I didn't see the point. Everyone, including me, was sweating.

Watcher stood with his hands on his hips looking over the immense wreckage. "What on earth happened here?"

"Thirty-five malfunction."

"This was the Basin thirty-five. What were you doing down there?" He turned to face me.

"Visiting a friend."

"Did your friend live at 667 Templeton in the Basin?"

"No, why?"

"There was an accident there last night. We discovered a nest of … individuals hiding there. It was very unpleasant, and some good men got hurt. Some punk was playing with an old Zippo lighter, probably caught a gas leak, and the whole place went up."

I couldn't help but notice the use of the word "nest." Maybe I should check out what was there before.

"Was anyone else on the ride?"

I shook my head and told him it was an empty bus. The image of the young blond woman flashed in my mind, but she couldn't have been on the ride. I would have noticed a woman wearing nothing but her secrets. The five mysterious burn marks made me think, but the link escaped me.

"Any news about blondie?"

The question caught him off guard. "The stiff in your room? Forensics said it was a heart attack, a massive coronary shock with complete neurological collapse. She had the life sucked right out of her."

"That's all?"

"That's all I'm telling you."

"Can I go?"

His eyes did another pass over the wreckage. He squinted back at me. "I can't find an angle where you caused this, so I can only label you a victim, an exceedingly lucky one. Where were you heading?"

"Down to the Terrace."

"Well, you're not going there now. The whole central line's shut down. The Terrace isn't an appropriate place for a casual visit. Where were you going exactly?"

"The Vinyl."

"You have to be joking me. If I find you've been there I'll throw you straight in the cells. You're not to go there under any circumstances." He stepped in close to me. His breath slapped me in the face. I could see the meat from his last feed stuck between his teeth. "If you do go there I'll find something worse than the cells."

"It's a free country."

"No, it isn't. This is my city, and I'm telling you to go home." He pointed that damn finger at me. He flinched as he raised his arm, his shoulder in obvious discomfort.

I got up, gave him a dark look, and walked away.

"Give the blanket back," he shouted. "I've seen your bed and you're not stealing our blankets."

I pulled it off my shoulders, bunched it up and threw it at him. It landed on his head and he struggled with it before he flung it on the ground. My nerves were bouncing around like a bad check from a Basin hooker. I needed liquid Valium, urgently.

Another thought had occurred to me while I was waiting around. Hugh was a singer, and in this city the reprobates knew each other.

CHAPTER 8 ...

Wonderboy sat behind the Opera, pounding the keys like he was on a personal vendetta. His old friend Jay took up the double bass and for about five minutes they hit the groove. Perfect. The Stylus was spinning like a raccoon. They looked over at each other and Jay gave Wonderboy a nod, followed by that million-dollar smile.

A group of excitable young ladies had formed a queue on Jay's side, waiting for a glance. I wondered if he slept with all of them and they kept it a secret from one another. The set finished, with Danny on vox saying something stupid. The women started to fight over who was buying a drink for Jay.

Wonderboy gave me a nod and made his way over. "What happened to you?"

"I had a date."

He laughed. "You know, I know some nice girls. They do things like talk, dance and kiss, not beat three kinds of hullabaloo out of you. It wasn't one of those foreign brides?"

I shook my head. It didn't fall off.

Wonderboy called Jackson over, then threw some ice in a dishcloth and poured me a shot while adjusting his glasses.

"You know this guy?" I handed Wonderboy the photo.

He ironed out the creases with his thumb against the tabletop then tapped the face with his index finger. Its speed always impressed me. "Yeah, he was that singer who came out of nowhere. What was his name? Hugh something."

"Jorgen."

"Oh yeah, had a three-piece. Made a whole lot of noise and then went quiet. Played the Palladium a couple of times. Big gigs. Big cash." He nodded in appreciation of his own powers of recollection.

"You know his location?"

Wonderboy tapped his fingers against his lip and shook his head. "Didn't he lose everything? End up with no cash? Blew what he had up his nose and down his trousers?"

"Sounds like him."

"It's tough at the top. That's my excuse for never making the big time—too much temptation. You forget it's about the music."

"He's got some stolen cash," I said.

"Yeah? It ain't from us. We got no cash to steal. Danny drinks our profits."

"Where would he go?"

He looked over his shoulder at Danny, who was expecting his free drinks from the impressionable bartender, then turned back to me. "You remember when Danny got that inheritance and his thug-brother came after him?"

I nodded.

"I think he went to Limbo's, that dive over in Gayme. It's got a secret number, and a gate a mile high so you can't tell if anyone's there."

He turned and waved Danny over. He looked around conspiratorially and asked Danny, "What's the number for Limbo's?"

"Why?" Danny's thick voice rolled with the hint of an accent. He'd put on weight over the years, adding reasonable beef to his chords. But his hair hadn't liked it and had taken the first opportunity to split.

"Van's got a line on a good deal, but he lost the number," Wonderboy said. "You want in? Ten for a cray. We'll give you a free one for the number."

"Yeah, I'm in." Danny wrote down the number and passed it over. "Who's the source?"

"You remember Jorgen? You hung out with him for a while, didn't you?"

Danny nodded.

"He's pushing now. More money in it than gigging, especially for a has-been."

I left the two of them reminiscing about the old days and went looking for a phone, weaving between the dancers and the groovers. The Stylus has a phone concealed behind the cigarette machine, the only place that was quiet. I pulled across the curtain that fell to knee height, picked up the receiver and dialed. I kicked my heels against the carpet, looking at the patterns they made. The carpet was thick and red, same as the curtain. I felt like I was in a coffin.

It rang … and rang … and rang. I was about to give up when a woman of a certain age answered.

"Yes?"

"Mr. Jorgen."

"Are you the police? You have to declare it."

"No."

There was silence. A minute passed. Then another.

Then came a rustling down the line as the receiver was picked up. "Yeah?"

The curtain fluttered. I flicked it aside to see what the commotion was. A man was spinning around in the middle of the dance floor. He was crying for help, his plaintive voice lamenting the loss of a daughter, his, I assumed. He stumbled several times before a couple of Samaritans reached out and caught him, leading him back to a secluded booth. He didn't look that old; his blond hair was fighting courageously against the gray.

"Are you press, because you're going need a heap of money

to run with this story," Hugh said. His voice was clear and deep, and purred like a lion. I could hear why the ladies fell for his tones.

"I'm not the press."

"You've got three seconds to interest me."

I let the three seconds roll around. He didn't hang up. Maybe there was something in my voice that kept him hanging on.

"You took her money?" I said.

"Whose?"

"Mina's."

"Oh, you're a private dick. That makes sense. She'd be afraid to call the police." He let out a deep laugh. "Don't tell me you buy that victim crap. She's not as innocent as she seems. She might cry or look pitiful or even give you some sob story, but it's not the truth. You get to know her, you'll find out. Anyways, she can afford it. She's so loaded I'm surprised she hasn't pulled the trigger and shot. What do you wanna know?"

"Where'd you meet her?"

"At the Vinyl. I met some guy who said they got juiced-up ladies clustering for attention. I tagged along with him. He seemed to know everyone. Then I meet Candy-wouldn't-melt-in-her-mouth. Of course, with me it weren't candy. At least I think it was Candy. It's hard to tell the sisters apart. Hey, maybe I had all of them and I never knew. I'll ask if she comes back."

"She's missing?"

"Looks like it. She went out last night and I haven't seen her come back."

"Any distinguishing features?"

"Nope."

That was an odd declaration. "You sure?"

"You bet. It's weird. Normally when you get a woman down to her secrets she's got something, a small scar, some freckles. She's got nothing. She's got skin like porcelain. Trust me, I've been over every inch of her. Just a skinny blond girl."

"Why does Mina want her money?"

"She doesn't want the money. She's only saying that. She's afraid because you-know-who's coming down."

"Who?"

"That, my friend, will cost you. But she's after something else I got. Something she shouldn't have had."

"What?"

Hugh let out a low laugh, followed by a tut-tut-tut.

I flicked aside the curtain. The dancing man was looking at me, staggering around, his fist clenching and unclenching. At least he was in time with the music. The in-between act was doing its best, and Danny and Wonderboy were giving them the occasional nod of approval while talking to Jackson and taking a drink.

"You want the truth, you come find me," Hugh was saying.

"Maybe I will."

"Take some advice, Mr. Dick. If you want to go on hanging around Mina and her friends, get something shiny and reflective. You might need it. It's a broken record playing down a path laid from the seeds of truth."

The phone went dead. I replaced the receiver and stood staring at it. The guy was annoying beyond rationality. I didn't know him beyond a few minutes of listening to his voice, but I harbored a desire to see his throat slit.

I made my way back to the bar. Jackson had an icepack ready for me. It stung as I placed it on my face. The others laughed. There was a tap on my shoulder. I swung round, reluctantly. It was L. Mallory. I lowered the icepack.

"Jiminy Cricket, what happened to you?" She brushed her hand over the bruises and I flinched. "Don't be a baby."

Wonderboy gave me a nod and turned back to Jackson.

"Are they your friends?" she said.

"No. They're the band."

"Are you going to introduce me?"

It seemed like a bad idea. "Band, this is L. Mallory."

Wonderboy sat back, grinning and enjoying the show. "Hi, L.," he said.

Danny activated sleaze mode. "What a beautiful name, Elle,"

he said, putting on his thick, exotic accent.

"It's Laura." She gave me a sideways look as she extended a hand toward Wonderboy.

Danny whipped in and wrenched it to his mouth, coating her knuckles with saliva-excessive kisses. She extracted her hand while continuing to smile, but her eyes told a different story as she surreptitiously wiped her hand on her dress.

"Let's go," I said. I grabbed her arm and pulled her over to one of the tall bar tables.

(HAPTER 9 ...

She was class. Most women would have dealt with Danny with far more repulsion and physical confutation, yet her language had remained civil.

I watched as she spun herself up onto the seat. Her heels clipped into the low rail circling the chair's legs. The emerald-green dress hugged her curves. She wasn't like Mina—an atomic bombshell that could flatten a continent—but she dazzled in a million other ways that meant a whole lot more.

She released the squirrel, and her locks twisted down around her shoulders. She had dark roots, meaning she wasn't a natural skinny blond thing. I liked that.

"Why are you here?"

"I asked around the tank to see if anyone knew where you hung out. This seemed the most common answer after all the rude ones. I thought I'd give you a try. Some people said you were worth knowing." Her hair fell over one eye, and she shook it away.

Jackson appeared with a couple of plated drinks. He slid them onto the tabletop and disappeared in a blink. We both took a sip and watched as the bands switched over. Wonderboy gave me a wave as he stepped up onto the stage.

"Laura." I tried out the name in my mouth. It came easy.

"That's me." She looked at me. She had large, deep-green eyes, full of sadness. They offset her lightly tanned complexion, but matched her get-up.

"It's a good name."

"It's just a name."

"Your father is Mallory."

"My father's always going to be Mallory, it being my name." She took a sip of her drink.

"Head of District Nine?"

She let out a long sigh and looked away, clutching her glass in both hands. "I was hoping you wouldn't know that."

"Why? He's a good man."

"Not everyone thinks so, especially the ones with something to hide."

"District Nine's tough."

"No, growing up with Commander Franklin Mallory as your father, and his three outstanding sons, is tough."

"Then why be a cop?"

"It's all I know. Everyone in the family is a cop. Didn't you follow in your parents' footsteps?"

I recalled broken memories of unknown motherhood, and a domineering father who commanded more than engaged. All I could offer him was disappointment.

"My feet went elsewhere."

I looked up at the band assembling on the stage. People were milling around on the dance floor. Something must have flashed across my face, because Laura leaned over and rested her hand on mine.

"Do you dance?"

"No. I drink."

"And no dancing after the drinking?"

"Not the kind you'd enjoy."

"I bet you do really, or did once. Come on, I'm not your biscuit. I think you do."

"I'm not a floor flusher. The only way you'll get me giving a knee is in your dreams."

A sad expression settled on her face. And in that moment she looked undeniably vulnerable.

"I don't like dreams," she said. "I had one more than ten years ago that scared the living daylights out of me. It still does. The most beautiful girl came into my bedroom. She had short, spiky blond hair, vivid blue eyes, and the most amazing figure. And she was so friendly, and full of joy and happiness. We were talking, and she was telling me about herself, when she leaned in close and reached out to me. Suddenly I felt a dog bite me. It hurt so much I woke up. I cried for a week. I was sure it had really happened but there was nothing there, no sign of a bite. The doctor said it was in my head. Even now, when it's a full moon and I hear some baleful dog howl into the night, I feel the teeth."

"Time heals all."

"Time heals some things."

I looked at her sad face. "Do you have friends?"

She shook her head. "But I have you now."

"I'm not reliable."

She looked away from me, toward the bar. "No one is. The only person you can rely on is yourself."

I sighed. I don't get that answer when I look in the mirror.

I looked around. Some old lady pushing the wrong side of a Cadillac was buying into Danny's *technique de l'amour* routine with change to spare. She was glowing from ear to ear. Wonderboy was shouting at him to get back on stage.

"An old friend of my father's is coming down from the north with his daughter, who's about my age and doesn't know about my past. Maybe we can be friends, talk on the phone for hours about boys."

I raised my eyebrow. "How old are you?"

She laughed, covering her mouth with her hand. "I missed out on all that."

"Not every experience is great." I took a long slug of the

whiskey and a moment of silence descended.

She played with her hair, something obviously digging away inside of her. She threw back the rest of her drink and spoke just as the band started up. She gave them a sideways glance as though silently castigating them for the bad timing.

"You said you'd loved and lost," she said. "What happened?"

I let the question rest for a moment, feeling the grip of the memory aching around my heart. I wondered how much to tell her. I had the feeling those big green eyes could look through any fabrication. After all, she was internal audit.

"Another man's wife chose me."

Her face registered surprise. "You must've been young."

"We all were."

"It's too loud in here. Can we go somewhere quiet?" She ran her finger around the rim of her empty glass.

"Where to?"

"How about your place?"

I gave her a low look. "What if a client comes?"

She gave me an unsettling smile and pulled me up by the jacket collar as she wheeled off her chair. "How often do you get a client?"

The answer was easy: never. Unless I wanted a piece of privacy and then there'd be a queue around the block.

As we made our way past the staggering, dancing man, he lunged at me. He gripped my collar and looked desperately into my face.

"They say you can make people forget," he said. "I have to forget my daughter and what they did when they came for her."

"Not me," I said, shaking my head. "Try Jackson."

I pried his hands off me and twisted him away. He collapsed to the floor in a ball of tears and wails, which faded into the background hum as the door swung shut behind us.

A few steps along the sidewalk and she had her arm entwined in mine. I heard the swooping of wings close by. I mentioned it to Laura, but she shrugged. To her, the night was still and quiet.

I'd barely unlocked my office door before she was accelerating through it. She sat down on the edge of my desk, with her hips twisted sideways, and stared at me, biting her lower lip.

"You've done this before."

"I never said I was a nun. In this city, even a lonely girl can find a few minutes of comfort if she's prepared to—"

"I don't want to know."

I woke up to the twittering of the birds hyped up on discarded coffee beans. I rolled over and watched the dance of disguise as L. Mallory, Laura, pulled her dress down over her head. Her hips swiveled and twisted as she peeled the tight number down, and I felt blood coursing through my veins. She made me feel full of life again.

"You leaving?"

"It's six. I've got to get home, shower and change for work."

"Stay for coffee?"

She leaned over and gave me a kiss, one that burned deep into the bonds tying back my grief, and for a moment I was freewheeling above the clouds. Then her lips were gone and I fell to earth with waxen wings dripping away.

Her hand wrapped around the door handle. Her eyes danced around the room as she pulled the door open. "This place feels strange. Eerie." She smiled and slipped away.

CHAPTER 10 ...

I pressed the buzzer on the enormous gate in front of Limbo's. Gayme was a decent 'burb, compared to the Basin anyway, where hardworking people lived who didn't have the imagination or backbone to be criminals.

It had taken me a while to get the day going. I was never a morning person, but it had been getting harder lately. Maybe it was something to do with all the violence.

A voice crackled through the deteriorating speaker.

"Here to see Jorgen."

After what seemed like forever and a day, the gate clicked open and I made my way through a rundown garden, parts of which were tending towards towering jungle needing a machete. The path twisted and turned on itself so many times you'd have to spend an eternity in there trying to get out if you were lost.

Eventually I found a series of cracked marble tiles, corrupted by weeds, that stepped up in front of the building. I followed the tiles through an elongated archway full of portraits with eyes that followed as I passed. A member of staff was putting up a new portrait. The face was half concealed and I didn't recognize it.

The foyer was black marble with gold inlay. A crazy chandelier hung above my head, threatening to fall and pull the roof down with it. Most of the lights were broken. The place had been sweet once, but now it looked like boredom had sunk its teeth in and then fallen asleep.

There was a lady of a certain age standing behind the desk. She was dressed for cocktails, with her hair done up beauty-queen style. A pair of gold-rimmed half-moon glasses were chained to her head. She was scratching a pen across an old ledger. There was a brass desk bell next to her.

I removed my hat and cleared my throat. After she reached the bottom of the page, scribbling what appeared to be a series of meaningless words, she looked up.

"Are you the phone lady?"

"If I answer it."

I flashed my badge.

She lowered her glasses and squinted at the small card. "What's that?"

"My badge."

"Badge for what?"

"Licensed investigator."

She raised her nose in the air and presented a face of disgust. "You need a badge for that? I thought the only requirements were a healthy disrespect for other people's privacy and a conscience that dissolved at the sight of a handful of sweaty candy."

I shrugged. She was allowed her opinion. I was sure her attitude would serve her well when the time came, as it would in a place like Limbo's, when she was looking down the wrong end of a homemade weapon wielded by an out-of-town thug with orders and no understanding.

"Is Jorgen in?"

"We don't have anyone by that name."

I gave her a flat look, the kind she'd get from a squashed lizard. "I spoke to him on the dangler yesterday."

"We've got no one by that name," she repeated through clenched teeth. Her hand moved beneath the desk.

I rolled out a couple of handshakes and placed them on the desk next to each other, all neat and symmetrical. I could see the greed in her eyes. Limbo's was a place where the candy talked, especially if it was sweaty. Considering the heat of the day, I hoped Jorgen was the same.

She lifted her hand and whipped it across the old marble. The handshakes were gone. "Are you sure you're not a cop?"

"I swear."

"You can have fifteen minutes before I send down the heavies. Your time's already started."

I gave her a dark look. "Where is he?"

She nodded vaguely in the direction of the east-wing exit. "Room nineteen sixty-nine. It's the California suite. Thirteen minutes."

The room numbers were random so I had to check every one. I had the feeling that if I backtracked they'd all be different. I put it down to the heat. The minutes ticked by as urgency grew. I found the room. I checked my time. I had barely eight minutes left. I dispensed with formalities and pushed open the door. In the end I didn't need the eight minutes.

The room was all Hollywood, dedicated to love of the self. It was plush and sumptuous, with mirrors on the ceiling and a bottle of champagne on ice by the bed. The ice bucket was frosted and looked like seven kinds of temptation in the midday heat.

Hugh Jorgen sat in the middle of the room in an oversized chair that had ambitions to become a throne. Behind the celebratory figure was a set of iconic relics from every faith, each given its own space in the expansive shelving.

Hugh had a fat cigar in his mouth, the smoke curling up around the solitary light. He looked pleased with himself, grinning like the Cheshire cat. A fat, diamond Rolex encircled his wrist, and his fingers were loaded with gold and jewels. He had sharp clothes, sharp hair, sharp shoes, twinkling eyes, and looked a million bucks.

So it was a surprise to see his throat slit.

"It's not how it looks," Mina cried. She dropped the red,

eighteen-inch-long dagger from her hands, its end slicing through the rich carpet into the floorboards. "Please, believe me."

There was a sudden movement behind me and all went black.

All was dark. I felt the stretch across my shoulders. I opened my eyes. There was a dark, tiled floor several feet below me. My eyes closed.

I felt the stretch across my shoulders. I opened my eyes. There was a dark, tiled floor several feet below me. A couple of blurs, possibly people, shouted. I felt a blow to the side of my head. My eyes closed. All was dark.

All was dark. I felt the stretch across my shoulders. I opened my eyes. Time had loosened its grip on perspective, leaving me in a dizzying state of semi-awareness. The large room wheeled in front of me. The smell of blood filled my nose.

My clothes were gone, a situation made apparent by the cold chill of steel pressing into the back of my body. Ropes had been tied to my wrists and my arms stretched out on either side of me. I was standing on a small metal plate. I could feel small holes with my toes. I stretched and stood up on my toes, and the burning in my chest eased off. My calves started to cramp, then shake under the strain.

The room was deathly quiet. Light, such as there was, crept in via a sliver of a crack under a door to my left. It hinted at things in the room rather than illuminated them. There was something big and solid in the center of the room.

At the edge of hearing I could make out the slight wheezing of someone fighting for breath. It was coming from the right. I stared into the darkness. Eventually the glow of a slight young woman's porcelain skin came into focus. She was hanging from a huge cross. Her wrists were tied and arms outstretched like mine, and her head hung down.

I called out to her, but there was no response. I could see that she didn't have long. My own breathing was a struggle against the pull of the muscles across my chest. My nose started to itch. Involuntarily, my arm tried to reach up. The rope held it in place, but I noted some flex. I worked at the ropes, wrenching and twisting my wrists until they burned.

I could hear the bonds begin to fray, which meant they were against a metal edge sharp enough for cutting. I continued, with my body crying out in agony until white spots wheeled across my eyes and red descended over my vision. The intense burning in my arm pushed through into numbness. My strength was draining, but I could feel the give in the rope.

I squeezed the fingers and thumb of my right hand together and gave an almighty pull. The hand came free. I swung down and forward. Sweat had run down my body, and my feet slipped off the plate. I hung from my left arm, still tethered to the rope that was holding me. The pressure on my shoulder was intense and I struggled to get back up onto the metal plate.

Once my feet were on the plate I was able to work away on the remaining rope. Within minutes I had it loose enough to pull free. I lowered myself into a sitting position and reached down with my legs until my toes touched the floor. As soon as they found the cool stone and I was standing free, relief flushed through me. I shook life back into my limbs. I made my way over to the door, my feet slipping on occasional wet spots. The door was locked.

I felt around the doorway until I found a light switch. It made a heavy clunk as I flicked it. A couple of lights in the far corners slowly brightened. They were at floor height, and sent shadows up the walls. The room was big enough to hold a hundred people. They were lined with pieces of livestock equipment, similar to what the Vinyl had on display. But these were worse.

The Vinyl equipment was about herding.

This equipment was about killing.

CHAPTER 11 ...

There was a small table near the center of the room. It held a plate of food. Someone had been having dinner while watching the show. And in the dead center of the room was a great stone altar—and this time I had no hesitation in using the word. A great winged demon was carved at one end, its claws reaching downward. Stone half-heads perched on each corner, and channels ran from the center of the stone slab to each half-head mouth. The thing looked older than time and more evil by half.

Pools of blood lay around the room. On one side, where I had been, were three large metal crosses. Crucifixes. Two were empty. The third held the skinny blond thing, still fighting for her life. She was naked except for the secrets wrapped around her vulnerability. I looked down. I was the same. Underwear was all I had. And a pair of bloodied and exhausted limbs.

I spotted a sharp knife-like tool on the wall and wrenched it off. I clambered up onto her small metal plate and our bodies squashed together. Her head rolled around, fighting against unconsciousness. I could feel the heat of her body against mine as I reached up and hacked at the ropes. One hand came free and fell over my shoulder. The second was easier and she was soon draped over me.

I hitched her up and she wrapped her legs around my waist. Her face fell against mine and her mouth brushed my ear. She whispered something inaudible. I twisted around, and slowly, with some considerable discomfort, eased us down onto the plate. My legs burned as I lowered her to the floor. When her feet touched the tiles, I let her go and she collapsed. I jumped down next to her.

Shaking her face yielded no response. Her breathing diminished to the shallowest of gasps. Her eyes fluttered. Life was draining away from her.

I ran over to the wall and wrenched off a long pike. I slipped the end into the doorjamb and put all my weight on it. Wood splintered and metal creaked, and the great steel door swung open. It was a good two feet thick.

I ran back to the young lady. Her eyes were closed and her body was still. I checked for a pulse. I checked again. I checked a third time.

I sat back. The urgency was gone. I had another dead, skinny blond thing.

Her arm shot up in the air. Her fingertips glowed white and irradiated an intense cool that penetrated my skin and deep into my bones. Without flexing, she stood up. Her eyes snapped open, and she turned toward me. I scrambled back and fought for purchase on the bloodied floor. Her body, smeared with dark blood, moved toward me.

I'd be a liar if I said I saw her legs move.

I'd even swear she wasn't touching the ground.

I took a couple of steps backward and she continued forward, pushing me toward the corner, past the table. Her hand reached out toward my chest. I could feel the burn, the crushing pain on my heart, as though she was sucking out my life. She squinted, and her face twisted like she was in trouble. I wrapped my hands around her wrist and tried to force her away, but she was as unyielding as cast iron. She pushed forward and I staggered backward, tripping and stumbling.

My hand landed on the table and searched for something to use as a weapon. My fingers wrapped around a butter knife. I grasped it and thrust it toward her. It bent and broke against her shoulder, useless. I flailed for something else. In desperation I grabbed a handful of food and threw it at her, catching her in the face.

I ran for the door. She leaped after me, pushing me to the ground. I lunged forward, but she grabbed my ankle. The burning was intense and shot all the way up my body. I cried out in pain. I grabbed the pike. She was up and leaping for me, her glowing hand fully extended. I raised the pike just as she started to descend, and it punctured her stomach. She collapsed to her knees, eyes blank. Her limp, impaled form hunched over and started to shake. The twitching increased. Her arms snapped forward and grasped the shaft sticking out of her body. She pulled on it until she had ripped it out, and then threw it to the floor.

She grabbed me around the throat and flung me across the room. I landed heavily on the altar. Before I could blink, she was standing above me; feet planted on either side, looking down with those deathly blue eyes. She reached behind her and pulled a red, eighteen-inch dagger from the mouth of the stone demon.

I scrambled to my feet and wrestled with her impossible strength. She braced with the dagger in her hands and we stood locked together, both unyielding. Then I felt the slightest flex in her arm and pushed—hard. When she spun around I smashed her hand into the face of the stone demon. She roared and spun back. I used her momentum and twisted her around, thrusting her back into the statue. I pounded her wrist into the ancient stone repeatedly until she cried out and dropped the dagger.

She leaped off the altar and I lunged for the weapon. I ran for the door. She stood before me, barring the exit. She hissed at me. Her face had lost whatever beauty she once had, and she looked half animal. Her fingers had the form of claws. She leaped.

I brought the dagger around and she scrambled to avoid it.

She was too late. The dagger sliced into her chest. Her eyes went black and her head lolled to the side.

Then there was an explosion, so bright, so loud, that it seemed to emanate from the air itself. In a moment where the entire fabric of space exploded, the room turned into a raging inferno. I dived for the doorway and just managed to roll to one side as the ball of flame roared through the opening and up the stairwell.

I jumped to my feet and ran up the steps, still with the image of the demented girl impaled on the dagger, her eyes a combination of rage and sadness. I burst into another room, a large room, a party room. One I'd seen before.

Welcome to the Vinyl.

CHAPTER 12 ...

The phone rang. Times had changed and I wasn't interested in what it had to say. I sat staring at the door. Was I expecting someone to burst through it? Probably. I had to round up some thoughts and herd them into the what-the-hell-happened rodeo. I wondered how I'd explain it to Watcher without him calling in the men with straitjackets. Maybe this was one I could leave behind. One thing was for sure; I needed some expert advice.

Limbo's was where it had all gone wrong. The lady of a certain age owed me a few answers.

I caught another thirty-five down to the Basin. As soon as I got there I knew something had happened. The entrance was busted open, but not from the outside. I went in through the gate. A clear path had been blown from the front door straight through the overgrown garden. Plants in the line of fire had been charred into a blackened mess, allowing an unbroken view of the sky.

I went in through the front door. The marble had met the same fate as the garden. The smoking remains of the recently hung portrait were in pieces on the floor, but I could still make out parts of the face. Hugh Jorgen. I looked over the other portraits. I pulled out my Leica and took some snaps. It would be interesting to find out who they were.

Phone-lady was dead, her burned body crumpled on the ground, her hands up in front of her, like she was a stone statue. I shuffled through the keys until I found 1969.

The corridors were eerily quiet. I knocked on a couple of doors but there was no response. I made my way through the maze and eventually came to the California room. This time I opened the door cautiously before looking around. The place was empty of life. Hugh's body was lying on the floor. He was still smiling, but he didn't have much to be happy about.

The trash monsters had visited. Most of the room had been turned inside out; whoever it was had definitely been looking for something. Pillows and cushions were slashed; drawers pulled open and upended. Stuff everywhere. What interested me were the artifacts in the shelving unit. They looked untouched, which seemed odd considering the rest of the chaos.

I took a closer look. Each object was offset from a ring of dust, meaning they'd been slid over but left in roughly the same place. That seemed strange. I lifted up an old totem head, a piece of wood created to keep superstitions at bay. It didn't explode. It wasn't particularly heavy. There was a hand, dead as a doornail. It looked creepy. It didn't spring to life and try to strangle me, or answer a telephone.

I guessed there were sixty-odd hundred compartments in the shelving unit, each space occupied except for one, bang in the middle of the structure. The space was long and thin, with a circular clip on one side. I took some more photographs, on the lookout for someone sneaking up silently behind me.

I sat in Hugh's chair, hoping to see what made him look so happy. The sun was creeping across the sky. A high window above the roof was letting in dull light. I squinted as the sunlight fell into my eyes. I saw what he was smiling at. By the door were two framed gold records. His hits before people realized he wasn't any good.

I grabbed one of the frames. It contained his first hit: "You Got Me." I flicked around the edges. The back was a patchwork of yellowing tape that held the frame together. I sat down in Hugh's chair again and ran my eye over the tape. Written on one small piece was the name *S. Cain*, followed by a number. It was the kind of thing you'd miss if you were in a hurry, or not particularly delicate. I carefully peeled off the tape and shoved it into my pocket.

I picked up the second frame and started to examine it. On the edge of my hearing I picked up a distant crack. I ran over to the door and glanced out. Shadows fell over the entrance to the corridor. I bolted out of the room and tried the opposite door. The handle turned under my grip and I slid into the room. It was dark. I held the door open a sliver and peered out. The angle was bad. All I could hear were heavy steps trying to sound quiet. Whoever it was stopped in front of Hugh's door and looked around before pushing into the room. I made sure I didn't gasp. The solid, tall body with the long black hair was unmistakable.

Levi.

I closed the door and waited. In the darkness of the room my senses picked up. What they picked up was a particular, familiar scent. I heard a smashing of glass from the other room, like a frame containing a gold record being busted open. I glanced down at the one in my hands. It had suddenly become a lot more interesting.

The scent hit me again. Its familiarity gnawed away at me. I put the frame down on the floor and walked further into the room. I could see the outline of a bed in the center. I fumbled around it until I found a side table. I turned on the lamp and the room was filled with a dull golden glow. I stood back and took in the scene.

The bedsheets were tucked in tightly; the bed looked neat, shipshape and ready for action. The rope coiled in the center of the bed was a little unexpected, but not unheard of in a cheap or discerning hotel. The end had been cut and burned for incarceration rather than for freedom. But was the person tied up here, or released here? Why leave the rope neatly coiled?

The walls caught my attention. I stepped back and took in the spectacle. Blood had been sprayed in large letters in a foreign language over each wall. I couldn't read the words, but I could guess what they meant.

Still that familiar scent lingered in the air. I followed it to the source. My nose ended up hovering over the bed. I picked up the pillow. The scent was strong and reminded me of Desire. Something fell out of the pillowcase and bounced on the taut sheets. A broken-heart hairpin.

Mina.

The sound of a door being expertly and silently opened clicked delicately through the still air. I grabbed the hairpin and went back to the door, picking up the frame. I cracked the door and saw Levi look around before stepping out and heading down the corridor. His face was full of fury. Perhaps he didn't find what he was looking for. Perhaps because it was in my hands. One of two objects.

I eased open the door and crept down the corridor after the big man. He was easy to follow with his great stomping feet crushing all sense of discretion into dust. He made his way back to the Terrace, but went west rather than toward the Vinyl. I tracked him by hanging off the back of his thirty-five. He was a guy who never looked back.

When he got out at his stop, I cruised onto the next one and made my way back. I slipped behind a building across the street. Levi was engaged in a heated exchange with another large man. I'd describe the stranger as a bear; he was covered in hair and had a set of arms that could crush small vehicles. From my observation point it was easy to see they weren't friends. They weren't even enemies; the anger and spit ran way deeper.

Levi poked bear-man in the chest.

Bear-man let out a shout that could be heard all the way to the bay: *"Betrayer!"* He took a swing at Levi, who ducked out of the way easily.

Levi pushed Bear-man, who stumbled backward. Levi turned and ran. Bear-man recovered and put in a couple of long strides before giving up. He let out another shout. I spotted a thirty-five approaching and dashed over to the bus stop. Bear-man strode back. He slowed as he passed me, giving the gold record and me a strange look, but he didn't stop and his long, loping strides took him down the terrace.

I jumped on the thirty-five. Hanging off the back, I could see Levi ahead. He slowed, looked around and ducked into a small alleyway. As the bus slowed, I jumped off and ran back to the alleyway. Eden Lane. It was as empty as a Basin hooker's mind. I wandered down to the end. Brick walls ran down both sides and ended with another brick wall. No doors. No windows. No exits other than the way in. I kicked various points, but nothing happened other than my toe protesting.

I took the gold record and went back to my office.

I was pulling apart the frame when there was a knock on the door. I slid the frame behind my chair.

"Yeah?"

The door creaked open and Laura looked in. I waved.

"You up to much? I was passing and thought I'd see if you wanted to go out."

I looked hesitantly around the room.

"You in the middle of something?" she said.

"Yeah. An investigation."

"Oh." The disappointment in her voice was solid, and her face fell.

I couldn't let her be a warren for the sad bunnies. "How about dinner, tonight?"

"Okay." She brightened, which made me feel better. "My choice?"

I nodded.

"I'll do some paperwork down at the tank until then."

"Is your friend not here?"

"Something happened. She got ill or something, and she can't come. My dad's friend said he'd say more when he got down here, but he was all weird and refused to talk about it."

She disappeared, probably to plan some difficult night out that involved too much dancing and not enough drinking. It was a troubling thought, which I had to put out of my mind.

The strange woman in the Vinyl was banging around inside my head. I wanted to know if I was crazy or if I was real crazy. I flipped open the pages and searched for possible assistance. Among all the shysters and con artists, it was hard to find an honest man. I grabbed a couple of names from the more interesting ads and stepped out into the afternoon.

I was worried that my place was becoming too hot. I went by the yellowbox, where I'd hired a locker to secret the few things in my life that held any kind of value to someone other than myself, and dropped off the gold record. It would be safer than concealing it in the special flap in the floor.

CHAPTER 13 ...

The first two ended up being less substantial than a puff of opium through a broken hookah, nothing but unwashed men with excessive beards and weird eyes, and a misplaced belief that they were something more than ten-a-decimal wannabes. The third didn't even have a glitzy sign. The building only had a small silver plate screwed into the wall. The letters had been scribbled over by a demented person with a crayon.

I pushed my way in, accompanied by the tinkling of a small bell above the door, and was immediately struck by the aura of the place. There was no showbiz here. It was a plain dark room with nothing but a couple of chairs and a small table up against the wall. There was a strong scent of garlic, like someone was cooking up a storm. I spotted several cloves on a small shelf above the table.

"Is this a shop?"

"That would imply I have something to sell," came the voice. It was hollow, full of defeat.

"What do you do?"

"I protect myself, and educate those of an inquisitive mind."

I looked around the small room. It seemed devoid of any

educational equipment. As my eyes became accustomed to the light, I began to recognize the outlines of various religious artifacts, painted black, hung against the wall. It reminded me, disconcertingly, of Hugh Jorgen's California room.

"What has glowing fingers?" I asked as my eyes drifted around the room.

"Are you talking about the skinny blond women?"

"Yeah."

"God, I hate them."

A young lady stepped out of the shadows. She looked normal, unlike the other people, and was dressed in the "city" outfits all the uptown ladies were wearing—a white shirt, short black skirt, and a long set of white socks pulled up to her knees. Her long, dark hair was pulled back into a squirrel.

"They're vampires," she said.

I didn't say anything, but my expression conveyed it all.

"No, really. I don't know where this whole myth of sinking fangs into the neck of virgins comes from, but these creatures, they turn into these large winged beasts and they suck the life force out of their victims—young girls." She reached forward, her eyes going wide and her fingers questing out.

I'd seen that before. I took a step back.

She focused on her hand, seemed to realize how it looked and lowered it.

My mind flicked back to the food at the Vinyl, the strong herb aroma, and the effect it had had on the skinny blond thing. "What's with the garlic myth?"

She took a clove down off the shelf. "It's the scent. Animals rely heavily on scent. If you wave garlic under the nose of a dog, the dog will shy away. And it fights mutated antibodies in blood, their blood." She rotated it in her hand, mesmerized by it. "It's like it was created to hurt them. A vampire hand grenade."

"How do you know this?"

In one swift movement she ripped open her top, which was unexpected, and pointed to the five burn marks on her chest.

"One was sucking the life from me when a dog came along and scared her away."

"What kind?"

"A big one."

"Why you?"

She hesitated, standing there with her top hanging open and her breasts visible. "I ..." She drew the sides of the shirt around her front. "I met the right criteria."

"Is that all?"

She nodded but I knew she was hiding something.

"Why are they appearing?"

"I don't know," she said. "They've been around forever, but only rarely are they spotted. Maybe something important is coming."

"Something like the change?"

She hesitated. "What do you know about that?"

"You tell me."

A moment bounced around the room as she stared at me quietly. "What do you know about people?"

I gave her a quizzical.

She cocked her head to the side. "Do you know where we come from?"

"Storks?"

A manic energy entered her voice and she started waving her hands around frantically. Her eyes grew wide. "What if what they've told us has all been a lie? What if there'd been no evolution, only mutation? Those creatures consider themselves the next step. We're like monkeys to them. They're going to wipe us out." She stopped. "That's the change."

"You're crazy." I shook my head and turned to leave.

"I've seen things. When they were sucking the life out of me, I had visions. I know what they're doing." Her eyes were wide with desperation. She lunged at me, grabbing my jacket lapels and dragging me closer. "They're vermin, draining the life from people, spreading disease. They're vicious and relentless. Nothing stops them once they've targeted you. *Nothing*. Until you're dead."

"What's your name?"

She hesitated, her eyes half full of tears and doubt. She drifted off into a recollection that gave her a small smile. "Angelina," she replied.

"Angelina, am I a target?"

"They don't target men." She looked at me uncertainly. "Do those little skinny blond things come to you offering dreams and promises?"

"Not really."

"Once they've targeted you, they won't stop until one of you is dead. And they don't die. You have to wrap yourself up in all this"—she indicated the superstitious artifacts around her dark, pokey room—"and take it one day at a time."

"Why only women?"

"To stop us breeding. They want to replace us. Wipe us out."

I reflected on the information. It was utterly fantastical and completely unbelievable. This woman seemed to be as whacky as the other fraudulent shysters. I nodded to her and moved toward the door.

"You can't leave me like this. They'll come for me. Every day for the last year has been torture. I've seen the pain, the madness that sits inside the head, like a brain half rotted away. They're animals. I need to be ... reclassified. I need my flowers potted," she said, struggling for a metaphor.

All she had to do was shut her mouth for five minutes and any eligible partner would be throwing himself at her. That had also worked for Jorgen.

"It's not me you want," I said, as I turned to leave.

There was the sound of a hammer being pulled back and a bullet dropping into a chamber. I raised my hands and sighed.

"Guess again."

CHAPTER 14 ...

Angelina was all right. A little weird, I'll grant you. And she sure gave herself permission to release. I thought about her desire to forget her past, which included me.

When I left her little shop of horrors, at gunpoint, she had let her dark hair down and she looked relaxed, as though a great weight or curse had been lifted. She had collapsed back into her great gothic throne, her top still hanging open and her skirt up around her waist like some delinquent schoolgirl. I hoped she would find happiness. Preferably not at gunpoint.

I was getting a little annoyed at being considered a machine. Although it had its upside, I was beginning to chafe, and I needed to do some serious walking.

Eden Lane was a mystery. How does a guy the size of cow disappear into thin air? I considered the options and figured there was something I'd missed. I jumped off a thirty-five when it shunted into Gayme, and I trailed down the drag until I found the insidious street. It took several attempts, the lane being deceptively dull.

I crawled over every inch of that lane, taking a good couple of hours to do it. It was nothing but a cleanly swept alley with nothing but bricks and mortar. As the sun started to diminish into late afternoon, I gave up. I was sitting at the stop, waiting for a thirty-five, staring at the vacant little lane, when Levi stroke out.

I blinked in disbelief. What was going on? There was no way he could have come out of the lane unless he'd descended from the sky, probably on wings of fire. He hitched his size tens down the street and I took off after him. He cut through the city park out toward the Hill. He strode with purpose, never looking back, hair flowing and shirt flapping.

Behind the Hill was the old chameleon church, the Grand Hilltop, sitting behind an old city graveyard, having been desacralized decades ago but left quiet since. Dark windows punctuated the worn stonework that towered into the sky in true gothic-style architecture. I caught a glimpse of him disappearing in through the front doors after throwing a casual glance over his shoulder. I waited, hidden behind a stone angel, to see if he'd stay or not.

Ten minutes came and went. I heard the scuffing of feet and dived for cover. Someone else was coming up the ancient path. He looked a lot like Levi, but younger and not as big. Mini-Levi approached the door, also looking back over his shoulder, and rapped a quick tattoo on the old oak. A few moments later the doors opened and Levi stuck his head out before motioning for the guy to enter. The doors closed. I could hear voices.

The door opened again. Levi walked up the path, with various items of clothing flapping glamorously in the breeze, and disappeared into the city park.

The sun started to descend behind the church, casting its shadow over the graveyard. I extracted myself from behind the angel and approached the great doors. Everything seemed quiet. I placed my hands against the old wood. It felt slightly warm. I pushed and the door creaked open. I stepped inside. It was difficult to see in the dim light, but the interior had clearly been trashed.

The pews had been destroyed and lay smashed and toppled. A couple of side windows, formerly stained glass, were smashed out, with the shards lying around on the floor. They crunched underfoot. The place was class-A creepy. Musky smells, dusty eddies, desolation, hardly enough light to see by.

Wings erupted from beneath me. They swirled and flapped around, battering me, then were gone. There was an aggressive squawk. Just a bunch of pigeons. I sighed with relief. Then there was a gentle sob. Distant and muffled. I moved toward the rear of the church. The old masonry crunched under my feet.

As my eyes accustomed to the low light, I could make out the details of the place. The floor was covered with thick dust, marking the footsteps of previous visitations. My eyes followed what looked like the most recent, and drifted up onto the walls. The place hadn't been desacralized; it had been polarized.

Effigies and symbols of adulation had been erected to the darkness. Disturbing pictures of people in unnatural situations adorned the walls in a macabre slideshow of disfigured anguish, with one constant theme: blood. People bleeding it, drinking it, bathing in it. The images added more and more deviations, with a variety of instruments and animals, culminating in a horrific spectacle placed above the altar. Square in the center of the image were two winged people, beautiful beyond compare, surrounded by winged animals, just like the ones I had seen in the tank.

Behind the picture was a small staircase, which disappeared into the rear tower of the church. The sound of gentle crying was drifting down from the spire at the top of the tower. Mini-Levi had disappeared, leaving the church in silence except for my footfalls and the weeping. There was only one set of prints leading to the steps.

The steps, bearing worn hollows from a million footsteps over thousands of years, wound tightly around a center stone column, which was also worn smooth by time and a multitude of hands. There were no windows in the walls, making the walk darker and more dangerous the higher I got. A breeze gusted down, blowing a cloud of dust into my eyes. I wiped them, momentarily losing my balance as a wave of melancholia swept over me. The tunnel effect of the tower seemed to amplify my senses. My hearing picked up every little groan and cry coming from above. My eyes craved light and sought the faintest of rays illuminating the edge of the stairs. I made it to the top of the tower, and was now in total darkness.

There was a solid door barring the way. I ran my hand over it. It felt like metal. I pushed it. It was locked tight. I felt around the edges. There was nothing. The metal door sat solidly in a metal frame that felt like it was cut sharply into the stone. I placed my ear to the door. I could hear the weeping on the other side. I ran my hands over the cold metal again, slower. I could feel a slight, raised circle on the right side of the door. As my left hand swept over the metal, my fingertips made out a second circle.

I stepped back. I placed the fingertips of both hands in the centers of the circles. There was the faintest of clicks, more a detection of the low frequency of something moving rather than the actual sound of it. The door swung inward silently. Light exploded from the room beyond. The sun shone directly into my eyes, forcing me to shield them with my hand. I felt like it was burning my skin away.

I stepped into the small round room.

Her hands were tied in front of her around a post. She was gagged and on her knees. Behind her was a large stone altar, just like the one in the Vinyl, with its stone demon and four stone heads at each corner. This altar had a twelve-inch spike sticking up from the center.

Her head was lowered, but she sensed someone was there and looked up. She tried to rise and fell back, sobbing, her hair falling forward to cover her face. I didn't need to see any more to know who it was.

Mina.

(HAPTER 15 ...

I ran over and shook her. She cowered, turning in on herself, afraid of facing her assumed assailant. I knelt down and gently held her face. She looked up slowly. Her eyes were full of fear. Tears streaked her face, which was smeared with dirt. Her arms were bruised. Her dress was torn, showing glimpses of her divine body.

Her eyes brightened, then went wide. In their reflection I caught Mini-Levi looming behind me like a cheap wrestler, all show no curtains. I spun around. The stone statue of a demon wasn't a stone statue. Or a demon.

I dodged to the side, catching his arm and twisting him onto the floor. He landed with a heavy thump, but rolled easily onto his side and back onto his feet. He let out a strange hissing sound and leaped back up onto the altar. I was impressed. It was a four-foot vertical jump, and he did it without effort.

He pulled an eighteen-inch-long red dagger from within the altar. We all looked at it, with various levels of emotion. Mina looked terrified. Mini-Levi looked confident. I looked fed up. I was tired of being the only one without one.

He leapt onto the floor, tucked into a roll, and jumped up,

ready for combat. It was a bit showy for my liking. He swung it at me, clumsily. I ducked out of the way. A couple of poorly aimed stabs later and I grabbed him by the hand. He seemed taller now than when he'd walked in. But he wasn't tall enough. I wrenched his arm around behind him, running him forward toward the spike in the center of the altar. He dropped the dagger and it bounced away. I kicked his legs aside and he collapsed, banging his head on the stone.

I picked up the dazed fool and gave him a couple of sharp slaps across the face. His eyes rolled as he fought for consciousness. I held him up by the collar. He sagged to his knees, blood trickling from his nose. I raised my fist to give him the countdown. There was a soft cry from Mina. I looked over. There was a twist within my grip. I looked back to Mini-Levi.

He leaped up, but I used the momentum to lift him high over my shoulders and slam him down onto the altar spike. It drove up through his body, leaving him dead. Limbs hung over the stone edges, and blank eyes stared at me. I felt momentarily sorry for the young guy. But then I remembered that he'd been trying to kill me.

I picked up the dagger and sliced through Mina's bonds. The dagger felt hot under my touch and it grew hotter. I threw it aside; it just added to the overall weirdness of the place.

She was lighter than a delicate soufflé. I lifted her easily and cradled her in my arms.

"Who is that?" I indicated the fallen man. Blood had pooled underneath him, spreading out from his shoulders toward the demented stone heads. They looked like wings of blood.

"It *was* Phoenix. We need to go before he …"

I looked back at Phoenix as we left the room. It didn't look to me like he'd be doing any "before he" ever again.

The metal door slammed shut, leaving us in near perfect darkness. I waited for a moment for my eyes to adjust to the blackness.

"Take me to your place," she whispered.

"It ain't safe."

"He can't find us there."

"You did."

I descended slowly, feeling for each step as I went. She lifted her hand and gently stroked it down my face. I sensed rather than saw her eyes glowing in the dark.

"You don't know how long it took me to find you," she said.

The sun had set when we left the church and early night crept in like vengeful molasses. I kept to the backstreets until I could grab a dimbox. The discreet ones ran off the main drag. It was going to cost, but privacy did these days. I bundled Mina in and gave the cab driver, in his crisp, charcoal uniform with yellow banding, a sorry excuse about her drinking too much and a husband on the warpath. He gave me an understanding nod and hightailed it to my office. I asked him to stop around the corner and tipped him on the courageous side.

I carried her up to my office and laid her down on the stretcher. Thankfully there was no sign of the rent monster.

Mina was a complete mess. I unzipped her dress, peeled her out of it and threw it in the machine. I tried to not look at her secrets, but damn she was seductive. And she had taste so expensive and classy her secrets were nearly art. I placed a blanket over her and she stirred briefly, wrapping herself into it.

Time ticked by, and she drifted in and out of some haunting dream. In the deepest sleep she started to perspire heavily. I rinsed an old cloth under the kitchenette tap and wiped the grime off her face, and then folded it across her forehead until the disturbance had passed. She opened her eyes when I removed the cloth.

I offered her a glass of water and she drank from it greedily. She was living without an ocean, running hot and cold, currents going nowhere. Then her eyes focused and she made all the sense in the world. I swept her hair back from her face and looked into deep blue eyes as wide as the Pacific.

"Are you all right?" I said.

"You're a man, and I'm a woman. Honey, you're never supposed to understand." She looked down. "You seem to have relieved me of my clothing. Well, some of it."

"It's in the machine." I hiked my thumb over my shoulder. The sound of the ancient Bendix echoed through the paper-thin wall.

"At least you left me something," she said, glancing down at her underwear. "There's nothing like the lure of anticipation to get people hot and bothered."

"Start talking."

"Are you sure there isn't some other use I could put my mouth to?" She raised her hand and stroked my knee.

Some things never changed. Her desperation for attention was so deeply ingrained it was never far from accentuation.

"Start with Levi."

She sat back and sighed. "He's a mob boss. Second from the top."

"Who's the top?"

"I don't know. They're all hidden. You don't know they exist until they decide to let you meet them. You know what these underworld figures are like."

"No, I don't. Maybe you can fill in the details."

"They've got something going down where there's going to be a challenge between some of the lower heads. Whoever's left can challenge for the top job. Then they get to run the city."

"Why are we safe here?"

"In your office? Well, honey, as delectable as you are, you have no idea about this new-fangled thing called advertising. And in a big city, if you don't want to be found you got a million places to hide, above or below ground."

"We should lie low."

"I thought you'd never ask, but taking off my clothes was a pretty good hint. How low do you want to go?"

I closed my eyes and fortified myself. "Do we need protection?" It was too late; I'd spoken without fully analyzing the consequence and potential of the sentence.

"Get your gun out, big boy. I'd like to see you pump out a few rounds."

"Stop it."

She let out a sigh and for the first time—while fully awake—looked vulnerable. She clasped her hands on top of the sheet. "I'm sorry. I thought you liked that kind of thing. I thought you were a tough guy."

It was almost a question. But I knew that if she was asking it, there was something she was missing, longing for. Maybe she was looking for a tough guy for protection so she could stop pretending.

"Maybe once, but not anymore."

"No one ever takes notice unless you chase them down. Especially the good ones."

She sighed again and gave me a half-smile while reaching out for my hand. I took it in mine, my two hands wrapping around her delicate hand completely.

"How did you get involved?" I asked her.

"You'd be amazed how easy it was. They offered so much, and it was all very exciting. In the beginning there was so much fun in being bad. Then it was a slippery slope straight down. I soon got tired of it and wanted to turn it around. But you can only go one way, unless you deal or betray your way out."

"Who are you going out with?"

She let out an incredulous laugh, covering her mouth with her hand. "No one. I wouldn't have shaken the tree with you if there'd been someone else. Who said I was going out with anyone?"

"Levi."

"He said that?" She laughed lightly. "I'm amazed you got him to talk. He's a tough guy."

"Yeah." I nodded at the recollection of his right hook.

"I'm a free robin, sitting on a branch until I get bored." She made a small flapping motion as though flying toward the window. She watched her own hand, mesmerized by it, then quietly folded it on her stomach. She looked down for a moment.

"I'd been trying to get out for ages," she said. "I met Hugh, and he seemed like someone with the confidence to get me out. It never occurred to me that he was a plant."

"What?"

"They were trying to trap me, prove that I wanted to sell them out. I wasn't. But then Hugh stole something of significance to Levi and his thugs, and they went all out to get him."

"Why are you so important?"

And that little hesitation let me know there was something she was hiding. She tried to mask it with her widest, most sinful smile.

"Honey, look at me. How can I not be the most important thing in your life?"

She was a whole bagful of mental delights that could melt your resolve out your ears, and she played harder, quicker and more deviously than a star throwback in the championship league. But she was locking something away with such strength that even my Remington picklock wouldn't have worked on her. Although I was sure she'd want me to try.

I sat back and scratched my chin. I let a few moments tick by, seeing if she'd get uncomfortable. Then I realized this foxy lady could probably lie on a bed of nails and think it was a princess's mattress, whether someone had pea-ed on it or not.

"What happened at 1969?" I said.

"I found out and felt bad for him. I wanted to warn him, but he'd taken off. I had no idea where he'd gone. I found you, but Levi was also looking and he has fingers everywhere. Levi was out when the messenger came with the news that Hugh was at Limbo's. I went there straightaway, but Levi was only a few minutes behind. He found us together and killed the poor guy. One swift motion, straight across the throat. I jumped on Levi and grabbed the knife. He threw me to the floor, but I managed to twist that dagger out of his hands. Then you opened the door."

She paused. A look of concern flashed in those baby-blue cheaters. "I'm sorry."

"What did Hugh say?"

"You know him. You can guess. He was full of his own self-importance, just like the rest of them. He said he had something that would defeat them all. I asked what it was. He said he'd put it somewhere safe, as protection."

"What was he hiding?"

She sighed. "Don't we all have something to hide? Except at this moment there's not a whole lot I'm hiding under this sheet. See?"

She went to whip up the sheet, but I put my hand on it and pushed it down.

"You're pale. You look tired." I got up and made my way to the door.

"Please don't leave. I'll make it worth your while ..." She reached out to me. Her smoky eyes filled in the rest of the sentence—all the prose required to fill the top five erotic bestsellers.

"We need supplies."

"You mean food?" Her eyes lit up. "I haven't eaten in days."

"Sure." I gave her a smile and flipped opened the door. A woman was standing there poised to knock.

CHAPTER 16 ...

Laura gasped in surprise. The light from the desk lamp shone out into the corridor, casting her seductive silhouette onto the opposite wall.

"Van! How did you know I was here?"

She was dolled up as high as a skyscraper, looking like she'd stolen all the credits from the city bank. The soft light made her glow. Her features were flawless, highlighted by her elegance.

"Are you going to invite me in?" she said, after an embarrassing amount of time had passed without me giving any sign of being conscious, or even alive. "Or how about breathing or blinking?"

The reality of the location and the occupant behind me socked me in the face.

"What's the matter?" Laura asked.

Mina coughed.

Laura's face morphed into excitement. "Have you got a friend here? I'd like to meet one of your friends."

She pushed past me as I struggled for an explanation. The first thing she saw was Mina lying on the stretcher, showing way too much skin, and a hint of the high-end secrets Laura could only dream of on standard police salary.

"Who is she?" they both said at the same time.

"She's a client," I responded. "And a friend." I let them decide which one was which.

"A client?" Mina said. "I'd better be more than that."

"She's here, lying low," I said.

Mina let out a low, seductive laugh.

"That's not helping," I said.

"She's in your bed," Laura said. "And she's not wearing any clothes."

"It's not how it appears."

"You said you'd take me to dinner." Laura stood with her hands on her hips. "I was told you were a man of your word."

"You promised me food," Mina said.

Laura turned to leave. I grabbed her and pleaded with her not to go.

"Please," I said.

She hesitated at the door. The look she was giving me was none too pleasant.

"Honey, we've got to eat something," Mina said, "and you've got nothing here except cheap booze and no space."

"Fine," I said. "We all go."

"All of us," Laura said. "To dinner?"

"I'm injured and physical activity is too taxing for me," Mina said.

I looked at her. "What about a few minutes ago?"

She had the decency to look flustered.

"A few minutes ago what?" Laura said.

"It's not important." I looked at both of them.

"What do you mean it's not important?" Mina said. "Hey, where are you going, sunshine?"

"To get your clothes."

I left them together in the room, hoping at least one would be gone by the time I returned. No such luck. Mina was strutting around in her secrets, showing no embarrassment. I ironed Mina's dress while Laura stood awkwardly, having trouble deciding where to look. In the end she just stared out the window. I saw her watching Mina's reflection, which probably didn't help.

Once Mina was suitably clothed, and Laura's ears were glowing pink, we all went out into the moderately cooler night air.

"Are you sure?" I said.

The door swung in on Jimmy's. It was on the down side of the Turnstile, but it was good enough in its own way—clean and stripped back to the essential elements of service, but food was food.

"No, we didn't hear anything. Stop asking," Laura said. She glanced inside. "Are you sure this is the right place?"

"You and flapping birds," Mina said. "It's a city. There are no great flapping birds." She looked around the cafe with a look of distaste. "Are places like this allowed to sell food? Jeez, Van, you really know how to spoil a lady. I actually feel sorry for Laura."

"I don't need your pity," Laura said.

"Looking at you, you're going to need someone's pity to get attention."

"Stop it." I glared at both of them before selecting a table.

"There's no bar," Mina said. "How am I meant to enjoy myself?"

"I'm sure you'll find a way," Laura said. "Maybe a pole instead."

"Have you got something against fun?"

"No. In fact, I'm going to make the best of the situation. I'll buy the first round of drinks. I'm assuming you'll drink anything. Van, what would you like?"

Mina looked shocked. "You buy your own drinks?"

"Don't you?"

"I've never paid for one yet."

"That says more about you than you realize."

The two women sat down across from each other. Laura glared. Mina looked indifferent. The silence was electric—dark and dangerous. I sat in the middle, looking from one to the other, my spirits dejected. To distract myself I reflected on Angelina's crazy ramblings, and how they could possibly tie into the bizarre events

I'd seen recently. Maybe I'd been sucking too hard on the stupid juice.

Laura reached over and placed her hand on mine. "What's the trouble? You look like something's on your mind."

I looked into her eyes. "Do you believe in the paranormal? Ghosts, spirits, ghouls, elves … vampires?"

She laughed. Then she saw my expression. "No. Although strictly speaking, an elf is mythical rather than paranormal. But you can't believe in them."

Mina pitched in. "You have to believe in something." She looked at me. "Right, honey?"

"People are always saying they see ghosts," Laura said. "And there's always stuff we don't understand. So if there are ghosts, why not vampires? They say belief is good for children's imaginations."

"It's not a belief," I said. "It's facts."

"Don't make fun of him," Mina said.

"He's not serious," Laura replied. "His head's probably out of shape after the excitement of the day."

"At least it's got a shape."

Laura narrowed her eyes at Mina. "What are you implying?"

I leaned forward and put my head in my hands.

Mina squared her shoulders and brought out her big guns. She gave me a dismissive glance. "You've got no shape—"

"Calm down," I said calmly. It didn't work.

Mina leaned forward and glared at Laura. "Are you sure you're a girl?"

"It's better than being fa—"

"That's it!" I got up and made my way over to the restrooms. They both watched me go.

"What were you going to call me?" I heard Mina hiss at Laura.

"Well—"

That was all I heard as the door mercifully closed behind me, shutting out the aggravation. The room was cool and starkly white. Its cleanliness, simplicity and peace provided an oasis in the unpredictable maelstrom of warring women. I took a couple of deep breaths to calm my nerves. The bright strip lighting reflected off the tiles, bouncing around me in my contemplative solitude. There were a couple of cubicles, matching sinks, and a small window on the other side of the room that opened onto a quiet and dark street. A fine mesh covered the glass. I wondered if it was to keep people in or out.

I ran the taps, enjoying the sound of the babbling stream. My hands were shaking and my nerves were on edge. I splashed the water over my face, taking a moment to stabilize my thoughts. The cool water ran down from my eyes. I looked in the mirror.

Levi was standing behind me in the reflection.

I blinked my eyes and turned around. There was nothing there. I shook my head. The small room was empty, the pristine tiles still reflecting bright light into an empty room.

I checked the cubicles; each was empty and partly disgusting. You'd think humans would have got the hang of shooting straight by now. The lights above flickered. I closed the door of the last cubicle after giving it a flush, and sighed. I was afraid my mind was beginning to slip, seriously. I leaned back against the wall.

Levi was standing in front of me.

The lights went out.

A voice danced in the darkness. "Where is it?"

CHAPTER 17 ...

The first punch came from the left, predictably. I managed to avoid the bulk of it, but it still knocked me reeling across the small room into the wall, cracking the tiles. Shards fell to the floor.

"Where's the rood?" The voice bounced around me, like it was coming from the walls themselves.

He pulled me back across the room and smashed me into the mirror. It shattered and crashed down into the sink. Light leaking in under the door and from the streetlight outside reflected off the broken glass, highlighting a large triangular shard. I grabbed it and swung my arm around in a wide arc. The end of the glass speared into Levi's shoulder.

He remained silent as he pulled it out and threw it to the floor. I could see the anger in his face. He threw a bunch of hamfisted blows in wide from each side, all easy to block. A blow came in from the right and I caught it under my arm. I brought in a roundhouse swing, landing it on his jaw. I unleashed a couple more, driving him to his knees.

He twisted free and gave me a strange look. Almost like fear. The room felt real small in that moment, or I felt real big in it, like the transcontinental smashing into the thirty-five.

I picked him up by the collar and threw him into a cubicle. Porcelain shattered and water sprayed everywhere, rushing over the floor. I glared at him. In the low light he seemed to glow; it was child's play to pick him out. I wrenched him up off the floor and sent him sprawling across the room, crashing into the far wall. His head cracked against the tiles, leaving a crater in the wall. He slumped to the floor.

The room was quiet. The lights came on. The place was empty. I sagged against the wall. The restroom was a mess, and Levi was gone.

I staggered out. Another guy entering gave me a stunned look. "Give it ten," I told him.

I limped over to the table. Laura was laughing and Mina was talking, waving her hands around. The table had a large collection of small, empty glasses huddled in the center, some with the remnants of thick, sweet spirits of varying colors. Both women's eyes held a distant disconnect.

"What happened to you?" Mina said. "Do you need more fiber in your diet?"

They looked at each other with a knowing look and laughed in unison. Or was it a giggle? Whichever, it seemed inappropriate.

"This place isn't my scene. Take me to the Stylus," Mina said.

"I know a great couple of places to go on the way over there," Laura said. "Small, low key, great bands."

I sighed. It was going to be a long night.

It was close to two-thirty. The two women, looking the worse for wear, staggered out into the street, singing loudly. They tottered along the sidewalk arm in arm. I longed for the Stylus. At least there'd be someone there I could talk to, and who would listen. I herded them away from the roadside, keeping them from catapulting themselves into the traffic.

I was trying to keep Laura from climbing a bus stop, and holding Mina up so she didn't collapse with laughter, and I didn't hear the footsteps. Some snatcher ran up and before I could grab him he had knocked Mina into the trashcans. Laura was still giggling as she slid down the pole, but Mina was quiet.

I ran over. She was staring up at me, holding her stomach. She raised her hands; they were covered in blood. A knife wound sliced across her stomach, and it looked deep.

"We have to get her to a hospital," Laura cried when she saw the wound.

"No," Mina gasped.

"Laura's right," I told her. "You have to go to the hospital."

She shook her head. "They'll find me."

Laura knelt down beside Mina and examined the cut. "Can we take her to your place?"

"I don't have medical supplies," I said.

Laura thought for a moment. "I've got first-aid supplies at home from a work course. They're pretty basic but they're better than nothing."

Mina raised her hand and placed it against Laura's face. "You're a good girl, honey. It's been a pleasure to meet you." She closed her eyes and drifted off into unconsciousness.

"This is becoming a habit," I said, lifting her up and cradling her in my arms. She felt lighter than before, like a ghost hanging onto its body.

We made our way back to Laura's place. The haunting image of the assailant was lodged in my mind. I'd swear to a preacher that it was Phoenix.

I followed Laura into a small room with a single bed covered in her clothes. I was surprised. I thought she would be neater. She wiped her arms over the bed, knocking the clothes to the floor.

"I tried on several outfits before I came out," she said sheepishly.

She ran out to get the first-aid kit, leaving me alone with Mina for a few moments. In her state of unconsciousness, she looked angelic. Golden curls rolled around her slender face. Her skin was perfection; there wasn't one blemish. Her features were calm.

Laura reappeared with an armful of medical supplies. She cut through the silky material of Mina's dress and peeled back the folds to reveal the cut. She soaked up the trickling blood with cotton balls. Once the area was wiped clean, we could see it was a fairly light cut and not fatal, but it was still deep enough to cause concern.

I left Laura to it and went out into the living room. The sight of Mina's injury had shocked me, more than it should have. My hands were shaking and my head was spinning.

Laura had a nice place. She lived up above Fernando Drive, which edged along the Westlands scarp between the valleys before trailing down into the Basin. The apartment was worth a whole load of candy, but then Daddy Mallory was rich and knew the right people in the right places to get this zip code for a steal. Maybe it wasn't even legal.

Laura had the sleek, squared-off furniture that was all the rage, sliding over the concrete and marble flooring. Designed by some overpriced Italian designer, it was slick, elegant and refined.

I looked out the window. The Basin lights, always in a state of being browned out and dimmed by the high level of diesel pollution, flickered occasionally as politicians demanded more electricity to keep their chardonnay chilled. You could see their constitutional collective trying to lie low behind the Hill. You could see all of the rich diversity of life from here. It was like a secluded hiding spot where you could spy on the depravity of humanity.

Right in the middle of it all, high on the hill, was the Grand Hilltop church, now firmly etched in my memory.

I went out onto the deck overlooking the city to get some air. I took in a couple of lungsful of the clean air rushing in from the desert. The war had taken its toll on outlying areas, forcing us all into this dustbowl of diesel particles and malcontent ideology built around the worst of human distraction.

There were still the occasional scavengers out on the plains, scraping together a subsistence living until the rogue mechwarrior monsters designed by the war geniuses came and ripped them apart. But the air was clean and people could grow fresh food in the small allotment of time life dealt out to them, usually off the bottom of the deck. This was their choice. The uncertainty of daily existence was apparently better than living here in the city. No one made them go, and no one made us stay in this cesspit. From this height I could see the flares from the occasional mechwarrior as it toasted some trapped folk. What had we done to our world? What were we doing to ourselves? My hands were still shaking.

I turned away from the city and went back in to see how Laura was getting on. She had the wound cleaned and dressed.

"She's been rambling. She said some pretty crazy things. I think she was delirious from the blood loss. Don't worry, she'll pull through."

Mina's face was as pale as a sheet. Laura tried to give her some water, but she was out for the count.

We left her and went out onto the deck. Laura poured herself a drink measured in inches in a glass that could take a standing umbrella, and then did the same for me. We stood for a few moments wrapped in silence. Laura was staring into the middle distance. It would take a better man than me to know what she was thinking.

"You know what I'm thinking?"

"It's all a mystery to me."

"Who's the 'they' she keeps talking about?"

I took a sip from the bucket and leaned forward onto the balustrade. "She says it's the mob."

"Makes sense, they've got people everywhere. Worst place you can be is somewhere where there are records and a phone. But you don't think it's the mob." She glanced at me, placing her hand between us on the balustrade.

I shrugged. I didn't know much anymore, not after the last few strange days. Mina said it was the mob, but the mob didn't wrap itself up in the occult. The words bouncing around my head were *death cult*, some group of delusional loons with a righteous attitude and an overzealous approach to a disproportionate distribution of essential fluids, mainly blood.

"She was saying that Hugh had some kind of weapon to use against them. Maybe one of those old mechweapons from the war." She glanced at me. I made no response. "She said he'd hidden it. That sounds a bit strange to me."

"We're living in strange days."

"Better than the end of days," she said, and laughed. It wasn't overly funny and she seemed to realize that. "I guess we all have to face our end of days. Mina was lucky. It could've been her turn tonight."

"She's tough."

"Her talk sure is. And she's funny." She had a distant look in her eyes.

I gave her a sideways look.

"Sometimes I wish I could be a bit more like that. Funny girls always get the best guys."

"I wouldn't change anything at all about you."

She gave me a smile and a slight bump, shoulder to shoulder. "It would be funny if she and I ended up friends."

"No, it wouldn't."

"No need to get jealous, lover boy." She knocked back the rest of her drink and went in for a refill. "You want one?"

I declined the offer, still having a gallon left in the glass. To put more in, the glass would need another story.

She turned on the wireless and some old-time jazz filtered out into the night. "We didn't get to dance," she called out. "That was going to be my mission tonight."

The tinkling of glass on glass floated out as the bottleneck bounced off the rim of her bucket, and the quiet of the city rolled up the scarp. She reappeared with her engorged vessel filled to the brim. It looked like she was on a mission.

"Tell me about the Vinyl," I said.

"We don't know much, but it's a violent party house run by the mob. They use it for illegal dealings."

"You can't shut it down?"

"No. Their influence runs too deep in the government and

services. It makes IA a joke half the time. Most of the corruption's at the top, and we can't do anything about it."

She had an expression that was half anger and half futile despair. She was being forced into a life of no consequence that would drain the goodness and charity out of anyone. She was also succumbing to the effect of her drinks. She leaned in closer, either for support or in supposition. She ran her hand down my arm, feeling it, the curve of the muscle. She closed her eyes as if remembering a distant memory.

"You're a big guy, but you hide it well." She let out another of those inappropriate laughs that told me exactly what she was thinking.

We needed a diversion. "You heard of a rood?"

"A rude what?"

"Just that. Something called a rood."

"Oh, a rood. Isn't that one of those old words, Latin or something? I'm guessing it means rod or pole." She giggled in a way that was more menacing than innocent. "My classics education was waylaid by my interest in boys, especially when the Greeks started wearing sheets. And when the Greek gods came out, well, I don't recall anything else until my sixteenth birthday. Except flushing a lot when I read the things those old guys used to get up to. Most of it's illegal these days, but I'd still like to try."

Her low chortle was very unladylike. Her mind was dropping below the waistline faster than a knoch free of its lure. Then her head drooped and she collapsed forward, catching herself and theatrically opening her eyes wide. She needed a bed.

"I have to go."

She reached out and placed her hand on my arm. "Oh, don't. Please stay." Her eyes started to close again.

"You'll be asleep in a minute."

"No. No. No. Bed, yes. Sleep, no." She shook her head with passion, but she knew she was on a losing stretch.

I went back inside and headed for the door to let myself out.

"Give me a hug before you leave," she said, following me.

"Give me that."

She tottered over, closed her eyes, and purred like a contented kitten. It felt like every inch of her was touching me; she was wrapped around me so tightly she could've kept an Egyptian mummy fresh for centuries. She stepped away, recovering her composure. I opened the door.

"I always keep a key under the pot, the small one," she said, indicating a ceramic pot. "For special friends. If I'm out, just come in. Make yourself at home. But I'd prefer it if you didn't use the key, because if you stayed, well … it might mean something important to me, and you don't need that."

She leaned forward, her hips swaying gently. In the moonlight there was no denying her angelic beauty, wrapped around a vulnerability that would make weaker men weep. There was no greater vision of perfection on the planet than her. She appeared to float closer, almost reaching out for me, crying for that human touch that we all need, that gets us through the darkest hours of the night.

My father once told me our greatest regrets are for the things we don't do … just before he threw me out onto the streets.

We stood in the doorway, staring at each other. I looked into her deep green eyes and felt everything slip sideways. The world stopped spinning and we were caught in that blissful moment that every tortured soul quests an eternity for, dreams of, and would ultimately die for.

I turned away and walked out. She deserved better than me.

CHAPTER 18 ...

You walk the streets at night, you hear things, you learn things. You listen out for people talking, and sometimes you walk away a little wiser. And a little dirtier. Sometimes, buried among the small talk of client hotspots and new diseases, you get the insane or those so drunk they don't make much sense, and then you don't learn things but at least it's entertaining. Tonight was different. Everyone's mouths were zipped tight. People were scattered in the darkness, with dead eyes and haunted faces, sheltering from the demons that their imaginations made solid.

And always at the edge of my perception was the constant flapping of those damn birds.

The moon, still as large as an incoming baseball, was lobbing its way across the clear, dark night sky. A bat swooped past, its wings outstretched, silhouetted against the glowing orb of the night before it dove away, screeching its traditional mating call. I was drawn back to the words of Angelina: *They won't stop until one of you is dead.*

I had seen a diaper-dispenser's worth of disposable skinny blond things all come to rest at the foot of the reaper. To this point I'd assumed they were all different ones. How do you kill something that's designed to kill you, and that's unkillable?

I stopped in my tracks. You don't.

It was all a butcher's worth of baloney. I shook my head at the preposterousness of it all. I was getting wound up by some highly strung women, over-caffeinated, over-emotional, and lost in their lives. They were dragging me down with them and had me looking for a lazy explanation to a bunch of coincidences.

The wind picked up, blowing dust in my face. I held up my hand, shielding my eyes from the dry, blustery wind. A couple of penny-hookers lined the streets, flashing whatever wares they had. More often than not they were peroxide-enhanced surfboards skinned down through whatever addiction kept them there, more examples of lazy solutions to difficult predicaments. Probably the only course of action an addled brain could choose.

At first I didn't take any notice when they turned and stared after me as I wandered by. That was common practice—until they realized you weren't looking for a good time and were blocking their trade. But these skinny blonds stood there draped in oversized leather jackets and durable secrets with their torn fishnets, looking after me with dead, hungry eyes, wanting and craving. They seemed to be hanging in space, almost timeless, waiting, but for what?

I made my way cautiously along the street, trying to keep as far away from the freak show as possible. There was a commotion behind me. I glanced back over my shoulder. Something flashed past me on the opposite side of the street. I spun around, but nothing was there. The hooker directly opposite flashed me a smile devoid of humor. I glanced at the one next to her and was knocked back by a sudden blow to the shoulder. I took a couple of stabilizing steps backward. The first hooker was gone.

There was a powerful blow against my back. I took a step then spun on the spot. There was a flash of white behind me, leaving the scent of cheap perfume and sweat. There was another blow, straight to the back of my head. It drove me to the ground and made my mind spin, like someone had taken to me with a piece of the transcontinental railway track. I shook my head and spat a mouthful of blood onto the blacktop.

There was a sudden intake of air, a gasp of excitement ... of shock ... it was hard to tell which, with my ears clanging from the full volume of the cathedral ringers.

I looked up. The hookers were forming a circle around me. They took a step closer, in unison. Then another. There was a high-pitched squeal at the edge of my hearing. They stopped and, as one, turned and looked back down the street. A distant figure was standing on the corner in the perfect darkness beneath a burned-out streetlight. I squinted toward the corner, but it was too dark to make out the face.

There was movement around me. A couple of eddies blew dust into my face. I blinked a couple of times and looked up. The street was empty. I thought of the sinister figure. It was impossible to be sure, but it sure looked like Phoenix.

I sat back against the brick wall of a liquor store, directly underneath a streetlight, and nursed my head until there was some life back on the streets. I wondered if Phoenix had a twin brother. The records bank wouldn't be open for hours. I'd have to wait to check on his family. I glanced at my watch. The government wouldn't be awake for hours, but nosy neighbors might.

The line of hookers haunted me. A scented-lace network of trouble. Or a nest. The word "nest" triggered a recollection but I couldn't grasp it.

I hitched down to Templeton Drive on the night thirty-five. I was relieved that this one had a guard, a solid fat man with a face full of scars. He said nothing and just stared at me, but his eyes were full of hatred and suspicion. Regardless, his presence gave me a sense of security.

I wandered down Templeton, counting off the numbers as the early-morning sun blinked above the horizon. I felt lonely without jamoke-man, and his magnetic smile and entertaining dialog tagging along. The joe would've been a welcome jumpstart-juice; my eyes were beginning to feel the weight of a painful night and the deprivation of a decent slumber. The sun crested above the

Westlands scarp, pouring daylight over the land like molasses in a billion-year-old death match.

The places I passed looked like they were in lockdown. One old building, looking the worse for two hundred years of wear, was set back from the blacktop. The occupant, currently sweeping his mean strip of green and acting as a clothesline, was in a position to leer at and be abusive to the passing trade.

I stopped and lifted my hat to him. He wore nothing but baggy old-timer pants with braces, and a sleeveless undershirt that I guessed did double time as a tablecloth and napkin. Wild gray hair matched his eyes. He chewed his upper lip as I approached.

"You were here before, wasn't you?" he said. "Yesterday. You and that darkie." He leaned on his rake and spat on the ground.

I ignored his slur, putting it down to the influence of a bygone age and an enfeebled mind born of ignorance.

"You know anything about 667?" I nodded toward the pile of rubble.

He gave me a suspicious onceover with a withered eye. He stared at my face. "I ain't seen anyone as beat up as you before. And I seen the match between Jandice and Wellcott when they came through town on the championship circuit, when this place was just a town. There'd never been blood like it before."

"It's been a bad day." I gave him a smile. He did not reciprocate.

"I can see that. I'm guessing the night ain't been your friend neither. Lady trouble?"

"You're an observant man."

"I keep my wits about me when I needs to."

"Tell me about 667."

"They had a whole heap of them hookers."

"You sure they were hookers?"

"They were dressed like 'em. Wandering around in barely more than trashy secrets, with their hair done in that fancy thing they do to make it all white. I didn't have the minding of it, because an old man doesn't get much in the way of silky smooth skin. I ain't got long left on this planet so I get what pleasures I can."

"You take any pictures?"

He let out a low laugh and shook his finger at me. There was a faint glint in his eyes. I figured that meant he had a whole box full of them but was never, ever going to let them out of his grubby little hands.

"What about the explosion?"

"It was a loud bang, rattled the windows, but they was built in a time when things was *built* instead of prefabricated. Then there was a sucking sound. Then a few moments later the police was all over the place with the sirens, trucks, and them big sniffer dogs."

"Are you sure it was a few moments?"

"Yeah, it was real quick. When I call them they take hours to get here, if they bother to turn up at all."

"What'd they do?"

The old-timer stared at me before unloading a mouthful of phlegm onto his sorry excuse for a yard. "Kicked around the rubble, looking for survivors, finding witnesses. Tried to catch the landlord, him being the only survivor, but he ran away. They'll never catch him. He runs like the wind."

"Who is he?"

"Dunno his name." The old man's eyes flicked around, until he pitched his balls over the fence into Crazy Town. "He was cursed," he rumbled. "Something was up with him, like the devil. I watched him as I grew. Man and boy, I've lived in this house. He was always the landlord of that house. And he never aged a day."

There were plenty of reasons to go back to my office, the foremost being to escape the deranged ramblings of an old man.

CHAPTER 19 ...

I cruised past the yellowbox on my way back to the office. I thought of my recent visit from the trashmen and knew they'd be back. It would only be a matter of time before they started to unearth things in their ongoing efforts to redecorate the place in the award-winning style of *nouveau vieilleries*.

The morning was in, sitting around the day with a sour expression, as I made my way into the building. Generally the place was quiet, except for the few occupations that needed the space and freedom of the early hours to work. I caught the occasional squeak from a beam when the local tax enforcers, finally looking at themselves in the mirror, had seen the truth and decided to do the only civil thing, which involved said sturdy beam and a thick rope.

The man in the lemon squeezer let out a low grumble that I guessed was some kind of salutation, creeping out of the bowels of his throat before rolling over me in a cloud of ingrained nicotine pollution. Spikey the cleaner was vacuuming the corridor. He didn't look up as I stepped over his thrusting hands and maneuvered around him awkwardly with my cargo.

Inside the office I put the parcel down on the desk and poured myself a shot of stress relief. I opened the window to let in some air, sat down and put my feet up. All was quiet except for the vacuum cleaner.

I unwrapped the parcel and looked at the framed gold record. I was hoping there was a clue in Jorgen's death gaze. I ran my hand over the smooth glass. The prize underneath, so slender and inconsequential, meant so much to so many.

Gold. We were a race of magpies, collecting shiny trinkets when all we needed was food and shelter. I wondered if there was a reason gold was only one letter away from God. Once we got past the superstitions we created to guide us through our desperate fear of the night, huddled there in the back of the cave, we flipped and became crazed hoarders driven by a deep-seated hunger for excess. Maybe we used it as a buffer to stop us falling back into the darkness of those primal fears. The more we had, the more we could lose and still be safe. The mightiest *more* of all was the lure of gold, and we'd do anything to get it, selling out our most precious ideals for a few flakes.

But what did we really worship? To be nothing less than we were yesterday?

I suddenly realized that the rhythmic phasing of the vacuum cleaner had faded to an unvarying, steady hum. No one was pushing it. I got up and quickly slipped the gold record into my secret hiding place under the floorboards.

I opened the door and looked down the corridor. The vacuum was lying on its side. The cleaner was absent. In his place were two people. When they saw me they walked up to my door. The tall woman was wearing black pants, a set of loafers, and an expression as sour as dough from hell. When life gave her lemons she shoved them in her cheeks.

The even taller, thin man, with a smile as wide as a canyon and small eyes too close together, wore a pinstriped zoot suit that reeked of cheap cigarillo smoke. His head twitched with distracting regularity. An occasional giggle slipped from between his thin lips. He took in air through large nostrils in a hooked nose that could double as a boat anchor.

"Where's Spikey?" I asked them.

They looked at each other. Eventually the woman spoke, lifting her nose and closing her eyes. Her thin, angular face emanated calm and assurance, and her voice was more suited to commanding than conversing.

"Are you Mr. Avram?"

I nodded. She shifted her focus and studied the lettering on the door.

"What does the H stand for?"

"Halitosis."

"Counsel, perhaps, for the uninitiated and unanticipated? Or perchance a method of entreating sympathy?"

"A warning. Don't stand close."

"We shall risk the sea of uncertain, dread exhalation, and hope we can converse in words comprising a minimal collection of hard consonants." Her face wriggled around. I assumed she was cracking a joke, and her mouth was trying to join in on the excitement. "May we intercourse with you in your multipurpose abode?"

I shrugged and let them in. If nothing else, maybe my vocabulary would expand in unusual ways.

The lady sat in my visitor's chair. The man twitched around my office chair. I gave him a warning look and he retreated to the safety of the corner behind his captor. I looked at them. Even though they were as different as warring neighbors, there were some facial similarities.

"My associate recessed into provision is Mr. Bird. As you see, he is divertingly petulant due to the circumstances."

"You got a name?" I said.

"You may call me Ms. Early. I hope we're in time."

"In time?" I gave them a matching set of quizzicals, one each.

"We're experiencing undue distress with a particular individual who has been causing difficulty for an extended duration. A difficulty that's apparently embedded within the descent of her genealogical fraternity."

"Nepotism can often be like that." The two people in front of me looked like perfect advertising for the fact.

"I, we, are the recipients of a cavalcade of commentaries and interpretations, even descriptive intelligences about said individual, with whom you may be associating. Do you know this woman?" She handed me a photo of a young lady who was throwing a scared glance over her shoulder. It was Angelina. "And are you aware of her current locale?"

"I haven't seen her."

She handed over another photograph of the two of us talking.

I looked at it and spun it back at her across the desk. "It's not me."

Ms. Early stared at me, tapping her long nails on the old desktop. Mr. Bird seemed to be experiencing his own kind of trouble. Behind Ms. Early's back, he danced in a bizarre movement that looked part ritual and part drunken wedding guest. It was distracting, but not as distracting as Ms. Early's next line.

"We believe she may be in possession of some particular family heirlooms that she has acquired without going through the appropriate procedures. It has been related to me that the monetary reward is handsome, if you find yourself able to contribute to our knowledge of said individual."

I'm always a sucker for that kind of argument.

"Monetary reward?" I tilted my head, trying to block out the distracting behavior behind her. But only partially. It never pays to completely block out a psychotic who might be carrying a weapon.

She withdrew a battered leather purse from a cracked and brittle handbag. She opened it and took out a century, waving it in front of me. She laid it down and smoothed it out.

"This is an untithed gift for you. Consider it an expression of regret over our unexpected appearance."

Ms. Early then took out another nine bills and laid them across the desk. They took up the entire width of the wood. It was almost enough to buy the office outright. It was two-thirds of the way toward a bungalow out past the 'burbs, a peaceful place where I could live out my existence in a bubble of serenity.

Mr. Bird continued dancing his bizarre steps, his arms flapping over his head. In its own mesmerizing way, his actions made her request reasonable. That's when I knew something odd was up.

I slowly opened my lower drawer and took out the silver-plated cigarette lighter in the shape of an illegal Luger 311. I knew it was out of fluid so there weren't going to be unexpected flames appearing and ruining the illusion.

"You know what this is?"

Mr. Bird stopped his insane flapping and focused on the gun. His beady eyes tracked the barrel with intense concentration. Ms. Early pulled a face of disgust and peered down her extensive nose.

"I haven't heard or seen her." The reiteration seemed to sink in.

"You could've just said that," Ms. Early said. "The offence initiative with the hand-held weapon is not a requirement of the expedient completion of this interaction."

"I was born that way."

"I will leave the money for you, as authorized. It will guide your decision."

There was a moment again, like with Silbi. It hurt to decline the temptation. Saying yes would make all the troubles go away, and I'd be content in that little bubble of happiness.

"Take it with you."

"Are you certain?" Her voice dripped with honey.

The pain hammered down. Compliance wanted to slip off my tongue. What was Angelina to me? Just some bent woman with a broken understanding of her place in the world. The small seed of doubt at the back of my mind burned, and the spot between my shoulder blades began to itch like tomorrow was slipping off the menu.

"Remember my name." I cocked the pistol.

Mr. Bird went crazy, shrieking and howling.

"We won't forget, Mr. Avram." Her voice was as cold as yesterday's coffee.

"Who sent you?"

"That we can't tell you."

I wiggled the pretend gun at them. I could see their reflections bouncing off the silver. Both of them were damned concerned by it. I'd seen shakers before, and none of them were ever put in a flap over a gun being drawn on them. They all knew it took a big set of fluffy dice to pull the trigger. Normally the people with the dice don't wait. They extract their firearm du jour and shoot you. It's never a part of the conversation; it's the closure from a person who doesn't like to talk too much. Or doesn't want you to talk too much either. Up-state marriages used them a lot.

"What if I shoot you?"

"Then we definitely won't tell you," Ms. Early said.

"I didn't say both of you."

There was a moment of unfriendly silence in the room. I didn't like it, and it wasn't welcome. I put down the gun.

"Tell me or go."

"Will you take the case? She is not the person she says she is. Look into her past and you might be surprised by what you find."

Mr. Bird let out another high-pitched squeal that upset everyone in the room, including himself. Ms. Early gave him a sharp look.

"You might be interested to know that *most* people around you are not who they appear to be." She paused, momentarily lost in thought. Then she did her weird smile-thing at me. "It's for the greater good. Will you help?"

I picked up the photograph of Angelina. I flicked it back onto the table. "No."

"Then we shall go. Good day, Mr. Avram."

As the door closed, the pain lifted from my head. It was an interesting message they purveyed: threat and warning wrapped up in a warm burrito of candy. She had left a century on the table. I picked it up and looked at both sides of it. It could be handy down at the Stylus. It might even cover my bar tab.

I thought about the pair as strange as a set of joke spectacles with the wobbling eyes on springs.

CHAPTER 20 ...

I jumped up and ran out the door. Spikey was vacuuming the carpet like nothing had happened.

"Where'd you go?"

He gave me a blank stare. "I ain't been anywhere."

The two weird ones had obviously slipped the three of us into a parallel dimension; while they were here the world had continued to spin without us in it. Or maybe Spikey was only saying it to cover a quick smoke with the lemon-squeezer man.

I sprinted down the corridor and forced him to express me down to the first floor. I ran to the front of the building and asked the doorman which way they'd gone. He looked at me blankly. The parallel dimension theory was gaining credibility. I described a sour-faced woman all in black and her towering, thin offsider.

"How could you have missed them?" I said.

He shook his head.

I ran out into the busy sidewalk traffic, then into the road, much to the annoyance of the diesel dimboxes smoking past. A couple honked. A couple swerved. I scanned the sidewalk both ways. Then I saw them.

Ms. Early glanced over her shoulder at the hullabaloo going

on in the road. I ducked behind a thirty-five, avoiding her gaze.

I moved down the opposite side of the street, tracking them in the crowds. They hitched onto the back of a bus heading toward Gayme, and I jumped up onto the following one. Twenty minutes later they slid off the back and made their way into a deserted old building. Ms. Early's confidence ensured they didn't look back. I followed them in, stepping through smashed walls and fallen ceiling beams. Puddles wept by malfunctioning plumbing were dotted around the broken floor. I could make out their footsteps, two sets winding their way through the debris.

They had ventured up a set of stairs that were barely more than rusted beams held together with the hope of slow decay. I placed my foot on the first step. It crunched under my weight. I wondered how they'd gone up without falling through. I stepped carefully on the beams at a point closest to the wall. There was some solidity there, and I crept up one step at a time. With a sigh of relief I made it to the top. I made my way out into the remains of the upper floor, following the damp footsteps.

I slowed when I heard voices ahead. A deathly quiet enfolded the place. Ms. Early's voice pierced the broken spaces, echoing around the building, making dust fall from the beams like construction dandruff. I leaned against a wall and a series of pigeons took off, screeching into the air.

The voices went quiet. I stood stock-still. After an agonizing few moments they continued. I crept closer. They were hidden behind a short wall. I crept to one end and glanced around the corner. I could see Ms. Early, in her perpendicular deportment, with Mr. Bird standing to attention, looking at someone in between us. I moved silently to the other end of the wall, and glanced around. There was another man standing there anonymously, with his back to me. His hands were on his hips, like a commander of all he surveyed, but without the useful services of actually surveying anything. He wore a crumpled brown jacket and had wiry, curly hair.

His thick accent gave away who he was: Chief Inspector Rami

Watcher.

I kept my breathing under control, closed my eyes and focused on the conversation.

"He wasn't any help?" Watcher said.

"He has a ridiculous chip on his shoulder." This was spoken by a voice I didn't recognize but it was full of annoying tics and stutters. I assumed the speaker was Mr. Bird.

"What about the money?"

"He didn't accept it," Ms. Early said.

"Give it back to me, I'll return it to the evidence store. Those stupid internal-audit fools are always checking it out now. It was much easier in the old days."

A fattened and diseased pigeon with a disfiguring growth on its foot waddled up to me and started to peck at my shoe. I flicked it away. I tried to focus on the conversation.

"Does he have any idea?"

"About what's coming and his—"

The pigeon had come back and stabbed into my shoe. I kicked it away. It took to the skies and flapped out through one of the many holes in the rusted steel roof. I shrank behind the wall. I heard footsteps, and braced for a fight.

"Let's get out of here. I never liked this part of town," Watcher said.

I heard the footsteps retreat and diminish into silence, which wrapped around me. My heart rate eventually descended out of the stratosphere. I scouted the area. There wasn't much to see beyond muddy footprints and a few birdseeds. The glint of something caught my eye. I squatted down and found a small golden cross with an even smaller deity attached to it.

There was a deep growl behind me. I turned slowly to face a big black dog.

"Who's a good boy?" I tried to say in strong, deep and commanding tones.

It growled at me, baring its fangs. They were long and dark. They had seen a lot of meat. I hoped it hadn't been human. No voice would be strong, deep and commanding enough for this creature. Its sleek, shiny coat stretched across its enormous lean muscles. Every inch of it was a deep black. It would be impossible to see at night. I reminded myself to never go out in the dark again. Set against its dark hair was a pair of red eyes filled with malevolent intelligence.

It was a hound straight from hell.

I moved. Its muscles flexed like silk, and it moved in complete silence. It stalked around me. I scanned the area for the fastest exit. I could only see one way out, and it was going to hurt. But hurting was better than being eaten alive.

I faked a quick movement to the right. The dog intercepted me with a low growl. I twisted back and gave it a kick in its side, turned and sprinted toward the wall. It was decayed beyond any use and I smashed right through it, with the hellhound snapping at my heels. I plummeted to the sidewalk below. The hound stopped short of following me into the abyss.

It was a surprise to land on jamoke-man, although not as surprising as it was for him.

He looked up at the hole in the second-story wall. "Next time you want to drop in, let me know in advance. Maybe in writing."

Besides ruining his suit, I had to buy all the coffees I managed to spill. The century came in handy, and jamoke-man had the best day sales ever.

"If you wanted a cup of joe so bad, you should've called." He gave me an expression hitting up between damaged merchandise and light-hearted humor.

"Did you see two people?" I described Bird and Early. He shook his head. These two were slipperier than a basket of snakes in monsoon season.

The fall had knocked the small golden cross out of my hand, but I caught its glint and retrieved it from its precarious position above a storm drain. I gave it a polish on my sleeve and stared at it.

"You giving me more gold? I bought a house with that door

handle."

"I'll keep this one."

"I've seen those before."

He took it out of my hands, without so much as a free cup, and twisted it around. He sat down on the sidewalk, for a moment lost in thought. Eventually he came out of it with a snap of his fingers, like he'd woken from a trance.

"Those skinny blond hookers collect these," he said, handing it back. "I was in one of those nests a long time ago and saw a whole pile of them."

I still had a few hours before the city hit second gear, stuttering out of its bleary-eyed reveille and coming alive. I headed back to my office with a complimentary half-cup from jamoke-man. This was developing into a non-unilateral exchange.

When I got back to the office, lemon-squeezer man gave me a familiar nod, half tranced by the smell of fresh beans. My office door was open. I looked in at the turmoil inside. The first thing I checked was the gold record. It was still safely hidden under the floorboards. I spent the next hour cleaning up the office and fixing the lock. I made a note to get a new one.

Finally, I sat down at the desk with a fresh cup of coffee and examined the gold record in its exalted frame of prominence. Another little clue that we all craved popularity. I often wondered why we were so driven by a desire for acceptance. It was like something tragic had happened in human evolution and we were all afraid of being left alone, abandoned on the beaches of life. Animals handled it all the time. Humans? The exact opposite.

I looked at the title of the song. "Looking for Love." You had to laugh. The frame looked solid enough and the record was stuck on good and strong. I flipped the frame around and looked at the back. Fresh scratch marks around the screws meant they had recently been delicately extracted with uncommon finesse and replaced. I searched through my desk drawer until I found a screwdriver. I gently took out the tiny golden screws, laying them neatly on the desk in a row. There was nothing inside except the record, and some flecks of dirt and lumps of poorly applied paint.

I held my breath and flipped the record over. The reverse side was blank. Just a plain black vinyl record; there wasn't even any writing. I exhaled. I ran my hand over it, but there was nothing. I ran my hand over the inside of the frame. There was nothing. I sat looking at the collection of pieces in front of me, drumming my fingers on the desk. The record was lying flat on the desk. There was nothing under the label, no mysterious lumps. Except for the dust. I ran my hand over the dust to wipe it clean. The dust didn't move.

I took a closer look at the front of the record. All the lumps of dried paint were the same size and shape. I took a closer look. They weren't lumps of paint. They were seeds. *Seeds of truth*, Jorgen had said.

I spent an hour looking at those seeds, searching for a pattern or clue. The sun rose and slipped in through the window. I gave up. I threw the record on the desk and stared out the life on the street below. A couple of mouthfuls of tepid joe didn't help. A bird flew past the window, casting a shadow over the desk.

I glanced back at the record, hoping for a moment—or at least a seed—of truth.

The seeds were casting shallow shadows over the record's surface. Something odd caught my attention with some of the outer seeds. I twisted the record slowly. The shadows stretched and spun until some, in a certain fashion, formed the shape of an elongated number. I picked up the record and looked along the flat edge. I tilted it slowly. I rotated the disk, and before my eyes the seeds lined up, making a number, a phone number.

I picked up the receiver and dialed. It rang. It was answered by an early-morning voice. I hung up.

Angelina.

CHAPTER 21 ...

The phone rang. I gave it a dirty look, but it didn't get the message. I tried to ignore it by drawing moustaches on the photographs on page one of the paper, but curiosity was always going to win. Curiosity sat everywhere lately, in every person I'd met to every place I'd been. An undeniable veil of obfuscation and complication lay over every move, every word, and every breath. I wouldn't answer the damn phone.

I picked up the receiver. "Yeah."

"Hey, boyo, I got a report here says you were at 667 Templeton."

Watcher. Alarm bells rang in my head. This was one yellow brick road I had to tread down carefully.

"Thought I'd visit the place and see what all the commotion was about."

"I didn't recommend it as a vacation destination. What was your reason for being in the area?"

"A client asked me."

I glanced out through the blinds to the street below. Someone was standing by the corner phone box. I squinted but couldn't make out much beyond the brown clothes the person was wearing. A diesel dimbox pulled up at the curb and a woman stepped out carrying several boxes.

"Did your sneaking ways find anything?" Watcher said.

"Nothing but blind neighbors," I muttered.

"Do you know anything about the landlord, this Phoenix guy?" There was a hint of inquisition in Watcher's line, like he was being force fed the question.

"Not much. He runs fast."

"No mistake there." He let out a light chuckle. "I've done my fair share of chasing the madman."

"Why are you calling?"

"To see if you know anything."

"You guys don't use PIs."

"Times are changing, my friend. We're looking for a competitive edge."

"Against who?" I hung up and grimaced at the receiver.

I glanced back out the window. The person at the phone box hailed a diesel dimbox and kicked off the curb.

Despite what Watcher had said, I knew that nothing ever changed with those bureaucratic blimps in case they lost their pensions and ancillary benefits. He was sniffing around, after something. Something he thought only I knew. If only I knew.

I left the office, slamming the door behind me.

Angelina's little shop was quiet. I flicked aside the sign on the front. The door was unlocked, after I'd applied the Remington picklock. I opened it slowly, reached up and muffled the small bell. I stepped into the room.

I had a quick look at some of the items on the shelves. Flipping over a small totem revealed the Sandleford Plastics Manufacturing Co. had made the item. The same went for the other artifacts on the shelves. Mystery by catalog. Or maybe just another woman with an illusion to peddle, a net to cast, a veil to drop, a trick to sell.

I made my way through the small entrance at the back of the shop that was closed off by a couple of draping black curtains.

Angelina was absorbed in grinding herbs or similar. She had a book open and appeared to be reading a recipe. She turned the page and read on, oblivious to the world beyond her table. There was a steaming cup beside her.

"You know Hugh Jorgen."

My voice caught her as she was lifting the cup to her mouth. She froze mid-raise. Her eyes darted from me to a gray metallic piece in the corner, too far to grab, and back to me.

"I'm not sure how to answer that. Was it a question or an accusation?"

"He had your number."

She lowered the cup. She looked at me thoughtfully, not as a predator this time but as a witness. Then she made up her mind. "I have no idea what you're talking about."

"Don't lie to me." I stepped closer.

She stood up with lightning speed and lunged for her contraband gun. I grabbed her wrist before she had it in her clutches. She struggled with surprising strength, trying to stamp down on my foot, but she was too slow and obvious.

"Is this how you treat all your women? Rough them up then have your way with them?"

I couldn't tell if it was an accusation or some deep-seated fantasy, but she was so tormented I wasn't about to play Russian roulette with a tank load of rattlesnakes as crazy as a month-old bolognaise.

"I don't have any women." I pocketed the piece and let her go.

She rubbed her wrist and gave me a dark look.

"He left another number." I handed over the number I'd hastily scrawled down.

"I have no idea what it is," she said, dismissing the paper.

"Why did he call?"

She let out a theatrical sigh, which fitted with her current behavior. "Maybe he was lonely. Maybe he wanted company, someone to while away the afternoon with."

"You, of all people?"

"You liked me, I seem to recall."

"At gunpoint."

"But it didn't stop you, did it? Maybe there is something between us. I find myself having funny thoughts when you're near me."

She stepped in close and I could feel the heat of her mouth as she hovered in front of me, hardly an inch away. It wouldn't take much and we would be touching. I could also feel her hand making its way into my pocket, after the piece. I removed her hand.

"That's nothing to do with me," I said.

The slap left my ears ringing, but I'd had worse.

"Did that hurt?" she whispered.

I shrugged. "If you want."

She brought around her other hand and opened it in front of me. Some of the ground herbs lay in her palm. She pursed her lips into a bright red O and blew. I coughed. My head spun and the whole world exited stage right. I took a couple of staggering steps, lunging out for the wall for support and missing. I collapsed to the floor and darkness closed over me.

I came to and felt rope bonds holding me in place, the thin binding cutting into my chest. I couldn't tell how long I'd been out because the room was in near darkness, with complete separation from the outside. There could be an apocalypse going on, and no one would ever know in here. Cool and quiet.

"Would you like a drink?" came Angelina's voice.

"Yeah." It was probably still early in the morning, but when you're faced with the sheriff of Crazy Town, you generally ride along.

"Are you a straight man, or do you like to mix it?"

"Straight."

"Of course. I bet you're as straight as they come."

"There's easier ways of dating."

She sat down on my lap, straddling me like a Clydesdale. She held the drink in front of me, twisting it, letting the minimal light bounce off the ice. Her fingers ran over my chest, tracing the outlines of my muscles. She'd swept back her cloak, revealing bare legs. I could see that the rest of her was also bare. She leaned forward, reveiling in the whole Lady Godiva act, and whispered in my ear.

"I'm exhausted. So worn out. So very tired. It all has to end."

Then she poured the drink over my chest. Nothing spoiled the mood faster than a wasted drink. I watched the liquid run off onto the floor and noticed the strange markings surrounding me. The familiar five-pointed star had been drawn around me, in white. It smelled suspiciously like raw garlic, but in the dark you can never be sure, which is why restaurants have their lights so dim.

"Why did you do that?"

"Sterilization," she hissed.

Her face took on residency from a demented fairy. She raised a knife—I could only guess where she'd hidden it—and stabbed it into my chest. It was a shallow wound, but it still stung, especially when she twisted it. But I kept my nerve and stared straight back at her. She focused on the knife, extracting it and stepping up and away, balancing a few drops of blood on its tip.

She ripped a dark sheet off a small plinth to my left. It held a small bowl suspended over a tiny burner. She shook the drops of blood into the bowl and fired up the burner. The smell of paraffin drifted around the room. She stared intently at the bowl. After a minute, it exploded and sent a small, green cloud into the air. The flickering flames cast an eerie light over her face; the green plume tinged her features witch color. A cackle would have fitted right in about now. She stood there looking slightly confused until the flames died down and then returned her focus to me.

With an exaggerated air of theater, she lifted a large cleaver from a lower shelf on the pedestal. Her face was dark and distant. The chopper was heavy in her hand, and her arm flexed with the weight of it. At least it wasn't one of the red eighteen-inch blades, which meant she wasn't one of *them*. But that didn't mean she was right in the head.

Her eyes sparkled in the light reflecting an unknown intent—at least unknown to me. Possibly it was just desire or ambition.

Her gait was slow and steady, marching to some inner beat. Each slow step revealed a bare leg, smooth, silken and untouched, except for once. Then the fabric claimed it back into seclusion. Her ceremonial march led her around behind me.

She took a deep breath. Letting out a guttural cry, she lifted the cleaver and brought it down.

CHAPTER 22 ...

The ropes severed and fell free. I snapped my wrists around in front and rubbed some life back into them. She knew how to tie a knot. I pitied her husband, if she ever found one, but I knew she'd at least keep him, with or without his consent.

There was a click and the lights flickered into life, revealing the room to be a dissolute basement, somewhere quiet where the debauchery could unwind. I glanced around the room, looking for potential weapons or general weirdness.

"I'm sorry. I needed to be sure," Angelina said.

"Why the lap dance?"

"I have to be careful who I choose as a friend. Make sure they're clean."

"Can I have my shirt back?"

She stood stock-still in front of me with various bits of her body peeking out from underneath her cloak. "Eventually," she said.

I could feel her eyes crawling down my body. She was as highly charged as a penthouse on the bay.

I nodded toward the burner and bowl on the pedestal. "What's with the mini barbecue?"

She glanced over, seemingly reluctant to withdraw her gaze from my torso. She had to stop cutting herself a piece of cake, put on the brooksy, and get herself a goof.

"It was a test. If you were one of them, it would've burned red. Their mutated blood does something to the garlic."

"So green means I'm okay?"

"Normal people have no effect. All you end up with is cooked garlic. Green's a new one on me. But it wasn't red so don't have to cut your head off. Not yet, anyway."

I stood up and flexed my shoulders. It was good to get some movement back into them again. I cast the question out quick to slide in under her defenses. "You heard of a rood?"

Her eyes widened, like she'd been busted doing something indiscreet.

"Want to tell me?" I said, after waiting in vain for an answer.

She let out a semi-deranged giggle. "How can you not know what a rood is? Especially with those people flapping around."

"Let's pretend only you believe."

She sighed and packed away her utensils, but not the knife, I noticed, which she hid someplace about her person.

"It's the crucifix. Born from Adam's mouth. It's an old English word from the Middle Ages. It signifies the True Cross, the actual wooden cross used in Christ's crucifixion. But phylogenetics isn't my strength."

After a few moments of silence she got the message.

"The seed? From the tree of knowledge of good and evil?" She waved her hands around. "Adam and Eve got kicked out of Eden for messing with the tree. Everyone knows that story. Adam starts to die, being about a hundred and thirty years old, so he sends his third son, Seth, back to the Garden of Eden to get some of the juice of life, or whatever it was called. So much has been lost in translation. Seth's refused entry by an angel standing guard. The angel gives him a seed from the tree, saying it'll ease his passing. Place it in his mouth and all will be okay. On the way back Seth's attacked so he hides the seed in his mouth, but the seed makes people forget. As long as it's in your body, you can't remember. So he forgets what he's doing, gets lost in the desert, collapses and vomits up the seed. Then he remembers, so he runs back to Adam, who's now dead. He buries Adam with the seed under his tongue.

"Seth goes off and does more biblical stuff. A tree grows where Adam's buried on top of a hill. Jesus turns up, annoys the government, and is sentenced to crucifixion. They cut down the tree and make the rood from it. Then they nail him to it and raise him up so all can see. We all know what happened after that but no one knows what happened to the rood. Some believe it was fashioned into a weapon too powerful for mere mortals. Some believe the Templars took it and hid it deep in some dark cave. But then some people will say anything if you give them the right drugs and stick a bag over their head."

"Where is it?"

She shrugged. "It could be anywhere in the world."

"I think Jorgen had it."

"That man? Then we're all doomed. How did he get it?"

"He stole it."

"That makes sense."

"He called you."

"Yes, so? He probably wanted to get into my panties, trying to impress me with his large pole."

At this juncture, with our brief shared history, that didn't seem like an impossible task. Given the opportunity to meet the man with the large pole, she might've been eager. In which case he would have been the prey. But she could play the desperate-damsel card if it kept her talking.

"He blabbed on about how it was going to make him rich. His mouth was having a party, but his brain lost the invitation."

I picked up one of her precast relics and pushed it at her. "Is this real?"

"No."

I nodded. "How much if it was?"

"Several hundred thousand credits."

I picked up the one next to it. "And this?"

"About the same, but slightly less due to the regressive cultural appreciation."

I replaced it, wiping my finger along the shelf. It left a small trail in the light dust. Without looking back at her, I asked, "How much is a rood?"

"It's priceless. How much is the Ark of the Covenant? Or the Cup of Christ? These things can't be measured in credit value."

I turned to face her. "But they can."

"No, they can't," she bridled.

"Someone will always buy."

"It's valuable. It's symbolic." The indignation was dripping off her.

"And that's why he called."

"What, over money? I can't believe that even a fool like Hugh Jorgen would be shallow enough to see it as just a pay packet. All the myths say it has immense, ancient powers. Maybe it controls people. You know how the Bible stories go. That seems more of a reason to me. Ultimate power."

"They're all fairytales," I said.

"Not all of them. Many are warnings. Terrible admonitions of what's to come if you don't heed the tales. It's one thing that can bring Armageddon."

"The end of everything?"

"No. The end of this." She threw her arms wide, indicating the room. "The end of us, civilization, people. It'll clear away the past so the next evolution can start. The vampires think they're the next step in evolution."

She was skipping on the spot, so agitated and tense she was having trouble staying focused.

I grabbed her and pulled her in close. She loosened like jelly in my arms. Her eyes fluttered and she pursed her lips. A small sigh left her mouth. As vulnerable and hungry as she was, she was still a good and innocent, lost woman looking for the wrong kind of man. Her cloak fell open and she crushed her naked body against me. Electricity flew back and forth between our bare skin. I thrust her away, her cloak spinning up and around. She stood like a rock with the cloak settling around her, her eyes on fire, and probably her body as well.

"Get changed," I said. "You're going hunting."

We cruised past Limbo's, hoping to scratch the California suite, but the police were there and their excessive demarcation identifiers left no way in. We watched them picking through the blue-plate take-outs and mugs of joe, joking with each other and not paying much attention to the world passing by.

Angelina stood next to me. She was dressed in the upmarket fashion all the free-thinking women were wearing; tight leather clothing more in tune with flying a crop duster than shopping the strip. It almost looked like a uniform She'd calmed down and was focused on the scene in front of us. With her obsession abated, now looked like a good time to bring up my morning interactions.

"I've got people asking about you," I said. I didn't bother to look in her direction.

She kept watching the slowhands straight ahead. "Who?"

I shrugged. "Bird and Early." I furnished her with a description of the whacky pair.

"I've never heard of them." Her response was measured and deliberate. "They could be using fake names."

"They gave me a card." I withdrew it from my pocket.

"That proves they must be real." She gave the card a dismissive glance and folded her arms.

I placed the card back in my pocket. "You're wrapped up in this."

"No more than you. Maybe even less when you look at the grand scheme."

"Do you know why?"

She gave an absent-minded shrug, still staring across the street. "I'd guess it's due to my specialist, expert knowledge. What did your visitors want?"

"They think you have something. Stolen."

She let out a small laugh. "Half the stuff I've got's fake. The other half's from my family and it's been with our name for generations. It's not the kind of thing you can fake. I wonder what they were really after."

The police were arranged in a close-set pattern, the slowhands nearly bouncing off each other. I couldn't see Watcher.

"How big's the rood?" I asked.

"It's a staff. I'm guessing it's about four to six feet. And made of wood …" Something had caught her eye.

"Anything else?"

"Hmm?" Her attention was elsewhere. "Like encrusted jewels? No. It was a big piece of wood that once had a man nailed to it. How decorative should something like that be?"

"Things change over time."

"Oddly enough, religious relics don't. Something to do with sanctity. You know what that means?"

"You'd be surprised."

"Talking about being surprised, do you notice anything about the entrance, besides all the fat cops?" She indicated the dance of indifference by the constabulary collection.

I stared at the scene for a full egg-timer's worth of minutes. I shook my head.

She pointed. "There's a warning glyph above the entrance, a small cross in a circle. It would've been tough for them to get past without it causing a lot of pain. I wish I could've seen that." A thin smile danced over her bright lips. "I have an idea."

Without so much as a cat to-do, she improvised a disguise. She reversed my jacket and put it on, and flattened my hat on her head. The leathers did a pretty good job of making her look like a typical slowhand.

She made her way across the road and through the police, and used jutting-out bricks to climb up the wall. She reached the arch and lifted the small object off the hook. She danced back between the slowhands, who were blind to her. The force was getting slack in its antiquity. She skipped across the road between the diesels and presented the circular object.

"What will this do?" I asked.

That devilish smile danced back for another go-round. She leaned in close and whispered. "Just you wait and see." Her eyes twinkled.

I turned it around in my hands: a circle of wood ringing a small wooden cross. The cross, more stone than wood, looked old.

"It's old."

"Even older than you. It's from the rood. It's a rood shield. There are only a few of them in the world, obviously."

She stepped in close, wrapping her arms around me. I could feel the hunger of her body as she pulled herself in tight. "I know you don't believe, but when you meet one of them again, think happy, pure thoughts."

She took it out of my hands and placed it in my shirt pocket. "And keep it near your heart, it'll keep you safe."

I could feel her breath on my neck. Her perfumed scent filled my olfactories, sending exquisite shivers down my back. And with that she skipped off down the street, swinging off the streetlights. I shook my head as she bounced out of sight. She had failed to return my jacket or my hat.

CHAPTER 23 ...

I couldn't walk a block without my hat, so I called into the nearest millinery and got sized up by the in-store Cavanagh, hot from his Milan training. While he was sizing and pressing, I went through my pockets and discovered the photograph of Huge Jorgen singing his heart out, with his adoring fans crowded around. It wasn't the original, so parts of it were a little blurry. I asked the Cavanagh if he had a magnifying glass. He nodded and slid one over the counter to me, then continued with his blocking and pouncing.

I ran the glass over the grainy photograph. It looked like the bizarre microphone stand was made out of wood. I pondered. Would Jorgen be brave, arrogant, or insane enough to have it right out in front like that, hidden in plain sight?

"Wonderboy," I said to the bouncy young girl at the Stylus door. I walked straight past her without waiting for a reply, and even avoided a double from Jackson.

Wonderboy was writing up the set lists, waiting for the crowds to arrive and start creating an atmosphere. He looked over his reading glasses.

"Van the ... gentleman? I see you've survived a better night.

You've hardly got any bruising. Not that I can see, anyway." He raised an eyebrow.

"You remember Jorgen?"

"Yeah."

"Anything odd about his microphone stand?"

He thought for a moment before shaking his head. "He's a singer. I'm surprised he had a stand. Don't singers generally steal them from the drummer?"

Jackson leaned over. "You remember his stand. He carried it around in that special black case."

Wonderboy clicked his fingers. "Yeah, I remember. I only saw it once. Like some old totem or something. Old carved wood. Cool idea, but it'd wreck your back carrying it around for too long."

"Anything special about it?"

He laughed. "You know what my memory's like after decades of drinking? I can't even finish the set lists."

"Where would it go?"

Wonderboy and Jackson looked at each other.

"With Hugh, I'm guessing repossession," Wonderboy said. He smiled at Jackson, who smiled back, big white teeth and coolness to spare.

Then I had the double.

I called in at a couple of repo places but got nowhere. They either stonewalled or didn't care enough to give me any information. If I had no proof the rood was mine, they weren't talking—"they" being men counterpointed by burly off-siders, all muscle, no hair or neck. I tossed around some ideas about who might find value in it. The repo men looked at it and all they saw was something that would be a heap of trouble to shift. Easier to grab a Gibson, or sell a gold record.

But there was something else a musician could do when the funds ran low, another place they could try so they could get their next meal.

"I didn't expect to see you," Laura said, opening her apartment door.

I looked past her. The place was looking a little disheveled. Her voice wasn't completely cold, but her eyes were distant. She wasn't looking the best. Her face was pale and her spark was diminished.

"I have a request." I clutched my hat in front of me, humbled and remorseful.

"I was hoping for an apology. Or a dinner invitation."

"I'm working on it," I mumbled. "Do you have PDB access?"

"Its official name is the National Goods Recycle Database and Register." Her voice slipped a few degrees.

I nodded. "Pawnbrokers." I felt about a thumb tall.

"Don't say that too loudly, Mina's still here. She might get the wrong idea." Her voice thawed. "But yes, I've got access."

"Could you run this number?" I rummaged in my pocket and extracted the piece of paper off the back of the first gold record etched with S. Cain's name.

She sighed and took it. "It'll cost you."

"I don't have anything valuable." I looked down at my battered boots.

She sighed. "You've got issues with self-esteem, that's what you've got. Come back tonight with a golden smile. Now make with the feet until you can take a hint."

I backed away, expecting her to close the door. She just stood there, looking at me. I felt like a teenager on a first date with my first love, and it had all gone wrong, neither of us certain what to do next.

She tucked her hair behind her ear and smiled shyly at me. I was guessing it cost her to do that, and I couldn't even give her loose change.

The records down in government central went back an eternity. Templeton 667 was included. It was a big house, owned by various people over the years. The current owner was Phoenix. Every fifty or so years the owner changed, regular. According to the paperwork, it was built three hundred years ago. There was an ancient photograph attached to the front of the file, taken not long after the place was built by the look of it.

In the picture was Phoenix, or as close to a relative as it was possible to get without relying on heavy-duty science or magic. I was no expert on skin care, but he seemed in good shape for someone outliving a deep-sea turtle. Or maybe it was a clerical error, considering general government incompetence and corruption, and someone had left the photograph out in the sun too long. I wondered if Phoenix owned any other property. People who owned one old place often owned others.

I unclipped the old photograph and got the elderly woman behind the counter to make a copy for me. She grumbled, glaring over her reading glasses with an attitude of disgust that muted her blue permanent wave. A smile had no currency here, and her gray world of bureaucratic ineptitude steamrollered over my attempt at lightness.

She charged up the xerography machine, an old Chester, cranking the handle until the room was humming with electrostatic charge, and the corona glowed blue. Her flabby arm, stretching the floral fabric of her dress, wobbled with the handle's oscillation. We shielded our eyes against the eventual electrostatic discharge.

She peeled out the copy and handed it over. I asked to see the other properties owned by Phoenix. She gave me a stare that froze parts of the tundra and kept it frozen until the ice age ended. She said it was impossible, that it would mean flicking through her entire book of property owners. She implied that I should come back in another lifetime. I said I'd be back in an hour.

I'd barely stepped out of the building before I felt the presence of someone following me, poorly. Amateur hour. A couple of quick turns and double-backs and I was able to make the fellow, not that it was hard.

I ducked in behind a bus stop and watched Mr. Bird strut past.

Then I followed him, an easy task considering how high his head stuck above the crowd. He stopped, glancing around wildly, when he realized I was no longer in front of him. It was all I needed as confirmation. I turned and headed off across town.

I walked into the tank. The desk sergeant watched me carefully as I strode past. He tried administrative bureaucracy, but if you pretend you're deaf you can get away with anything. The tank floor was full of bustling men and women, some walking around and others sitting at the sea of desks. The omnipresent naked globes hanging down on their extended wires swung occasionally, sending eerie shadows over the bare brick walls.

I burst into Watcher's office. "Are you following me?" I leveled my finger at him.

He spluttered out his beverage, and nearly tripped in his eagerness to stand. He didn't have the confidence to debate me below waist level.

"What do you think you're doing, storming in here like you own the place?" he howled.

"Asking a simple question," I growled.

"No, I am *not* following you. I was sitting down having a nice cup of tea and you've made me spill it. I'm working through my memory to see if I can arrest you for shouting and disturbing the beverages. You come in here properly humble, with your hat in your hand and your voice low and polite, and your eyes full of nothing."

"I've got strange people visiting me." I sat in his low-slung visitor's chair, barely able to see above the desk. Watcher towered above me.

"It's nothing to do with me. It's the people you types attract. I'm sure you're old enough to take care of it." He dusted his hand and looked indifferent. He slumped down into his plush leather chair and glared at me.

"How sure are you?"

"Look, what do you want?" He leaned forward on the desk,

resting his elbows in the spilt liquid.

There was a shout from outside. He sprang up and went to the door. He went to shout, sighed, and looked back over his shoulder. "Stay here." He disappeared into the milieu of the tank floor.

I quickly went to his filing cabinet and flicked through the files. I searched through L and M, and found Angelina's file. It would make interesting reading. I folded it into my pocket and sat down just as Watcher walked back in, loosening his tie.

"Are you tracking anyone I know?" I said.

He paused before he rose up tall and said, "You're asking about privileged police information that could be being collected by top undercover agents to bring down the city's biggest crime ring."

I tapped my fingers on the armrest. "What about Laura?"

"Malory's relationship with this station, or any special action she may be addressing, is of no relevance to you. Quite frankly, she's been difficult and unreliable lately."

"I was talking about her health."

"Oh. I see. Why?"

"I'm a concerned citizen."

Neither of us had an ounce of humor to weigh between us; the smiles were thin.

"If you've had enough of wasting my time, there are other people I need to see." He gave me a curt smile and indicated the door.

I left the room and stood next to the door against the wall, which was as stone-faced as Watcher. I heard him pick up the phone and dial.

"Yeah, he was just here," I heard him say.

There was a pause as he listened.

"What do you want me to do? Listen, L—"

"Sir, can I help you?" A young slowhand snapped my attention away from eavesdropping. Watcher's conversation was lost as the slowhand closed the door.

"No. I'm leaving," I replied.

The youngster gave me a smile, and indicated the exit sign.

I stepped out onto the main street. The day was passing, as were the people. My stomach growled. It was well past lunchtime but I didn't care. Another pain was stabbing at me. There was only one person besides Watcher who had come into my life and got to know me, who was also associated with Watcher. Laura.

Thinking of that angelic face, I couldn't believe she could be so deceptive. But wouldn't she be the perfect person? No, she wasn't a betrayer. It must be someone else. But who?

Laura had said mob connections went high, and that Levi was probably connected. I wondered if the mob also included Rami Watcher.

CHAPTER 24 ...

I went back to my office. I took Angelina's file from my pocket, flipped it open, and slipped the contents onto the desk. The first document was a photograph—good quality, in a plastic bag—of Hugh Jorgen. That was unexpected. He was singing out his, at the time, still-beating heart. He had no idea what was coming.

That was the thing with death—you rarely knew it was coming until the reaper tapped you on the shoulder. I'd lived a life of Watcher breathing down my neck, holding out against the inevitable final curtain. Now I felt like it had all been to meet Laura Malory. Even for the briefest of moments, it was worth the wait.

In the photograph, a crowd of excitable ladies was standing at the base of the stage, staring adoringly up at Jorgen. The microphone stand was clearer in this shot. It was indeed an old piece of wood, semi-disguised by the cable wrapping around it. It was a long pole, about six inches wide, maybe less—the detail wasn't that great in the grain. I wondered what was special about the photograph for it to be included in the file. Angelina told me she hadn't met Jorgen.

Hadn't met him.

I examined the photograph more closely. I didn't recognize anyone in the band, or in the crowd. I reached into my desk drawer and pulled out a magnifying glass. I went over each person in the crowd. There at the back was a pretty young lady, with her black hair tied back, looking tense, afraid, and staring straight at Mr. Jorgen.

She may not have met him, face to face, but she sure knew about him.

There were more pictures of a bedroom—a young girl's bedroom, possibly a teenager's. It had been trashed. There were police tags over everything in the photograph. There were a couple of close-ups of a small bed with dark patches. The notes on the rear of the picture stated that it was blood. It was dated a decade ago.

I picked up a photograph of a second bedroom, with a double bed this time but showing the same mayhem; possibly a parents' bedroom, full of memories. A picture of the inside of a closet showed a collection of weapons bound together by thick leather straps. The next shot had them spread out on the floor. The notes listed Matchlock muskets, custom Taurus model-85 revolvers, a mocked-up Remington 870, and a gas-operated automatic crossbow. There were also knives, medieval and ancient.

The weapons were a collector's dream, but all very illegal after the '39 senate ruling. Good stuff to have around the house with a teenage girl. I picked up a note that said: *Missing: Wooden Pole "rood"*. It was also dated ten years ago.

Angelina had lost her parents at the same time she was attacked. Someone had gone in and massacred her family, and taken the rood. Then she had either fended for herself through her teenage years, or someone had looked after her, watched out for her.

I checked my watch; an hour had flown past. I put everything back in the file and stashed it in the backup secret alcove above my closet. Then it occurred to me that if I hid it and the trashmen found it, they might consider it important. I went for the double bluff and hid it in the filing cabinet, in plain sight, under "M" for miscellaneous, or possibly misdirection.

Time to make my way back to the government records office.

Xerography lady gave me a short list comprising four city addresses and one other document, handwritten, I noticed. They were all temptations of the flesh: a couple of brothels, a bar, and an all-you-can eatery. One of particular interest was—ironically—an old church, with an undisclosed address. That meant it was a piece of land, his only one, not within the city boundaries, but out on the wastelands to the east. You'd need to be a brave parishioner to venture out there. I put it on my to-do list, at the bottom, under cleaning behind the refrigerator.

I pocketed the list and made my way to the first address. It was a skin joint out to the north, probably servicing politicians and other respectable notaries. It was on a green, leafy street, open wide for any bribes that came its way. Nestled between a jewelry shop—catching the guilt money from philanderers for their forgotten wives—and a wine bar made of marble and glass was a bundle of bricks and twisted metal; an imploded building feeling unworthy of its location and extracting itself from view.

I knocked on the doors of the suffering businesses on either side. A young lady in the jeweler's said it was like the place had died. They were going to be hit hard by the sudden lack of custom. She told me it had happened two nights ago. I put that in the same timeframe as Templeton 667.

There were rumors, the young lady said, that it had been full of the skinny blond hookers they seemed to employ exclusively, but there had been no evidence they were missed. No one grieving had come by. Only the businessmen and politicians had paused momentarily before finding interests elsewhere and striding onto new stomping grounds.

I headed out to the western districts, to the bar next on my list. It was roughneck country, where haulers brought in banned contraband from the more freethinking parts of the world, big meat-headed thugs who maximized everything for greed. In the food chain of depravity, they were the fat middle management, ripping off the small fry and lying to the top about profits being made.

It was a surprise, but not a total one, to see that the building had been flattened. It looked like it had been an old church at one point. Now it was just a pile of bricks.

The diesel station next to it looked deserted. No one was stopping. No one was buying fuel. I knocked on the door of the house attached to the diesel stop, and eventually a hungover-looking guy opened the door. He confirmed that the place next door had collapsed in on itself, two nights ago. He had been on duty when it happened. He said there had been an influx of the skinny blond hookers they got in to entertain people, then not long after midnight the whole thing had come down. Like the life had been sucked out of it.

The third address was in the south basin. A fast-food joint had been built on the site of an old graveyard, where the first settlers had been buried, and sold food so cheaply it had to be bad. The place was gone. Another pile of rubble, just like the others. Everything around it was untouched. Precision implosion. The block was big. It had been a restaurant, bigger than most. At the rear was a lot of twisted metal, the ruins of a large car yard. Truck tires were heavy on the ground. There was also a lot of blood.

I asked the neighbors when the building had come down. Two nights ago.

No one seemed upset about it. They whispered their concern about the kind of meat that was served. Trucks came in, but not from the slaughterhouse. One neighbor swore she'd heard quiet cries once when she was walking her dog past one of the trucks and the doors were open. "They were human cries," she said.

One old neighbor told me the landlord had never been brought to trial over it. "It was a disgrace," she said. "I challenged him about it one day when I was a young girl. I threw tomatoes at him." She said she'd seen him five decades later and he still looked the same.

Templeton 667 was next on the list, but I knew the story there. That only left one other skin joint in the northwest. I knew what I'd find there. You'd have to be three-parts Republican not to see the connection.

Sure enough, it was another old place that had been operating as cover for the oldest profession for longer than any of the neighbors could remember. Old people told me their grandparents had said the same thing: skinny blond things, all looking the same.

For centuries the good men of the city had been sucked into a well of deceit, which succeeded in turning men with golden hearts into politicians who wanted little else than to line their own pockets and hide the evidence. And then commit suicide when they were found out, leaving their grieving families with nothing more than a half-baked retirement benefit and a bucket load of foul-tasting lies.

Folks understood it, they even played along when it came to election time, but they didn't like it, so they turned the other way and watched the descent of society over their shoulders while tending to their marigolds.

Five places in the city, all nothing but rubble.

I went back to the lovely lady at the government office. There were lease dates. They all expired at the same time: tomorrow night. Phoenix was checking out.

I went back to my office. It occurred to me that I'd completed a circuit of the metropolis. I grabbed my old street directory, ripped out the pages, and stuck them together to make one large map of the city. I thumbtacked it to the wall and marked out the five demolished buildings. I stood back. It was easy to see what was going on. Five points in a ring, just like you might find on the body of a dead, skinny blond thing.

I drew lines connecting the five points. The lines intersected on the Grand Hilltop church. For the first time I felt the cogs clicking into place.

I checked my watch, and gave the tank a call. The desk sergeant said Laura had gone home for the day. She'd only been in for an hour, doing paperwork, and then left citing illness. This meant I could go see her again.

I got the kink out of my head and thought about all the ways I could say I was sorry. In a world where Laura couldn't do any worse than me, and I could never do any better than her, maybe it kind of balanced out. Maybe there was the possibility of a future where we could spend more time together. If she didn't set herself on fire when I suggested it, I'd take it as a good sign.

It had been a good day. Progress with clues, resolution of mind, and a good lunch all combined to lift me.

CHAPTER 25 ...

Feeling a spring in my step, I caught a thirty-five to Fernando Drive. The weariness of the days fell away and a smile cracked its way across my face. I rapped on her front door. My eyes flicked over to the pot with the hidden key, and I briefly entertained the idea of using it. But she had said it was for friends, and I didn't know if I currently qualified as one. Maybe within a few minutes that would all change.

A minute rolled past. I gave the door another knock. Then another minute rolled by. I turned away, feeling deflated.

The door unlocked behind me. I spun around, with a heart full of hope. Mina was standing at the door wearing a robe she hadn't had the inclination to fasten. She curled her finger and beckoned me in. I followed hesitantly. She moved, almost floating over the cool tiles, until she was in the middle of the living room. She spun around. Her wrap swung out, revealing parts of her that looked flushed. No secrets on her.

She looked down at her top, or lack of, and sighed. She clenched together the edges of her wrap, partially concealing her body. "Come on, stud, you've seen more playing in the berry patch." She stood tall with her head high. Her injury was still patched, but she was carrying her pain like a radio. "When life gives you melons, wear a low-cut top. What do you want?"

"Laura was getting info."

"Ah, dear Laura, always thinking of others. It's such an attractive quality. But then that's her. All pretty and pure, and so much fun."

Her tone was different. She was no longer selling her intent; her shop was closed. She wandered over to the master bedroom and pushed open the door. She reached into the room and picked up a small envelope from the dresser just inside the door. She sniffed it and smiled. She leaned against the doorjamb and held the letter out casually. I stepped closer and she brought her arm in to her side, causing me to move in even closer. With both of us standing in the doorway to the bedroom, she released her grip on the envelope. She bit her bottom lip. She let her wrap fall open again. She stepped in close and I could feel the heat of her body.

"Hey, big boy, I'd invite you in but the bed's already taken." She looked back over her shoulder.

The identity had me confused for a moment, but then a sick feeling stole into my stomach. I felt myself break out in a cold sweat as realization dawned.

"She had a few drinks and finally let her barriers down," Mina purred. She laughed as the color drained from my face. "Oh, look at you. You shouldn't keep all those emotions trapped inside."

Visions of the two of them wrapped around each other socked me in the stomach. I could feel an icy grip in my chest, one from long ago that I'd promise myself I'd forget.

"Of course, I could always change my mind," she said. "We could whip up a little party, just the three of us. We'd all get to know each other ... intimately."

My head spun and I staggered back. I pushed her away and turned to leave. "No."

"Honey, I've seen everything under the moon and heard every word there is. Nothing can surprise or offend me except being declined."

Her face turned sour and her beauty dropped away. All I could see was someone who had lived a life of deceit and manipulation. And now she had lured away the most precious person in the world to me. Love wasn't a competition, but I'd lost.

I staggered down Fernando Drive, barely aware of the thirty-five that nearly ran me down. Only the blast of its horn and the diesel fumes almost on top of me woke me from my misanthropic walk. All I could see were images of Mina and Laura. Everything was dark. I was surrounded by a callous forest of thorny recollections. Every memory hurt. Every breath hurt. A thirty-five running over me would have been salvation.

I sat on the top story of the bus with the envelope in my hand. A tear rolled down my face onto the paper. I wiped my eye and watched the world drag by. We were a good hundred feet up. I could jump. Knowing my luck, on the way down flight would reveal itself as a secret power.

There weren't too many people I could call a friend, or even talk to, but I found myself pushing through the doorway into Angelina's little shop. The bell tinkled its little sad melody, but it was the only sad thing about the place. It had been redecorated. The dark colors were gone and bright drapes hung around the room. The cheap knock-off relics had been removed and replaced by rows of flowers, herbs, and New Age books.

I went back outside to check I was in the right place. I was. I pushed open the door again, and there stood Angelina in her new outfit.

Her dark hair was tied back and she was wearing dark glasses. A long leather coat hung down to her knees that said one word to me: chafe. She whipped back her coat and, for the first time, exposed no skin. She wore dark leather pants and a dark shirt loosely buttoned up, showing enough to distract what the rest of her was carrying. She had a huge gun strapped to each thigh, slung low so she could pull them out quickly. She also had a sword strapped to her back, plus assorted weaponry hanging off her belt.

"Expecting trouble?" I said.

"I was thinking about what you said about the people looking for me," she replied. She gave me a sly smile. "Maybe I am."

"I'm sure you'll blend in."

She whipped out the oversized weapons and spun them around, obviously well versed in their weight and execution. If the mechwarriors had found them they would have exploded with the excitement of such provocative firearms.

She jumped around the room, aiming at various plants and pretending to shoot.

"How did you keep the weapons?"

"We hid them." She beamed with inner achievement.

"Where? On the moon?"

"Maybe I'll show you later, if you're nice to me."

A fan in the center of the ceiling was slowly ticking around with barely a sound other than the occasional whip of wicker through the pollinated air. The breeze rolled down gently and caressed the colorful petals. Her outfit was in stark contrast to her new shop, but then maybe that was Angelina: an enigma wrapped up in a conundrum that didn't even know any riddles to break the tension.

She holstered her firearms, folded her arms, and glared at me. My mind drifted away, thinking back to Mina, her appearance as nature intended, and the things she'd said. The thoughts made me feel numb and I had difficulty pulling my mind back into focus.

"Why the change?" I said eventually.

"I've been hiding for too long. It's time to fight back."

I looked around the room again. "With flowers and herbs?"

"You'd be amazed at the damage you can do with a well-placed chrysanthemum bomb." She cast a careful eye over me. "You look like you could use something uplifting. You've taken another beating. On the inside."

"I'm not talking about it." I waved the address at her. "We've got places to go."

"And people to shoot?"

I shrugged. "If you want."

Her face lit up. I hoped her enthusiasm for wonton destruction would rub off on me. At the moment I was tied to the bottom of a well with the water rising up above my chin. The questions of the morning were sitting in the forefront of my mind, ticking away like an unexploded bomb.

The pollen was getting to me. My throat constricted under the allergies. I coughed. "Can I have a drink?"

She poured a glass of water, looking impatient.

I took a sip and stared at her. "You said you lost your parents," I croaked.

"Yes, when I was a baby."

I took another sip. "Who looked after you?"

"I think I grew up in an orphanage until I could escape."

"You *think*? Do you remember which one?"

"Not really, it was so dull and uninspiring. All those sad faces, staring without hope, the futility of an empty life pounding them into submission. The need. The hunger. The washed-out eyes of disillusionment. And the children weren't much better."

"When did the 'vampire' attack you?"

She paused before answering. An odd expression crossed across her face, the struggle of recollection, not painful but difficult, as if too distant.

"About a year ago, but I remember it like it was yesterday. The lights. That evil face. Beautiful, then animal. The pain."

Intensity seemed to set into her like she was burning from the inside. I could only guess what it was like for her. She'd locked everything away in her memory and all she'd been left with was pain, which sat within her without reason or release.

"You sure you've never seen Jorgen?" The change caught her off guard.

"I haven't met him at all. I promise."

"I said 'seen.'"

"Do we have to stand around with the questions all day? There are bad guys to shoot. Let's go."

She nearly dragged me out of the shop in her enthusiasm for retribution. She locked the door and turned to face me. "Where did you park?"

"I don't have a car."

"Why not? Time is of the essence."

"Nothing important should ever be rushed."

"That's all fine and dandy, but you're not the one in the fancy footwear." She lifted the cuffs of her leather trousers and revealed a set of black, studded stiletto boots.

Sometimes the right words just aren't there and all you can do is look disappointed.

"Surely you don't expect me to wear flat shoes. What kind of message would that send? Killing vampires requires, I assure you, that you look fabulous."

"We'll take a thirty-five."

She looked down the street to the distant bus stop. "No. We'll take a taxi. You can sit in the front and do the stupid talk-thing with the smelly driver."

Hitching a dimbox was straightforward. The first one came to a screeching halt the minute she aimed her twin guns at the hapless driver.

We passed through the lowlife areas on the way to the broker's address. The depressing sight of destitute people who'd sold everything, and now were selling themselves, darkened my already pensive mood. They lined the streets and alleyways, but slid away as we rolled past. I watched them from within the sanctity of the metal cocoon of the taxi. The thin glass barrier didn't make it less real, and I could feel the desperation begin to seep into me.

The driver pulled over near the address and made haste with his overcharged fare, leaving us to traverse the final hundred yards on foot. Angelina bounced along with her fingers itching and her palms scratching close to her weapons.

CHAPTER 26 ...

The Cashing In pawnshop was closed, evident by the open/closed sign flipped around on the door. The metal grill was up out of the way, but the door was locked. Angelina knocked until the solid door shook, but there was no response.

I took a quick look around before whipping out the Remington picklock and slipping it into the lock. The door swung open into a dark chamber of an office. It smelled bad. Something despicable had happened here.

Angelina tried to squeeze past me through the door, showing almost uncontrollable determination and effervescent excitement. She flicked on the lights to reveal a room full of people's possessions, now scattered over the floor, and mostly broken. The glass on the central counter had been smashed. There were traces of blood on the jagged glass, as though someone had been thrown through it.

Angelina armed herself and stalked around the room.

"Will those guns work against them?" I said.

"You think these creatures are new? They've been around as long as we have, maybe longer, living in our nightmares, chasing us, torturing us. We had to learn how to fight back. Our survival depended on it. So now we have these." She wheeled around, leveling the guns at me. "Weapons that'll wipe their conceited smiles off their stupid, pretty little faces."

She gave me a small smile before continuing with her exploration. She hadn't gone a couple of paces before she tripped up on the dead proprietor and fell face down on the blood-soaked carpet. He had been badly mutilated: ripped open and disemboweled. Angelina gasped in horror. I doubted she'd volunteered for this kind of thing, but you never can tell what dark lessons they pedal down at the asylum.

"Do you think he's dead?" she stammered, scrambling backward.

"I do." I continued my search through a filing system, ripped open and now scattered over the floor. "Haven't you seen dead people before?"

"Not as such. I've seen undead. But he just looks like a piece of meat." She lifted up his dead hand and let it thump back onto the carpet. She did it again.

Remember she's on loan from crazy school, I reminded myself. Angelina was lucky she was easy on the eye. It allowed her to get away with almost everything.

"Careful," I said. "You might resurrect him."

She went to move away from the prostrate corpse, but something caught her eye. She crouched down and ran her finger around his neck. There was a gold chain so fine it was barely visible. She unclipped the tiny clasp and slipped it off. A small brass key hung from the chain.

"We'll take it with us," I said. "It has to have value."

"I was thinking the same. It's such a plain thing, but he kept it hidden."

"I've got it." I waved a piece of paper at her. "Jorgen's card." It had been trampled on, ripped, muddied and bloodied, but I could still make out the copperplate lettering of his name.

"Whatever the key opens must be out back." She slid aside a dark curtain and disappeared into the small room behind the shop. She called out, her voice distant and hollow.

I followed her voice. The small room behind the curtain was dark, but I could make out rows of shelves stacked to the ceiling, packed with thousands of items. Some were lying in the open; some were obviously secreted in severe steel lockers, all rivets, welding, and disenfranchised attitude. The aged patina on the metal indicated the guy had been in business a long time. There was a small table to the right with a half-eaten sandwich, and a knocked-over chair.

A few steps past the table was a wall of small drawers. I grabbed the brass handle of the closest one and slid it open. It was full of index cards. I pulled out the first card. It was dated seventy-seven years ago. I opened another drawer to the left. A hundred and twenty-eight years ago. No one was coming back for these possessions. Why had he kept them? There were several more drawers, also to the left but higher up. I wondered how far back they stretched. If historians ever found this place they'd have a field day.

"I've found some stairs," Angelina said.

Tucked away in the rear was a small opening that dived down into darkness.

"Come down to Cashing In downstairs," Angelina called.

"Is that a euphemism?" I called back as I took my first steps into the gloom. I stopped when I heard a creak in the room behind me, than continued down the stairs.

It was nearly pitch black in the stairwell. I could see her outline, strong and feminine, formed by the glow of a minuscule light. She wheeled around, and her face, illuminated by a match, jumped out at me. The flame went out and we were both left in complete darkness, with her pretty face and rebellious hair burning on my retinas.

Her feet scuffed the steps as she came up and reached out for my hand. I heard another scuffing sound behind me.

"Exciting, isn't it?"

She was still holding my hand, and I wondered who felt more secure.

Another match flickered into life and Angelina's friendly face lit up. The light caught the reflection of glass beside me and I turned to investigate. The glass was an old miner's gas lantern. It was full, and we soon had a soft golden glow creeping out into the darkness like liquid treacle.

In a room at the bottom of the stairs were ancient shelves that towered up to the ceiling, being called to the crumbling event horizon even as I stared at them.

"The whole place looks like it was built centuries ago," Angelina said. She ran her hand along the dusty shelves. "There are some very odd artifacts here."

"Like what?"

"Religious stuff. Really old bits of …" She stopped and picked up an old painting. "I know her."

I moved closer and examined the portrait she was holding. There was an unforgettable face dressed in the clothing of an early settler, and some vaguely familiar Joe Schmo standing directly behind her, although the background figure couldn't draw me away from the figure in front.

"Are you all right?" I said.

"I'm not sure where I've seen her. Would you think I was weird if I said I'd seen her in my dreams?"

Most of the things Angelina said were on the far side of deranged, so I said, "No weirder than before."

She gave me a sideways glance before continuing with her exploration of the portrait. "This painting feels really old," she said, picking up the painting. She ran her hand along the frame, feeling the carved swirls in the ancient wood. "Everything's so dusty. I wonder if it's dirt or dead skin."

"Has the painting got a number?"

She flipped it over and read the number scrawled on the back. It was a number three, and that opened up at least two more questions.

I checked the nearest drawers, which also contained index cards. The numbers stopped at twenty. Angelina searched deeper in the dark room. She found one locker slightly ajar. She kicked it until it opened. There was a small pile of aluminum. She scooped it up and let it dangle from her hands. It was a pile of jewelry, necklaces and rings, all made from the cheap metal.

"What's this all about?" she said.

"Aluminum was expensive once," I said. "Then they invented smelting. All this would've become worthless overnight.".

She laughed. "Listen to you, Mr. Encyclopaedia Britannica. I've got this image of a stuck-up old lady thinking she's oh so clever investing her family fortune in aluminum jewelry, then being left with nothing but scrap metal."

"We don't have time for this, admiring the glitz while we're searching for the grit."

"But there are so many of these lockers, so old and full of … things we used to believe in. In a way it's fascinating."

"And depressing," I said. "It reminds me of childhood."

I thought of the toys we have as children, and the ones we put away and forget about. They're so much of who we are and what we become, but we leave them behind so easily. Our beliefs are the same. We seem to want to cast aside the thoughts that kept us safe through those dark days of early civilization to show someone or something how grown up we are. Now we get sparkling idols.

I could see the desire in her eyes. Although the jewelry was worthless, it was still shiny and her attention was hard to dislodge, especially by someone whose life contained so little.

"Focus on the rood," I said. "You'll find it more rewarding than hoarding shiny trinkets."

"Maybe we should all have been doing that a bit more, rather than hoarding shiny trinkets."

At floor level in one far corner, Angelina found a small wooden case with rusted hinges. It was locked. She looked over at me and withdrew the brass key on the fine gold chain. I could see it faintly in the golden glow. The key fit. She turned it, and the box squeaked open.

"A dozen cards or so, and some ashes." She knocked the ashes out of the box and stood quietly for a moment, reading the cards one at a time. "I've got the card." She waved it in the air. "I wonder if this is a hoax." She came over and handed it to me.

The date read *March 24, 1624.*

I looked back at the painting, and flicked the card yellowed with age between my fingers. "It must be a descendant," I said.

"Do you know her?" She looked at me suspiciously.

I nodded. "I know someone who looks like her."

"As I said, so do I."

"That woman you saw in your dream. What was it about?"

"Dreams, hah. They're nightmares, of a cat-like beast that comes into my room at night and bites me on the chest. Then it turns into a female figure and disappears through the door without opening it. Weird, huh?"

"When did these nightmares start?"

"When that skinny blond bitch tried to suck the life out of me. But I still have the image of the dog biting her arm. Her look of pain makes me smile after the nightmare's gone." She stared back at the painting. "But the woman in the painting, and my dream, isn't the same one who tried to sucker me."

She continued to stare at it. "I think the ship in the background is the *Mayfair.* I remember the shape from school textbooks." She laughed. "Wouldn't it be funny if the pilgrims who were persecuted for their religious beliefs turned out to be vampires, and the New World was settled by them. Oh wait, what if they brought over the people to breed them and hunt them, like the New World was some big game park."

"Focus," I said.

"What number's on the card?"

"C."

"That's not a number," she said, as if no one else had noticed. "Yeah."

"Maybe … maybe it's like in a different dimension." Her voice suddenly pitched up in excitement. "You have to do something weird, or ritually, then the whole world twists sideways and suddenly up is down, numbers are letters, colors are sounds and—"

"I've found it."

"Oh." Her face fell.

I'd found several tall lockers labeled A to F. I tried the latch on C. It squeaked open and we both peered inside.

"So where's the rood?" Angelina said.

The locker was empty. The lock had been forced, the latch bent, and inside there was nothing but space that would disillusion any rampant optimist.

Angelina wiped her hand in the dust at the bottom of the locker. She examined the dust on her fingers, sniffing it and staring at it closely. She brushed it off her fingers and let it fall to the floor. It glowed. She sighed and slumped against the opposite wall.

"The rood's gone," she said. "That's a rood awakening."

"Are you taking this seriously?"

"You think this is the first time it's been stolen? It has a history of slipping through people's hands."

"How do you know so much? It seems like more than a hobby."

"I've got notes."

I gave her a look of few words.

"Okay, okay. I don't know if you know this, but I'm from a long line of vampire slayers. That's probably one of the reasons they want me dead."

"Probably?"

She glanced at me. "Okay, it's a pretty big one. My family's been doing this for centuries. At times we've been custodians of the rood. There used to be dozens of us, but now it's just me. If I don't have children there'll be no more vampire slayers. But there's something they've forgotten. I'm the only one who knows how to use the rood."

"Really? You've used it?"

"Well … I've read the notes."

"So you don't know how to use it."

"I know the theory. It's all in the wrist." She smiled at me. "Lots of things are."

I sighed. She was turning into a Mina.

I kicked the ground, muttering the words "vampire slayer" the same way someone might say "psychotic delusional." The rood was gone. Crazy-pants might not have been worried, but the way the staff had disappeared before we got there was ominous.

"How did they know?" I wondered aloud.

Somehow they must have worked out that Hugh had brought the rood to this pawnshop. I didn't like where this was heading. I'd only told one person about it, and that person gave me this address. Laura. Unless she told someone at work, there was no way anyone could have known so quickly. But she wouldn't have told anyone at the tank. Maybe someone overheard her, or was spying on her. The voice of the bear-man came back, ringing in my ears: *Betrayer.*

The pain speared into me, making my head spin. The weight of the world fell on me, and I sagged under the pressure.

CHAPTER 27 ...

"Where did you say you got the address from?" Angelina asked me.

"A friend."

"How sure are you that your friend's reliable? You know, not one of them." She was watching me carefully.

"Ninety-nine percent."

"So there's a one-percent chance your friend sold us out."

"No."

"There's a chance they could've found this place on their own. There's also a chance they didn't find it and it's in one of these other lockers. But I doubt it."

I couldn't wrap my head—or my heart—around the implication of Angelina's words; that Laura had betrayed me. I put the gas lantern down and opened the next locker. The lantern went out. We were in darkness.

"Why did you do that?" Angelina said.

"I didn't."

"*I did.*"

"I wish you'd make up your mind."

"I didn't," I repeated.

I had the feeling I'd missed something. The dust and claustrophobia were beginning to sink their fearsome claws into my resolve. I felt someone breathing down my neck. I was shaking. I picked up the lantern and relit it. It was still full. I placed it back down. When I turned back to the locker it went out again.

"Stop doing that," I said.

"I didn't do anything."

I bent down. The lantern was gone. "Did you take the lantern?"

"Why would I do that?" She'd found a long, thin rod and was using it to prise open another locker.

The lantern appeared at the far end of the small room. Relit. On its own.

"What the …" Angelina glanced at me, and turned and looked at the lantern.

We both walked to the far end of the room. As we approached the lantern, it went out again.

"How can that happen? Is there anything in your notes?" I said.

"Yes," she said sarcastically, "its energy mode's set to transport." We searched the floor in the dark, but it had gone.

"For sure, this isn't exciting," I said.

"Before you said it was," she replied.

"That was you."

"I didn't say anything." She stepped in close to me. "Who did?"

Then the lantern reignited at the other end of the room, next to the lockers, the flames licking up slowly and menacingly, starting small then growing until the whole corner was bathed in the strange glow. Shadows flitted around the edges of the pool of light.

The lantern went out again and we were left blinking in the darkness. Then it exploded. Flames leaped up, engulfing the ancient wooden shelves, which cracked and burned with a vengeful intensity.

I'd never heard such language before. Angelina went through every blue word available to the local community and outreaching lands. We turned back to the exit, but found it blocked by the solid oak door. I banged my fists against it. There were scorch marks on it. There was no handle or lever of any kind. I knocked on the walls. They clanged.

We were in a metal box, underground. The place had become a furnace.

The flames leaped up the walls liked deranged goblins. Old parchment and wood, brittle beyond use, exploded. Smoke coiled around us as the heat built. Angelina grabbed my hand and squeezed tightly. She gasped and placed her hand over her mouth. I turned. In the smoke, floating eerily in the billowing clouds, were five points of light hanging in the air. We stood mesmerized by the sight.

Angelina stepped behind me and looked over my shoulder. "No. Not again," she whispered.

Another set of five white lights appeared beside the first. Out of the shadows stepped two skinny blond things, their heads bent forward and their burning red eyes staring up at us. Their hands were extended and their fingers glowed.

"This is not a good day," I said.

I reached back and grasped Angelina closely. I tried to back away, but there was no space left. The smoke was starting to thicken. I pointed to the shelves.

"Use your weapons," I said.

There was no response. I turned around; she was shaking with fear. Her memories had come back and paralyzed her. I shook her and shouted, and slowly her eyes drifted away from the skinny blond things to my face.

"Forget them," I shouted, "you're converted."

"Then why are they here?" she cried. "They won't stop until we're dead. And they don't die."

She wasn't any good to me like this. I slapped her across the face. That focused her. She kneed me weakly in the groin, which I wasn't expecting, but, given the circumstances, it was a worthwhile trade.

"You brought weapons," I managed. "*Use* them."

"Yes, I did, didn't I?"

Her face changed as the security of heavy firepower washed over her. She smiled with the conviction of a gambler who's discovered that the four aces up the sleeve are still there. She threw back her coat and snatched out her weapons. A determined spark flashed in her eyes. She unloaded several rounds into the advancing bodies. Smoke poured out of her guns as the spent rounds tumbled to the floor.

The figures stumbled backward under the onslaught. The bullets thudded into their bodies, ripping them apart. Their shapes deformed as pieces of them fell to the floor. But then the bullets ran out and they came stalking forward again.

"I should've brought the silver bullets." Angelina pulled the pistol from behind her back and emptied it.

I wasn't thinking straight. It would have been better if she'd fired at the damn door.

"It's not easy, but I'm enjoying it," she yelled.

She slipped the sword off her back and brought it down in one graceful swipe, but one skinny blond stepped aside, easily avoiding the blade. Angelina swung again, and again the creature dodged easily.

Smoke had filled the small room, and we were both coughing.

The first skinny blond reached toward me. My feet slid backward and I struggled to gain traction. She closed the distance and her fingertips touched my chest … and she exploded into a howling ball of rage and pain. She retreated, clutching her hand and hissing like a demented cat. Her face twisted with pain and anger, taking on the qualities of a hideous beast.

I felt my chest. Under the shirt fabric I made out the round shape of the rood shield. I approached her, and she backed away, stepping into flames that licked up around her. I could barely see her through the smoke. My head spun and my vision blurred. Holding my shirt up over my mouth failed to keep the debilitating fumes out of my lungs. I took a last deep breath and charged at her.

I felt fingers burning into me, pulling the life from my body. I pulled her close so she couldn't escape. The pain burned through me. I slashed at her with the blade, opening up a large wound in her stomach. I grabbed her around the neck, pulled her close, and rammed the rood shield into the wound. She staggered back.

Angelina's earlier words came to me: *They won't stop until we're dead.*

"Today," I croaked, "*you're* dead."

The explosion filled the small room.

I tucked in under Angelina's wilting body and hitched her arm over my shoulder. She was barely conscious, fighting for breath. Flames roared toward us, and the heat seared into my bones. As the pressure built, the door buckled and a moment later blew free. The shockwave lifted us up and blew us through the open doorway onto the steps. We began to tumble down toward the flames.

I rolled up onto my feet, grabbed Angelina and threw her over my shoulder. I raced up the steps. I charged at the front door and leaped through the glass. We landed heavily on the sidewalk as the shop exploded over us. Glass rained down around us, followed by smoking and smoldering pieces of wood, and scraps of paper that fluttered down like bloated fireflies.

The glass cascaded off me as I moved. I rolled over and checked Angelina's pulse. It was there. Faint but regular. I shook her gently, and the glass fell from her. Her eyes opened slowly, then widened as she recognized me, well enough, apparently, for her to slap me.

"What was that for?"

"You lost the rood shield," she shouted.

I held up the small piece of wood. Smokey blood dripped from it, but it was still in one piece. "It's tougher than you and me." I gave her a smile.

She slapped me again. I put it down to habit. Then she gave me a passionate kiss. I reminded myself that she was on loan from crazy school. But you can always check the books back into the crazy-school library later. Just as I was enjoying it she gave me another slap. Crazy school.

"You're a tough man, Mr. Avram." She lay back and stared up at the sky. "Thank you for saving me."

I thought there might be another kiss in it, but she appeared to have progressed beyond that level of physical appreciation.

"The rood is gone," she said. "Those ... *things* are out during the day and attacking us, even though neither one of us is a female virgin. Something bad is coming. We should get out of here. Go to a church or something and hide."

"You need to face your fears," I said, coughing up smoke.

"Easier said than done."

I looked at her. She was someone I knew very little about. Down in the darkness, the skinny blond things had wanted to kill me, that was true, but only in a you're-in-the-way kind of way. They'd had a definite target in Angelina. Their anger had been intense, way beyond defense; it was revenge. There was no doubting the manic and hateful look in their eyes. I wondered what they knew that I didn't.

"Do you think anyone noticed, or can we sneak away without telling anyone? The cops are going to want a mountain of paperwork. Let's get out of here before people realize explosions aren't contagious."

She was right. The slowhands would stymie everything. We needed to flash the feet back to respectable streets. And I was thinking of the *real* respectable ones. I knew Angelina didn't want to believe someone would sell the rood, but I had to be sure.

We agreed that she would chase down potential collectors. She had big guns, a dark, scary outfit, and a demeanor that would get people responding. She agreed to call me at my office at sunset with any news. It gave us both a few hours to come up with something.

I was guessing that Levi was after the rood, since he'd killed Hugh for it and taken a shot at me. The Vinyl tallied up as his main hangout. With reality trying to make some sense of the current circumstances, he'd be using the rood like some hokum stick to spook his underlings into line. There was still some mileage left in the mob aspect, and it was worth chasing up. At least it gave me something real to sink my teeth into.

(HAPTER 28 ...

The Terrace was quiet. I recognized a few old faces, shady characters on the black market always looking for a deal. They nodded as I strode past, looking for an opening for a potential sale, a bribe, or general company in the loneliness. But I kept my head down and barged past them.

The usual vagrants that hung out in front of the Vinyl were missing. The place was eerily empty. Even the building itself sagged in some anthropomorphic way; the cool, brutal kid in school suddenly finding out he smelled bad and no amount of bullying was going to bring back the followers.

The side gate was open. The wind blew down the alley, scooping up leaves and tumbling them out onto the street. At the entrance I glanced back over my shoulder; the street suddenly seemed very empty. I made my way down the alley and into the strange, antiquated, cobbled courtyard, also deserted. The metal door was unlocked. I reached for the handle and pulled the door open. My fingers felt wet. I turned them over. They were red. The handle on the inside was the same, covered in blood.

The main room was quiet, empty, and neatly ordered. The stairwell was also quiet. I slowly crept down the staircase, unable to detect anything below. The gloom and quiet wrapped around me; all I could hear were my own footsteps and breathing.

At the base of the steps was the familiar crucifix room where I'd spent a joyful afternoon hanging around. The three crosses were still mounted against the wall. I wondered what the significance was of three crosses. Surely one would have been enough for the show. Maybe they were trying to form a band.

The gloom was intense. There was strange-smelling smoke in the air; a hint of fruit gone bad. I found the light switch and flicked it on. The lights flared then exploded, leaving me in complete dark while my eyes tried to recover from the brief intensity of light.

I went back up to the main chamber and grabbed two large candles. I scouted around and found a matchbox with two matches. The candles flared and I went back downstairs, now with dancing shadows jumping out at me as I descended.

There had been meeting in the crucifix room. Tables had been arranged in a group, looking in one direction. A large book, call it a tome, lay open on the table at the front of the grouping. As I approached I became aware of something on the wall. I raised the candle. The light crept up the wall to reveal words: names written in chalk on the ancient brickwork. They were written in groups, with lines connecting some of the individual names. Some names I recognized as notable people in the government, or public figures. At the moment it didn't make much sense to me.

I turned back to the table and examined the book. There was a tag in one of the pages. On the cover was a leather patch with the letter *A* printed on it. That at least answered one question from the pawnbroker's shop. The book was so old the pages creaked as I turned them. I wasn't completely sure they were made of paper, and the feel of them made my skin crawl.

A genealogy tree, printed in red, covered the pages. I didn't recognize any of the names except for the last one: all the names were crossed off except for Angelina's. There were heavy dents and scratches next to her name, some almost like animal claws. They really didn't like her.

I caught a glint of light from the wall, something reflective at height. Scrawled in still-wet blood was the name *Lucy*. Who was Lucy? And why didn't she deserve a last name? She must've been pretty important; the letters on the wall were big and written in obvious anger, as though the person who wrote them was obsessed. You'd have to be concerned if you found a small room somewhere with press clippings and distant photographs of the mysterious Lucy.

Why was Lucy, whoever she was, important enough to have her name scrawled on the wall in this dungeon in front of a group of people? Maybe she was a suspect or the object of hate. Or maybe she was in a vocal group, but that was the domain of teenagers, and while most teenagers would have given their indifferent attitude for a bedroom like this, I doubted that was the answer. My guess was that Lucy was the enemy.

Then I noticed two other names on the wall, much smaller. Mina's was there. And mine, in the center of a circle with five points around it, punctuated by a big cross. It looked like they didn't like me either.

I turned my attention back to the book, flipping the leaves back to the first page. There was a long text, in what looked like Greek, printed in large, gothic lettering. Someone had typed up a translation on an old IBM typewriter, by the look of it, and placed it next to the page. And someone had added handwritten notes on top of the translation: *There will be a new union, and the mixing of blood from two* [something I couldn't make out] *will release a new evolution. The chosen* [above this was a scrawled "M" and "s"] *in conjoined unification under the dark moon will bring forth the power. The channel will be open* [the word "rood" appeared to one side] *and whoever holds the channel will be the deity in the eyes of the evolution. And all shall kneel before him and do his bidding.*

The problem with demented cults, and this one was pretty demented, was they often came up with elaborate stories that verged on fantasy just so they could get the dames. Power, wherever you looked at it, was the aphrodisiac that attracted the people who thought they needed the aphrodisiac in the first place. And it corrupted everything. I blamed marketing.

I took a step forward and my foot slipped. There was blood on the floor. The blood led to a body lying face down in the red pool. I turned him over to reveal Mr. Bird in a sharp grey suit. Italian styling. His dark hair was swept back off his forehead, held in place by a combination of hair product and bodily fluids. I flicked open his jacket and had a search. A thin wallet was secured, briefly, in a hidden pocket. I eased it out and clicked it open.

Before I had a chance to look more closely I heard a deep, disturbingly familiar growl behind me. I spun around. In the corner of the room were dark eyes staring out from the shadows. I didn't wait. I fled, slamming the door closed behind me. I leaned against it. On the other side I heard the scratching of claws against metal. The growling continued, rumbling through the door and deep into my bones.

I made my way out and back to the office to calm my nerves.

CHAPTER 29 ...

The phone rang, adding to my headache-making list of problems. At the end of the line Angelina careened between topics with her usual irrepressible energy. She'd come up with many people who were eager to buy the hoodoo stick, she told me, and others who would buy the gold records, their value rocketing after the discovery of Hugh's dead body. But no one was giving any clues about whether they'd seen the rood. She said she would continue checking and hung up.

I had a couple of contacts on the Terrace that I could shake down. I packed away the booze, dusted off some brass assistance, and got ready to lock the office.

There was a knock on the door. I begrudgingly allowed an entrance. The door creaked open and Laura looked in. My stomach twisted. I stumbled to my feet. She looked terrible. She was emaciated and barely had the energy to stand. I carefully helped her into the visitor's chair. I wondered why she was here, especially after recent events.

"I didn't think I'd see you," I said.

She coughed lightly. "That's a funny thought to have. I wanted to talk to you."

I prepared for the punch. It was inevitable. She wasn't a dime dame, and therefore was out of my league. I'd always known that anything she saw in me was going to be fleeting. I swallowed, and my heart sank into my boots.

"My nightmares have started again."

I blinked. This was unexpected. "About the dog?"

"The beast. And the pain's returned." She clutched at her chest and coughed again. Her breathing was shallow and her head fell forward. She was barely conscious. Then I remembered.

"How are you and Mina doing?"

She lifted her head, invisible strings reviving her as though she was an abandoned marionette puppet discovered by a teenager who enjoyed it momentarily before discarding it because of its low credibility factor.

"Oh, fine. She's so much fun, and it's been great to have her around while I've been bedridden. She makes me laugh so much, and her jokes are so rude. And sometimes after a few drinks, well, she gets very friendly." The strings went limp again and she sagged.

I tried to block out the images from my mind. They brought down a dark veil over my world. I couldn't understand why she was tormenting me.

"What's the matter? You don't look happy."

"It's nothing, a bad day," I replied.

She continued talking about Mina. "She sure is a night owl. She stays up most of the night, but she sleeps late, which suits me fine at the moment." She coughed again and her eyes went wide. "Oh, dizzy."

"Yeah, she loves the night all right."

"A funny thing happened yesterday. A funeral procession passed by, one of the traditional ones, and the followers were singing, 'Dropkick me, Jesus, through the goalposts of life.' And Mina got really angry. I'm not the best of singers, but the language she used to express her displeasure was pretty bad. I realized then that I didn't really know much about her. So when she was asleep"—she glanced over her shoulder and whispered—"I looked in her purse."

She fumbled in her bag, extracted a small piece of paper, and handed it over. "I found this."

It was a photograph. Really old. It made sepia look like the new kid on the block. It was a picture of Mina with some guy standing behind her. They were on a boat. I turned it over. There was nothing on the back. I flicked it over again and stared at Mina, lying on a deckchair on the deck of one of the super-steamers that had powered across the Atlantic in the old days. I tried to make out the lettering on the stack, but all I could see was *TITA*. The rest was blurred. I wondered why Mina looked the same in this photograph as she had yesterday.

"You said you hadn't met her before," Laura said, her voice a combination of police inquiry and hurt lover.

"Yeah," I muttered, pressing out the creases.

"Then why are you in the photograph?"

I blinked. I looked at the picture again. I hadn't even noticed the chump standing behind Mina. I looked at the chump. "It's not me. He's better looking."

"Have you looked in the mirror lately?"

"When the razor dictates."

"You shave? I assumed grooming was just the icing on the cake."

"It can't be her. Or me."

"It's you. It's her."

I shook my head. "It's probably her parents."

"I've asked her about her parents, in fact, heaps of questions about her past, but she refuses to talk about it. She says she lives for now. *Carpe diem* and all that."

"Carpe what?"

"'How much better it is to endure whatever will be! Whether Jupiter has allotted you many more winters or this one, which even now wears out the Tyrrhenian sea on the opposing rocks, is the final one be wise, be truthful, strain the wine, and scale back your long hopes to a short period. While we speak, envious time will have fled: seize the day, trusting as little as possible in the next day.'"

I stared at her. She was full of surprises.

"I went to a very good school." She coughed and lolled forward. She closed her eyes and swallowed.

"I always preferred 'Gather ye rosebuds while ye may,'" she went on, "but that's the kind of thing Mina would cover in innuendo." She was forcing her voice; it was becoming ragged and hoarse around the edges, barely more than a whiskey whisper. She opened her eyes and looked up at me through her thick eyelashes.

"Well, Mina seizes things all right." I gave her a smile.

"She sure does. I can't tell you what she did last night." She laughed, but it was quickly replaced by a violent cough. All color drained from her face.

"I'll get you some water." I stood up.

"I miss you," she said. "Everything's getting so confusing. And strange. Reality's mixing with my dreams and I can't work out what's true and what I'm imagining. I feel like darkness is creeping in over my world from the edges. I wish you would come ..." She collapsed forward onto the desk.

I picked her up. There was nothing of her. I laid her down on the stretcher and tried to think what to do. Her father was the best bet, but I had no idea of his number. I called Watcher, holding the phone in both hands. The woman who answered sounded concerned, but said he was unavailable. All I could do was carry her home in my arms.

I hailed a private diesel dimbox and laid her on the back seat. I climbed beside her and put her head in my lap. Diesel-cab man wasn't happy. With less than an ounce of concern for his fellow human being, he kicked us out when I indicated the turn for our destination, suspecting her to be on the verge of vomiting. He flat out refused to go one imperial inch farther. I held her in my arms and carried her to the apartment.

I kicked on the door. There was no answer. I placed her feet on the ground and reached down to slide the key out from under the pot. I shouted out once we were inside, but the apartment was silent. I called out for Mina. No response. I noticed signs of a struggle; a couple of things had been knocked over.

I laid her on the bed, which was unmade. I could smell Mina's perfume, which she must have poured over the pillows, as I placed them under Laura's head. Her forehead was on fire. She tossed from side to side, and I wondered if she was agitated by the scent. I went into the second bedroom. That bed was also unmade. Who slept in here? The pillows didn't smell of Mina, so I grabbed them and placed them under Laura's head. She calmed down under the neutral smell.

I looked through the medicine cabinet, but it was completely empty, stocked by Misses Hubbard. Nothing but a toothbrush remained. I went to the phone. It was dead. I needed a doctor. I searched for family contact numbers, or anything that gave a clue to outside connection. Nothing. Not even any photographs. I didn't believe she denied her family, even if the connection had been frosty. The other option was that they'd been removed.

I reached into my jacket for her purse; there had to be something in that. I didn't have it. I must've left it at the office. I could've slapped myself on the forehead. I didn't like the idea of the photograph just lying around, especially with my visits from the trashmen. I had to find a drugstore, pick up the photograph from my office, and come back with the cavalry.

I locked the front door, pocketed the key and ran down to the main street.

The man in the drugstore gave me a strange look when I described Laura's symptoms, but eventually he handed over some unnamed tablets after making me sit in the hearing-aid-beige chair for an interminably long time. I also picked up the photographs I'd taken in Limbo's foyer. I flicked through them. Most of the faces I didn't recognize, except for the last three.

I raced to my office, and as soon as I was through the door I spotted Laura's purse on the desktop. There was a scuffling at the door. I turned around. A middle-aged man glanced through the open doorway.

"I'm just leaving," I said.

He stepped into the office. He looked nervous; his eyes were dancing around the room, and his hands were wringing his hat nervously.

"I know you," I said.

His hair was still grey. He drew his hand, which was shaking, over his thick strands, but he stood tall. He had the look of a man who had seen a lot of bad things. It was like looking in a mirror, except I had better hair.

"You were the dancing man at the Stylus."

The Stylus was an age ago. In many ways I wished it was two days ago, or even a week ago, when I was about to get thrown out of the office.

"I'm sorry for that display," the man said. "Grief got the better of me. I'm Derek Mitchell." He looked around nervously, dusted off the chair with his hat and sat down in the visitor's chair.

Apparently my message hadn't gotten through. I sighed. I sat down and scanned his body. My guess was he was an ex-service guy, once as stiff as his excessively starched and pressed uniform but now directionless, and conflicted by an inner discomfort about being outside of the system and inflicting it on his child—except he'd said his daughter had been killed.

"I'll tell you the story," he said.

"Make it quick. Give me the headlines."

"I retired recently. I was planning on moving down here to live closer to some friends—some old buddies from the force."

I gave him a nod and pretended to make notes.

"My daughter was looking forward to it especially. We've been moving around for years; every three years I get a new posting. You don't get much chance to make friends like that, and it's important for children to have a sense of belonging. It created conflict between us and we hadn't really spoken in recent years. I had hoped our move down here would bring us together."

I noticed he was leaving out information about any kind of wife.

He twitched nervously. "Then several weeks before we were to move I met this young lady, Milli. Wow, she was an atom bomb." He made a movement with his hand with the accompanying explosive sound effect. "She made the day sparkle and the nights purr. I was too old for her, but when a vision like her is around it's easy to forget you're not the person you once were. The mirror lies, and we get carried away with our dreams."

"Or fantasies." Still nothing about a wife. I guessed that meant something bad had happened between them.

"Milli started to become friendly with my daughter, Denise. At first I didn't mind, as it kept Milli nearby, and Denise seemed happy for the first time. But they began to get a little too friendly. Holding hands, whispering in each other's ears, wrapping their arms around each other, staying up all night giggling. That's fine when you're a teenager, but when you're an adult it's a bit … unseemly."

I shrugged. "I don't judge."

"Well, I've lived in a different time and world, with different expectations of behavior. Milli began to change, like she was jealous when Denise was near anybody else. And then Denise began to change, fading away, going pale and quiet, not being able to get out of bed. She started to have nightmares about strange creatures and would only calm down if Milli was next to her."

At this point I started to take real notes.

"I called the doctor, but he said she was fine, she only needed to rest. I called in the specialists"—he hesitated stumbling over his words, still wringing his hat in his hands—"but each shook his head and walked away. Each one had a darker and even more fantastical explanation than the other. None were able to help, but they all held out their hands for a supportive donation."

He coughed and asked for some water. I ran him a glass from the rusty kitchen tap.

"In the end I called in a priest, and he was the biggest joke of all. He said her life was being sucked away by evil demons from the netherworld. He asked if there was someone new in her life. He told me that person was probably a demon or creature of the night. What do you do with information like that? When all the experts fail and you're left with the ramblings of a crazy man, what do you do?"

I stopped writing and looked into his imploring eyes. "Believe in science."

"Even when it's failing you, and it's your daughter who's dying? I was coming down to the capital and Denise was so excited about meeting someone else who had the same life experiences. If I'd pulled her away from Milli she might still be alive today."

I had heard this before. The cogs suddenly started clicking into place. I sat back and put down my pen. I shook my head at my own sluggishness. I leaned forward and leveled my finger at him.

"You know Laura Mallory."

(HAPTER 30 ...

Yes. How did you know that?" He took another nervous sip from the glass. His face took on a waxy sheen, and he'd broken out in a light sweat under the stress.

"I know Laura."

His face fell, and clattered to the ground, weighed down by the guilt of failed promises.

I tore the page from the notebook and started again, this time paying attention. "Where did you meet this Milli?"

"She was in town attending a relative's funeral. I asked who the deceased was, because in a small town you get to know everyone. She said the relative was Mircalla Karnstein. I'd never heard of her so I let it pass. She looked like a dream come true, which made everything else irrelevant."

"Did you chase up this Mircalla?"

"Not at first. Milli got a bit funny when I asked and she threatened to leave, so I backed off the inquisition."

I sighed. He had some cockamamie story about a woman with a half-baked name, with the most desperate, and unbelievable, reasons to talk to me. He was acting like an idiot and expected some miracle cure from me. I put down my pen and folded my arms.

"Why are you here?"

"I've run out of options. I hate my life in all possible ways. I've got two options. They said you could help people forget."

"Me? Who said that?"

"Milli."

"I don't know your Milli." I leaned forward and stared at him, watching his face.

"She knows you. Not where you are, but she said she's been searching for you and had been all her life. And she said you and her were going to fix things."

"Never heard of her, never met her."

"You do know her. I have a photograph." He reached into his jacket and pulled out an old sepia photograph that looked deliberately arranged, and placed it on the desk in front of me. "She carried it around with her. I sometimes caught her staring at it when she thought she was alone."

I picked up the photograph and looked at it. It wasn't a mirror; I didn't get the impression that I was looking at myself. I threw it back at him. He scooped it up delicately and placed it back in his wallet.

He still had a crush on this woman. It flashed across my mind that he might see me as an obstacle between himself and Milli.

"I caught her sleepwalking once with it clutched to her chest. She didn't know I was following. Sometimes police training can be useful."

"What happened?"

"We have a big house with three floors and several balconies. The south end, where Denise and Milli slept, overlooked Monday Forest. One night I watched Milli leave their bedroom, walk out onto the balcony and stare up at the moon. She'd done that a couple of times. One night when she went out on a strange ritual, I crept into their bedroom with an old sword and hid in the closet."

"A sword?"

"I just wanted to scare her, not kill her."

"I've found that swords can kill."

"I must've waited an hour before I heard the bedroom door open. Even though it was a full moon, it was exceptionally dark in the room. Then I heard the door lock. I felt her pass the closet, a gentle breeze, and I kicked the door open. I don't know exactly what I saw, but it looked like a great winged beast. I charged at it, and as it turned it seemed to turn into Milli. I put it down to the dark, and fatigue playing tricks with my mind. She shrieked at me. She ran away that night, leaving everything she had behind. Before the morning, my daughter was"—the word caught in his throat—"dead."

He licked his lips nervously. The guy was a story of monsters and swords. I wished he was still drunk. Then I could buy the monolog and see some sense. And yet ...

"I went through the things she'd left behind," he continued. "The photograph was one of them. There was also a piece of paper with the name *Karnstein* written on it. I checked the records. There had been a Karnstein hundreds of years ago. There was an address, and something written in a foreign language, something I hadn't seen before. I went down to the church and searched through the graveyard. I met the gravedigger, whose family had been running the place for generations. There were numerous interesting records, but they were based on popular thought rather than documented evidence. The gravedigger related a story written down by one of his ancestors, saying that the tomb was relocated long ago by the town hero, who vanquished Karnstein and her daughters, who haunted the region."

"*Vanquished?*"

"I had questions about that as well. They were words, stupid words, from the minds of the uneducated."

"Yeah?"

"Vampires."

I rolled my eyes.

Derek nodded.

"It's a fine fairy story, but—"

"I've done some research, if you're interested."

I shook my head.

"Not even if it involves you?"

"Everything involves me these days." I stood up. He had unfinished business with Laura, and I needed some help from someone from the right side of the sanity tracks. One thing still bothered me. "How can I make you forget?"

Derek shrugged. "I suspected you might be a hypnotist, or one of those old herbalists who knows some strange concoction. I thought presenting my story to you would let you see how desperate I was to leave the past behind."

I sighed. I grabbed him by the collar. I wasn't going to let him get away with his stupid mistakes. I was going to cement him into the past he let happen.

"Laura needs you. Come with me."

"She needs help?"

I nodded. I didn't want to tell him her symptoms, mainly because in my own head it opened up a whole bunch of questions that had no sane answer. "I'm looking for someone who cares," I said. I pulled him out the door and we made haste back to her apartment.

She was in a bad way. Her face was pale and hollow. Derek's face nearly matched Laura's.

"This is what my daughter looked like before she …"

He couldn't finish and I couldn't blame him. Looking at Laura like this filled me with the same whirlpool of grief. She opened her eyes and looked at me. She held out her hand and I grasped it tightly. I sat next to her, stroking her head and tending to her fever. The time ticked past, and Derek came and went with water and towels. I steadfastly held her hand and listened to her delirium.

There was a knock at the door. I looked at Derek.

"I called a specialist doctor," he said. "Someone I thought could help." He looked geographically guilty when he spoke.

"The telephone is working?" I said.

I went to the front door and swung it open. There was a nurse standing there, straight out of the pages of a penny dreadful. Her white skirt was so short it barely covered her secrets. The front was unbuttoned so far I wondered why she'd bothered. Her white mobcap, emblazoned with a red cross, held back the masses of black hair. I knew those curves.

"*Ja*, I am the doctor that vas called for. Vere is the patient?"

I looked at her. She looked back. Her gaze didn't break. I had to give her credit for the sheer audacity.

"Quick. You must lead me to the patient urgently. I demand it." She clicked her fingers in the air.

I led her through the impressive apartment into the bedroom, to the pensive Derek and a barely conscious Laura. Derek's face lit up like he'd won the lottery, then fell as he took in the doctor's outfit.

"You're covered in a lot of blood for a doctor."

"I am the old-fashioned kind." Her eyes dropped to Laura. She moved to the bed and placed her palm on Laura's forehead. "Ah, the poor girl. I have seen this before. I must perform my tests quickly to see how long she has."

"Please don't phrase it that way," Derek said.

"Ve must face the grim reality."

She placed a large leather case on the bed and flicked open the latch. She pulled out various pieces of archaic equipment, and an aggressive-looking medical apparatus that she placed on the dresser. The last item out was a size-nine syringe. She held it skyward in one hand as she opened Laura's eyes and examined them closely.

"You're not going to stab that into her eye," Derek said. He had a dread expression plastered across his face.

"No." She ran her medical eye down Laura's body and then returned her close attention to her face. Without looking up, she continued. "I am ascertaining the best place to extract a sample. Of blood. Not the other kind."

Satisfied with her examination, she straightened and lowered the syringe. She took a swab from the case and poured some medicinal alcohol onto it. A quick wipe on Laura's neck and she plunged the needle in.

"I must varn you …" she started. A fountain of blood spurted up and hit Derek in the face. "There is sometimes leakage. But don't panic, you probably von't be infected."

Derek's face went into an apoplectic spasm as he tried in vain to shield himself. The spurt stopped and he wiped his face down with his handkerchief. The large syringe started to fill. He sighed. Another short jet squirted up and hit him in the face. He spluttered and wiped his face down again.

The doctor filled another syringe. Her face was full of concentration. She coughed, and another small jet landed in Derek's eye.

"Sorry," she said.

She filled another syringe. Derek opened his mouth and managed "!" as yet another jet of blood squirted into his open mouth.

"I vouldn't svallow that, if I vas you."

He spat out the blood into his bloodstained handkerchief. He rubbed it over his face, leaving more blood on than it cleaned off. "Could you please not smile while you're doing that?" he said.

"Sorry, I vas unavare."

She now had several small vials of blood. She put each one into the apparatus, which spun the vials. Then she crushed leafs and herbs into each one. I recognized garlic. She stood back and looked at the array of equipment perched on the dresser. She ran her eye over the line of red vials, her face distorted in the cylinders.

"Now ve vait."

"Doctor?" I said.

"*Ja?*" Her focus remained fixed on the experiment in progress.

"May I speak with you?"

"Speak avay, young man."

"Follow me, please." I indicated for the demented medic to follow me. Everywhere in this apartment was open, allowing nowhere to have a discreet conversation. I went into the only room with a door.

"You vant to speak to me in the bathroom?" she said.
"Angelina, why are you here?"

CHAPTER 31 ...

I do not know of this person you call Angelina."

"Stop it. I know it's you."

She folded her arms, which didn't help the cause of containing her escaping cleavage. "Very well. He called me. He needs my help."

"He's looking for a *doctor*." I looked her costume up and down. "By the way, that's the worst disguise ever."

"I *am* a doctor. I studied eternally for my PhD and I'm widely recognized in my field of expertise. The clothes have nothing to do with my ability."

"A *medical* doctor."

"Pah, what do they know?"

"A lot about medicine."

"She doesn't need medicine. She needs me. She needs to be healed. Spiritually. She's been syphoned by a sucker, and she'll turn into one of them if we don't save her. What's worse, now she's a target. Remember I said they never stop until you're dead."

"But she wasn't like you."

"There's more to purity than inexperience in the bedroom. It's about the heart and the blood that pumps through it."

I glared at her.

She placed a hand on my arm. "You need to trust me. Please. Just go along with me."

"But this is Laura."

"So? Is she so important?"

I wanted to ask if breathing was important, if the sun rising in the morning was important, if the universe was important. In the end I answered with a simple nod. It was all I needed to express.

She looked into my eyes and smiled. "I'll do what I can. You helped me, now it's my turn to help you."

I edged past her to make my way out. She stood without moving, resolutely stuck to the spot, a sad expression on her face.

"Are you okay?"

"Yes, I just need to use the facilities," she said, pointing to the facilities. She started to unbutton what remained of her costume.

I hurriedly closed the door. A few moments later there was a flush and she reappeared.

"She needs to replace the roll."

We went back to the bedroom.

"Now, vere vere ve?"

I indicated the various vials on the dresser that were turning a multitude of colors. She looked at them and shook her head sternly.

"That's not a cure," I said.

"She cannot be cured. She must be killed at the moment of her turning." She looked at me. "The instant she is taken to the dark side, you must drive a stake through her heart."

Derek looked shocked. "You cannot be serious."

"It's not going to happen."

"Othervise she vill spend all of eternity in searing agony."

"There *must* be a cure," Derek cried.

"No one has ever survived once the turning has begun. There is no proof that anything vill vork."

"Proof?" That was a strange word to use.

She let out a sigh and feigned melodrama into the corner of

the room. "There is only one thing that can cure her, and it is all mythology." Angelina, the badly disguised medic, raised her finger. "And that is the blood of an angel."

There was silence.

Derek looked at her. "Yes?" he said earnestly.

"Yes, the blood," Angelina said passionately.

"We get the point. How exactly does the blood of an angel cure her? Does she have to drink it?"

"*Nein!* Don't be disgoostink." She raised her hand in front of us. Her fingers uncurled as though releasing a delicate bubble. We both stared into her palm. "Under the full moon, in the markings of the ascent, she must have sex with …" She leveled a finger at—

"Me? Why?"

"It is written. Then her wrists must be slashed in the moment of ascension of desire."

"I'm not sure that drinking blood is worse than what you're describing," Derek said.

She gave him a sideways glance. "It depends," she drawled, "on how good the sex is." She looked at me. "And to make sure you are vorthy, I vill have sex with you first. I must make sure you are capable of completing the act appropriately. All in the name of science."

"No, I won't do it."

"Fine. But if her soul is lost forever and she burns in eternity in the netherworld, you only have yourself to blame."

I strongly reiterated, with a two-word response, my disinterest in conjoining with a madwoman.

"Are you sure?"

"Do you have a gun?"

"Nein."

"I'm prepared to risk it."

"Fine. Be like that."

"Why sex?" Derek said.

"As I said, it's her little death, the moment of freedom of the body. When she … dies," she said, raising her eyebrows, "her heart will open and the evil can be drained away."

I looked down at the bed. "She's hardly in the mood."

"This is not a dinner date. Ve are talking about saving the vorld."

There was a pause. "I thought we were saving Laura."

"Ah … *ja*, that too."

"You appear to be hiding something from us. No one mentioned saving the world."

Dr. Angelina, mad medicine-woman, looked at Derek and sighed. "There are stories, fables from long ago that talk of something like that."

She stepped back and I prepared for drama.

"There is a time coming very soon when an archangel vill stand upon the ascension markings in a place of vorship. At his feet, upon the altar, two people vill join and shape the very future of the vorld. I believe Laura has been chosen. If she joins with the dark, the forbidden love, humans vill end and the vampires vill reign." She pointed at me. "If she joins with a human, he purifies her and humans vill continue on the planet. Whatever the outcome, it will be decided by the two who join."

"It all sounds a bit suspect and extreme to me," Derek said. "Why does it have to be one way or the other? Surely there's some balance."

"It vas probably written by a man desperate for a date. You have a better idea?"

"We're completely at sea on this topic," Derek said. "It's not as though it's discussed in the pages of the press."

"It's a very old and vell-known story. Honestly, didn't either of you ever listen to anything at school?"

"School?" I said.

"Where else do you find open minds that vill believe in the possibility of everything? Old minds close, get stuck in their vays. The vorld vas born of belief. You need to believe you can save everything."

She turned to me, not ready to give up yet. "In that instant, the two of you vill join together in an eternal moment of love. She is your destiny."

Something occurred to me. "Are you sure it's her?"

"Quite probably," she replied.

"Quite probably?"

"Okay, I'm not sure at all. But she's been targeted and she's not dead, and that makes her a prime candidate. The dark moon vill be upon us tomorrow, and that is about as long as she has left. Sorry. You vant to fix it, then you need to orchestrate events so they happen the vay you vant. Join with her, save her, love her at the feet of an angel. And bring a knife."

"Just say this is true," Derek said. "How do we get a so-called archangel? It's not as if you can get them through a wanted advertisement."

"Phoenix," I said.

"Who is Phoenix?" Angelina asked.

I related the story of a man who'd lived for hundreds of years that I'd seen die then come back to life. Angelina nodded. I assumed the person I saw after Phoenix died was his brother or some other relative I didn't consider resurrection. Maybe in a snow-dome of a world quickly turning upside down, it was time to give skepticism a bit of a shake. Or maybe it was sleep deprivation.

"How do we get the angel?" Derek said.

"Angel cake." She smiled. "Ve set a trap."

"Trap?" Derek said. "How do you trap a ... what you call an angel?"

"In a gilded cage. Catching the first snow of vinter," Angelina replied.

Derek gave a deep sigh. "Besides the obvious point of it being mid-summer, and far away from any snow-crested mountain peaks, could we stick to some semblance of the world in which we live?"

"You called the priest," I reminded him.

"I was grieving, and my mind was muddled."

"You cannot trap a good angel on Earth," Angelina said,

"because it is a heavenly being with powers ve humans do not have. It can return to heaven at vill. Phoenix, because he is fallen, could be considered a demon that has established residence in a human being. That is one vay the demons are trapped until they're ordered to leave the human being."

"Exorcism?" I said.

"*Ja.* His spirit will leave the dead body and search for the nearest one. He vill morph into his old form and stay like that until he finds a new body."

Derek sighed again. "Besides the obvious point of this all being totally insa—"

"Ve have no other options. Ve need to lure him."

"What about a gilded cage?" I suggested.

"You want a cage made of gold?" Derek said.

"Gilded doesn't necessarily mean 'made of gold.' It's about representation. It's where you're served and protected. It's about keeping danger out as much as keeping contents in."

"I know of one," I said. I recounted the story of my time in the tank, when the winged creatures had tried to attack me but couldn't get through the bars, even though they mauled the man in the next cell easily.

"How do we find Phoenix?" Derek asked. "Where do they live?"

"They always have a lair, vere they catch people and do despicable things to them."

"The grand church on the hilltop," I said.

"That old church, if it is a church," Derek said. "It hasn't been used in decades," he added.

"I found him there," I said.

"Did he have some kind of strange artifact there?" Angelina asked.

I nodded.

"If it vas his lair, you were amazingly lucky to get out alive."

"I killed him. Nearly."

She shook her head. "You couldn't have killed him. They can

only be killed by an ancient relic or artifact. And appropriate religious rites."

"How do we lure him?" Derek asked.

"What these people vant more than anything is blood. Life source. That's what they suck out of you."

"Not me," I said. "I need mine."

"I'm thinking that with all this activity, and the change coming, maybe ve don't need to lure him anyvere. Maybe they vill be getting complacent."

We both stared at her, waiting for a moment of clarity. I hazarded a guess after no further information was forthcoming.

"You think he's in his lair?"

"He vill be there at some point, especially if he's been veakened. You said you killed him, then saw him later but he didn't attack you." She snapped her fingers. "If he's in his healing phase, he'll need to feast to get the life essence, and blood. Oh, that's going to be bad. Have you ever seen one of the rituals?"

"No, have you?" I said.

"No … but I have seen pictures, and they're not pretty." She shivered. She blinked slowly and shivered again. "Maybe you should see them."

"No, thanks."

"I might have a look, just as a reminder." She started to look through her medical case. A frown settled on her face as her hands came up empty. "Damn, it vould have been useful in preparing us."

"You still want to go?" I said,

"Yes, he'll be vaiting for us. Let's hope he's veak. Don't forget that. It may be the only advantage ve have."

"What about me?" said Derek. His eyes looked plaintive and pleading. He moved awkwardly next to the bed, lost without direction and application.

"You must stay with the girl and make sure she stays safe," Angelina commanded. She glared at him fiercely. "It's the most useful thing you can do."

"If her condition changes, call me." I scrawled down my office number and placed it on the dresser. "Let no one in. No one." I pointed my finger at him to reinforce the instruction. He nodded.

Angelina began to pack her medical apparatus away, and spoke suggestively to Derek. I crept out into the living room, quietly picked up the phone, and dialed.

"You want Phoenix?" I whispered as the call was answered.

There was a muffled reply. I rolled my eyes. "You know who it is."

A resigned confirmation followed.

"Grand Hilltop Church, two hours." I put down the phone, went back to the bedroom, grabbed Angelina by her hand and dragged her away.

"Vere are ve going?"

"Drop the stupid accent."

"You have no sense of fun or melodrama."

"You'll like me in a minute."

"Why? Will there be sex? That would make me like you."

I sighed. I ran the plot past her. She didn't seem happy.

"If I do this, I want sex afterwards. If we're both alive," she added. After a pause she clarified. "If *I* am alive. I can practice necromancy on some particular parts of your body if you don't make it." She snickered and muttered something that sounded like "raised from the dead."

CHAPTER 32 ...

We cruised past Angelina's store where she grabbed some oversized weaponry. Apparently she thought her nurse's outfit was appropriate even though it clearly lacked any pockets. She cited irony. I cited the fact that it was very distracting. This seemed to be part of her survival plan.

She strapped two oversized silver pistols, with chambers the size of pickle jars, to her thighs. She was a girl who believed that bigger was better. I suggested she leave the six-inch heels behind. She swore considerably before relenting with a stern look, and threw me a small pink toy that nearly disappeared in my hand.

"What the hell is this?"

"A water pistol." She slung a sword over her back and tightened it into place.

"I can see that."

"It contains holy water."

Angelina was a damn fine specimen of womanhood, with little I could ignore. But she was also a woman who, once an idea got stuck in her head, wasn't going to let go of it.

"Let's go kick some freaking freaks back from whence they freaking came."

"That could've been snappier."

The church was dark as we approached. No lights. The only sound was the occasional rustle of insects feeding off the bones of the dead. The night was still. Angelina stood close to me. The scent of her heady perfume wafted over me, annulling the smell of the decaying plants and bodies being reclaimed by the damp earth and sub-terrestrial creatures.

I kept my eyes away from her distracting outfit, and watched the scaly bugs crawling and slithering over the crumbling gravestones. People had been buried, and remembered, in the best material possible to survive the elements: stone. Now the stone had crumbled, the bodies were gone, and even those who wanted to remember had passed through in the same fashion. With all the intent and will in the world, it all came to nothing. Eventually everything crumbled to dust and clay.

We approached the door. It was closed. The lock was old, but I had the Remington. Within moments the lock clicked open and I eased the door inward. The ominous chamber opened before us and we stepped into the gloomy darkness. Minimal moonlight crawled in via the filthy windows. The place was an abandoned tomb.

"This feels different from before," I said. I felt like everything was closing in on us.

"The door just shut behind us," she whispered. "Silently, and without anyone actually closing it."

I shrugged. It could mean anything and nothing. I felt my way forward, arms outstretched, until I found the first row of pews. Angelina stayed close by, clutching my arm. We waited until our eyes grew accustomed to the gloom. The scent of extinguished flames, something burnt, hung heavy in the air.

"Something bad has happened here," I said.

"Let's hope nothing else bad happens here while we're here."

My eyes started to make out the objects in the room. All of the pews had been reversed so they faced away from the altar.

The ones at the far end, closest to the altar, had been destroyed.

We crept forward. Several paces in, I stepped on something slimy. There was a hiss and the sound of something slithering toward the front of the church. I could hear more slithering coming from the walls of the building, following us as we made our way down the central aisle.

Something pale lay ahead of us. As we approached, it became apparent that the paleness was someone's skin, drained and untouched by age or the elements. A girl, barely out of her teens, had been strapped across the altar.

"This was upstairs before," I whispered, indicating the great stone altar with the surrounding stone heads, "but without the girl."

The girl's eyes, glassy and vacant, stared off into the darkness. Her limbs had been chained apart. Her body had been slashed violently, with deep cuts over her stomach, and lower down. On her chest were five small burn marks in a circle. The same marks were duplicated on the floor, with a large candle placed on each respective point, all burned down to small stubs.

It all had an eerily familiar feel to it, not so much the circumstances but the intent. And that made my skin crawl.

We made our way past the poor girl and into the depths of the pulpit. There were several industrial devices, badly damaged and tossed aside. Imagining the horror was not necessary as the results of it lay behind us, stapled to the sacrificial altar. Several large images of brutality were depicted on hanging tapestries. The worst, most inhumane, were on either side of the stairwell entrance. Angelina made her way toward them.

The burnt smell was stronger in the pulpit. I searched in the various alcoves looking for the source of the smell. I found several long spikes, eight foot long and thin. I picked one up and examined it. It reminded me of a rotisserie spit. It was hefty and had blood smeared all the way along it.

Angelina gasped. She had pulled down the tapestries. On either side of the stairwell entrance, two charred bodies stood at attention.

I instinctively reached for one of the impaling pikes and walked over to stand beside her. We looked at the bodies. They sent shivers up my spine and set off alarm bells in my primal alert center.

As one, they opened their eyes, balefully yellow against their blackened skin. They lunged forward off their pedestals. I brought the pike around, spearing the first figure and knocking it into the second. They both exploded in a shower of cinders and rubble.

They had been as silent as the dead. I had to wonder if they *had* been dead. Or tortured to remind them to guard the place with what was left of their lives.

"You know," Angelina whispered, "anyone could walk in here the way we did. They've hidden here for centuries, only appearing when they need to feed. This is one step away from broad daylight. They're either desperate, or something big is happening, and soon, and they no longer care." She reached out and held my hand. "And that scares me, a lot."

Her shaking fingers gripped mine. I pulled her close and wrapped my arms around her. Her whole body was shaking.

"I feel so safe in your arms," she whispered. "You're my gilded cage."

I didn't want to tell her I felt the same. Fear doesn't need a companion.

She took a couple of deep breaths then eased herself away.

"His lair is up the stairs," I said.

She nodded. "I'm ready. Let's go."

The steps were slippery. I bent over and wiped my finger over the stone. Blood. The walls closed in as we wound our way up the tight staircase. Our breathing became labored as the air became thick and musky. The putrid stench of bodies that had relieved themselves of everything twisted the air into a dark soup of gut-wrenching fear, which clouded all but the next footfall. Step by slimy stone step we crawled up the rounded stairwell, accompanied by the sounds of distant screams of terror.

We came to the room at the top of the stairs. A large fan in the ceiling was spinning slowly. Its blades whumped heavily overhead, making us duck instinctively as we entered.

Whump-whump-whump.

We stepped into the room over trickling blood.

Whump-whump-whump.

The door slammed shut behind us, startling us both. Angelina covered her nose and mouth. The limb of a deceased person reached out toward us from the center of the room.

Whump-whump-whump.

The limb extended from a tangle of bodies, naked and bloodied.

Whump-whump-whump.

"Oh, the smell."

The words caught in Angelina's throat as she stepped up to the towering pile of torsos. She examined them closely. She gave another gasp, clutching her hand over her mouth as her eyes widened. Every single body was consuming, and consummating. They had all been struck dead at the same moment. Now they were nothing more than an interlocking lump of gnawed and broken flesh.

Whump-whump-whump.

"Their expressions are weird. Some are crying. Some are in ecstasy," Angelina said.

"It's the same thing," I replied.

"How's that?"

"Both signify a release of emotion."

She nodded. "A body will get to a point where it can't contain the emotion anymore, so it has a natural release valve. I wonder what's holding them up. I can see what's holding them together, but with all this blood and other bodily fluids they should be slithering down all over the floor."

I decided not to remind her of the great skewers I'd found downstairs.

We started exploring the room. There were small windows, but no light filtered in. I went over to one. The darkness outside was absolute. There was a city out there, full of life and bad attitude, but I saw nothing but a dark veil, and howls of pain and despair.

It was in another place, or so it felt.

The draw of the black void outside sucked at my consciousness. I hovered near the window, floating my hand over the opening. I watched as the life was drained away, out into the infinite. My mind began to fall forward, tumbling into the pit of eternity. The lonely crying and howls of pain filled me with sorrow, and a desperate longing to help. They called out to me to become one of them. They whispered that I could cure everything that was wrong if I did nothing more than hold out my hand. We would join and fall together, they said.

But something inside of me knew that falling would only make things worse. There was no forgiveness. There was no redemption or salvation. It was evil, and it would take everything.

With hands on either side of the window, I wrenched myself free of the powerful force. I snapped away, as though I was pulling myself free of deadly glue, and staggered backward. Shaking my head free of the darkness, I focused once again on the interior of the tower, searching for something that was less harrowing than the tormented, existential damnation of the infinite void. *Is not your wickedness great, and your iniquities without end?*

"Do you know what this means, Angelina?" I indicated the human pile.

"Assuming you're not being rhetorical and melodramatic, it looks like a ritual. Someone, or something, is trying to increase their power or control. Or it could be a summoning. Whatever it is, it can't have happened without attracting someone's attention."

And it occurred to me then that we should probably be worried about whose attention all of this was intended to attract.

"Or maybe it's just a naked ritual, with … sex and eating," she said. "Naked forms. The start. The end. Rebirth. But of what?"

We searched the walls, the floor, any crevice, but the place was clean. Apart from all the blood.

"There's nothing here," Angelina said in frustration. "This isn't the lair, or not the main part anyway. But it must be close. They wouldn't dare do anything as horrific as this in anything but a lair.

We must've missed something in the church."

We left the tower and made our way back down to the main chamber. Angelina started yanking the tapestries down. It sounded like she was softly crying.

"Wait," I shouted.

She paused mid-yank and looked at me. I pointed to the image in her hands. It was a picture of the church.

I went back to the entrance of the stairwell. The most graphic images were on the two tapestries on either side of the opening, the ones that had concealed the burnt guardians. I spread out the fabric. One was a painting of a ritual sacrifice, showing a pile of human torsos in the middle of consuming, and consummating.

Angelina spread out the other tapestry. We looked at each other. We spread out and examined the others. They all depicted acts of depravity. Then I found a tapestry in the form of a map.

"Look at this," I said, holding it up.

There was no response.

CHAPTER 33 ...

Angelina was staring at the center of the tapestry stretched out between her hands. She turned it away from me, hiding the imagery. "You don't need to see this," she said.

I reached out for it, but she pulled it away.

"No."

"We don't have time for games."

Reluctantly, she handed it over. It was serene compared to the others. There were two people in the center of the image, enjoying each other in a normal way in comparison to the others. They were surrounded by—okay, it was a bit freaky—the giant winged beasts Angelina wanted to call vampires. And the vampires were surrounded by lots of people who were running and turning into red. The sky was black, and there was a giant red eye looking down.

"It's just two people."

She stared at me. "One doesn't look familiar to you?"

I stared closely at the two figures in the center. A curvaceous blond and some guy underneath her, caught in an act that would earn good candy down on the Terrace. I shrugged and handed it back.

"Green," she muttered. "What did the green mean?" She stared down at her feet, lost in thought.

"Look," I said.

I gave her a prod with the tapestry, bringing her back into the moment, and pointed to the drawing of the church. It showed the main chamber, the spire, the pulpit, and another corridor leading out the back. It seemed to come from beneath the altar.

I grabbed her hand, and we walked over to the altar. The girl staked to it hadn't moved. I started to examine the various demonic faces carved into the stonework, running my hands over them, searching for something that clicked.

Angelina shook off whatever was distracting her and also ran her hands over the stone. She stopped, stood back, and moved around to the back. She spread her hands wide.

"I am a priest. What do I see?" She twisted her head one way then the other. "I am a priest," she repeated. She scrunched her face up in concentration and opened her eyes wide. "I am a priest who needs to escape quickly. Where do I go?"

She started searching, running her hands under the wooden floor of the pulpit. She stepped down, and dragged her feet over the stone floor of the main chamber. She paused, smiling, and pressed down with her bloodied boot.

There was a click next to me, coming from under the altar. I heard the sound of stone being dragged across stone. The altar swung aside slowly, revealing a staircase leading down into the pitch dark.

"It's dark," said Angelina. "And we have no lights."

"There's got to be something down there."

"Lights or monsters?"

We crept down the steps and the darkness folded in around us. We fumbled along the walls and found a couple of flashlights. I flicked one on. The batteries were low and the beam was dim, barely illuminating only a dozen feet in front of us. Angelina's wasn't much better.

I swung the beam around. It revealed three corridors, two

leading off on each side and one straight ahead. There was a metal box halfway down the middle corridor.

There was a small door to the right. I opened it and looked in. Buckets, mops, cleaning equipment. I guessed they had to clean up the blood somehow, or they'd be knee deep in the stuff.

I indicated for Angelina to go down the left passage while I went down the right. A few steps in I found another door. I opened it silently and peered in. The yellow beam swept over gardening implements: shovel, hoe, chainsaw. There were two other doors leading from the small room. I shut the door and moved on.

The smell of blood wafted up from the end of the corridor. I glanced in a couple more doors, each revealing nothing sinister. A small library. A tiny bedroom, recently used, with the sheets pulled free of the mattress. There were photographs by the bed. Several clerical outfits hung on a peg on the far wall. A deck of cards lay neatly piled on a small writing desk. This room also had two more doors leaving off it.

I crawled along the corridor until it turned sharply to the left. All three corridors converged in the same place, and I could see Angelina's dim beam ahead. The corridor that continued was narrower, and lower.

"Find anything?" I whispered.

"No, just ordinary rooms full of normal stuff. Normal humans living a normal life. Somehow it makes the horror upstairs worse."

There was a pause as we both thought about the bizarre juxtaposition.

"There are lots of doors."

"Yeah, same on my side," she said.

There was a scraping sound from the end of the corridor. We switched the flashlights off and waited for our eyes to become accustomed to the dark. We heard the sound of eating. I signaled for Angelina to follow me.

We ducked our heads as we made our way along the narrow corridor, which opened out into a wide but low-ceilinged chamber. I couldn't sense how big it was. It felt like it went on forever. I took a couple of steps into the darkness, and flicked on the flashlight. It shone directly into the center of the room, on a great winged beast that was eating something fleshy. Abruptly, it stopped chewing. It turned its head slowly and looked over its shoulder at us, baring its fangs. It was a dead ringer for Phoenix, if he'd suddenly become a great winged beast.

The beast wheeled around and leaped forward. It misjudged its size and the height of the room, and crashed into the ceiling. When it rose, it was Phoenix in his normal form. He charged at us.

"Run!" we both shouted as one.

We turned and ran back down the central corridor, keeping our heads down and leaping over the metal box. We headed for the stairwell leading back under the altar. Something was wrong. The stairwell wasn't there. A brick wall blocked the way.

"We must've triggered it when we came down. Where do we go now?" Angelina looked around wildly, fear overtaking her. I guessed that the situation was triggering memories of her haunting past.

I pointed down the left-hand corridor. "Head back to the chamber, go," I said.

I swung the butt of the flashlight at Phoenix as he crashed into me. I managed a couple more swings, denting the battery canister and breaking the bulb, before I managed to shake him off. I turned and headed down the right-hand corridor with the familiar rooms. He got back to his feet and charged after me.

I ran past the gardening room and the library, and burst through the door of the small bedroom. I slammed the door shut and smashed the lock closed. I stood in the dark, breathing heavily. The flashlight was useless now, so I dropped it. I made my way over to where I remembered the candles were and fumbled for the matches. The sulfur glow filled the room.

Phoenix stood in front of me. He ripped the cord of a chainsaw and it roared to life.

I ducked under another swing. I dropped the candle on the

bed and feinted to the side. He swung the chainsaw toward me. The dusty blankets on the bed smoldered and burst into flame. I ran out the door, dodging another slash, and kicked the door closed behind me. Moments later, metal teeth ripped through the wood. I ran along the corridor and into the library. Smoke billowed out of the bedroom behind me. Phoenix followed me into the library and chased me through the stacks. Shelves and books toppled around us. I ran back into the corridor and sprinted toward the chamber, following a dim yellow light.

Something heavy and solid cracked over my back. I collapsed to the floor with a sword at my throat.

CHAPTER 34 ...

O h, it's you. Where's your flashlight?" Angelina pushed the heavy block of wood off me and I jumped up.

"Bent over Phoenix's head," I said.

"I spotted a way out down at the end there, past the big room where he was eating," Angelina said. "If we stay down here, we're dead. We have to get out—and get him to follow us. Maybe there's something we can trap him with upstairs. Let's get out of this hell."

We turned. Phoenix roared toward us, bringing down the chainsaw as it once more sparked into life. I grabbed his hands as he came forward. The two of us stood locked together. We staggered back and forth, wrestling each other, with the chainsaw howling overhead. I could feel my biceps trembling.

Phoenix gave me an evil smile, which turned to a scream of agony. The chainsaw tumbled to the ground and he clutched his side. Angelina brought her sword around and sliced another blow deep into his leg. He lunged after her, but I had him around the waist. I picked him up and slammed him onto the ground. With amazing speed, he whipped his legs around and kicked mine from underneath me. I landed heavily on my back, winded.

He picked up the chainsaw and started to bring it down. I forced my hands up, catching his and throwing the blade wide. He dragged the chainsaw along the stone floor. I struggled to keep the blade from cutting into my neck.

"Hey, big boy. You looking for something?" Angelina ripped open her top, exposing her pure skin underneath.

For a moment Phoenix was distracted. I kicked him heavily in the shin, forced him away from me, and dived for cover. The blast from her gun erupted into a ball of splinter and flame, engulfing Phoenix. He rolled back with the fireball, tumbling in the turbulence and destructive force

"Nice try," he spat through his fangs.

He rose up and crawled over the metal chest, crouching on all fours. He leaped forward.

Angelina fired her second weapon. The blast caught him in mid-air, throwing him onto the flagstones. Flames roared across him. His clothes caught fire and his skin bubbled. And then the fire was gone, leaving nothing but a cloud of smoke.

I held my breath, staring into the dense smoke.

Slowly crawling along on hands and knees, Phoenix emerged from the cloud. His breathing was labored, and his wheezing audible. He lowered his head and stared at Angelina.

She checked her guns. They were both spent, and far from recharged. She dropped them, pulled out her pistol and fired at him. He leaped from the floor up onto the wall, then onto the ceiling. Her aim followed him as he dangled impossibly from the roof, jumping from side to side as she shot round after round at him.

The chamber jammed and she rocked the barrel back and forth furiously, trying to free it. She looked up, wide-eyed, as Phoenix ran along the roof toward her. She turned and fled, and I ran after her. We crashed into the library room, which was littered with broken shelves and tortured books, and locked the door securely behind us. Angelina checked her weapons. They were both spent. She holstered them and pulled out her pistol. She waited, breathing quietly, trying to get her racing heartbeat under control.

She closed her eyes and counted quietly, mouthing out the numbers. She spun around and kicked the door open. There was nothing there. The corridor in both directions was empty. I scrambled over the wreckage to reach her. An iron bar caught my trousers. I tried to pull the bar free but it slipped from my fingers and clanged onto the floor.

Something black and sticky fell on Angelina's hand. She looked up.

Phoenix fell from the roof and tackled her to the ground. She screamed and tried to dive away, but his arms were around her neck and his knees were thrusting into her. She pushed and twisted, but was locked within his clutches. He lifted her up and threw her against the far wall. She lay unmoving on the floor.

I seized Phoenix and wrenched him away. I grabbed him around the throat, locking down hard. He staggered over to the wall, placed one foot on it, and thrust himself upward, twisting out of my grasp. He brought a high, hefty kick into my shoulder, which had me spinning across the floor and crashing into the wall. In the blink on an eye, he was on top of me, gripping me around the throat.

I grabbed an iron bar and brought it down onto his skull with a resounding clang. He dropped me and staggered back, blood pouring from his head. I jumped up and planted my feet in his chest. He went down. I laid several hooks into his jaw and he screamed in pain. I felt the power of my punches driving into him as I pounded relentlessly, but the guy wouldn't give in. He howled and kicked at me without landing anything. Just when I thought I felt him weaken and was about to go under, he found new vigor.

He scratched and flailed with frenetic urgency until he landed a couple of swipes against my eyes. Then I was in the air and crashing into the far wall. His hands grabbed my clothes and hoisted me onto my feet. Again he swung me into the wall. I grabbed him and we both crashed into the wall. He swung at me. I tangled my foot within his own footwork and he lost balance. I ducked my shoulder, ramming it into his chest and pushing him into the opposing wall. He gasped for air as I pushed hard into his ribs. I spun around, bringing my elbow up and into the side of his head, jarring it back against the wall.

Blood trickled down and he spat at me. He kicked out at my knee, causing it to buckle. Pain speared through me. He brought his elbow down onto my shoulder, forcing me to my knees. He wrapped his arm around my throat and squeezed. I put a couple of hefty blows into his stomach, but he tensed his muscles every time I swung in.

I grabbed his hair and dragged him over my shoulder. I charged into the wall. He bounced off, and in the blink of an eye was back on his feet. He grabbed me and thrust me into the wall again. I twisted, spinning him into it next to me. We bounced down the corridor, crashing from side to side. I felt my energy draining away with the constant, unrelenting barrage.

We smashed through a door and into a tall set of shelves containing old books. Dust rained down as the shelving toppled, pages and bindings cascading over us. I feinted and twisted him into an arm lock. He pushed back, forcing me onto a pile of books. I slipped. He pushed his advantage and we crashed out into the corridor again.

He tripped me and pinned me down on the floor. He pushed down with his forearm on my throat. I struggled, but he had the upper hand. I could feel my muscles weakening. I'd given it my best shot, but the chambers were empty.

"Use the pistol," Angelina shouted.

I wriggled my hand into my pocket and inched out the small toy. Breathing was becoming harder. Effort to move … hard. Madman grinning. Big teeth. Vision dimming. Raised pistol. Eyes closed. Squirt.

Air burst back into my lungs.

Phoenix shrieked and flung his hand against his face. He rolled away, frantically wiping his hands across his eye. He writhed, thrashing on the floor and smashing into the walls. The shrieking was eternal and painful, forcing me to clap my hands over my ears.

Angelina appeared next to me, keeping one of her weapons trained on the thrashing form. Smoke was rising from his head.

"Are you sure this is holy water?"

She shrugged. "That or toxic, radioactive acid. I didn't stop to check."

I struggled to my feet and we ran for the alcove at the back of the chamber.

"No exit," she said, "but there's a big lever here."

She pulled down on it, and there was a grinding sound from the other end of the crypt. Bricks slid back and revealed the stairway back up.

"Oh great, we've got to get past him to get out."

There was a whimper from down the corridor, mixed in with a dash of anger. But I'd heard enough in life to know someone was hurt badly.

I glanced at Angelina. "Whatever happens, just run."

We charged forward into the smoking corridor before either of us had the chance to come up with an even more insane plan. There, in the smoke, I saw the evil, red eyes. They floated, disembodied in the fog. Then Phoenix was on me. I smashed him to the side, thrust Angelina toward the exit and shouted at her to run. Phoenix tried to leap past me, but I grabbed his leg and brought him down. He howled in rage, and turned toward me.

His fist came smashing down and I staggered back under the impact, collapsing to the floor. I rolled and came up on my hands and knees. My head was throbbing. Every part of me felt like it had been tenderized. I gave my head a shake, then staggered back up onto my feet, moving closer to the exit. I placed one foot back and beckoned him, and his duplicated images in my eyes, forward.

"Come and get it," I growled.

"Why won't you go down?" he shrieked.

There was a laugh to one side of him. "I was asking the same thing."

Phoenix's head snapped sideways. There was a lightning blur as something dark rushed at him. An iron manacle snapped down around his wrist. It locked with a resounding click.

"I've got you, boyo."

CHAPTER 35 ...

Watcher stood beside me, staring into the cell. Phoenix was lying on the small metal shelf that passed as a cot. His hands were behind his head and he was staring up at the ceiling. There had been cheers when Phoenix had been brought in. The men had applauded Watcher, and he had accepted all of the accolades without much, or any, referral to those of us who had actually fought the madman.

The medic had examined every part of me and said I was okay, just a big bag of bruises. Something of a miracle, he seemed to think. Luck was on my side. I wondered how far I could push it.

Angelina was probably releasing her own demons from her cage, and I'd see her when she finally acquiesced. She had been so wound up that she'd jumped on the first halfway decent-looking youngster and kicked him into the back of the ambulance. The rocking was disconcerting but she emerged fifteen minutes later. There was no sign of the young guy.

Angelina had left with a call-me wiggle of her fingers. She sure had embraced her change in criteria, and was enjoying getting her flowers pressed harder than a manic ornamental horticulturist discovering the wonders of Florentine découpage.

The hours had ticked away, pushing hard past the pumpkin hour. My eyes were so tired they burned. I rubbed them with the palms of my hands.

"He's a tough guy," Watcher was saying. "It took a handful of my biggest men to get him in there. And since he's been in there, he's been a wild one, stalking back and forth. He seems afraid of the bars." He gave them a kick and they hummed.

Phoenix snapped his head around and glared at us.

"He tried to touch one, then acted like it was on fire," Watcher said. "Is there such a thing as a metal phobia?"

I shrugged. "It works for me."

The desk sergeant called down the corridor. Watcher signaled back.

"We've been after this guy for decades, but we could never catch him." Watcher kicked the cell bars again. "But we got you now, boyo, haven't we?"

Phoenix jumped up and lunged at him, baring his teeth and roaring. He stopped just short of smashing into the bars. Watcher took a couple of steps back in surprise.

"You can't hold me. No cage can," Phoenix spat.

Watcher gave him a dismissive glance and made his way back down the corridor.

Phoenix stared at me. I stared back. It was definitely the same man who'd been impaled at the church, with the same scar on the neck.

He saw me looking. "You know where I got it from? The scar?"

I shrugged. I didn't really care. I watched him pace back and forth in his cell. It was strange to think that I'd seen him killed twice.

"I saw you die," I said.

"You sure? You sure you hadn't been drinking? You sure you hadn't been drinking a lot? I know about your drinking." He let out a manic laugh.

I turned away, in half a mind to let him rot in the stinking cage. His laugh cut through the air so loud and sharp it nearly hurt. My mind became clouded with dark thoughts, things I'd like to do to him.

He leaped up onto the bars and swung from them like a deranged monkey. His laughing turned into the mock chatter of a gibbon, and he screeched, and screamed, and smoke began to seep out between his fingers. He landed back on the floor, showing me his burned hands. He stepped toward the bars again, and his hand shot out between them, trying to grab my jacket.

I stepped back. He pressed against the bars. He tried to grab my throat with his other hand, the smell of burning flesh drifting up into my nose. His face was flush against the bars and they burned vertical lines into his skin. Finally his burning face made him shriek and he let go.

I struggled for breath, keeping him at bay. I had visions of grabbing him by the throat and squeezing until every drop of life had drained from his sorry existence. Watching his eyes pop out of his skull, slamming his face against the bars and watching him burn. It would be cleansing. The world would be a better place without him. I felt angry and old, as though the world had been dragging me down every moment my mind was awake.

I stood back, horrified at the thoughts in my head.

"Anything coming back to you?" He stood close to the bars again, but without touching them. His red face looked demented in the light. "I'm telling you, as soon as I'm out of here I'll rip you apart. And I don't care who you think you are. Or were. Because from what I see, you ain't even a fraction of the person we all once feared."

My anger flared at his ridiculous comments. He was just a punk with a broken mind, full of self-conceited thoughts and irrelevant nonsense. I cleared my mind and tried Angelina's pure thoughts.

The laughter stopped. Phoenix was staring at me, half in a trance, with death in his eyes. "What are you doing?" he said.

His voice drifted away, as did the feeling of extreme confrontation. There was peace. I no longer felt old, but refreshed as though I had drunk a glass of cold water in the middle of an unbearable night.

Something clicked behind Phoenix's eyes. "The change is coming."

"So I hear."

"Levi has a plan. He's challenging for the top job. The previous boss has broken all her promises."

"The previous boss?"

"Lucy."

He seemed to be a calmer man. He scratched at his burns; skin fell to the floor. Small bugs scurried out to eat the skin. With a blank face, Phoenix stamped down on them until the crunching stopped.

"People are like bugs," he said. "They don't come back when you crunch them."

I wasn't buying into his shock tactics. "You've got a church."

"Politics demand it. You can't get anywhere if, in the eyes of the public, you don't believe. You own a church, everyone thinks you're pure and great. Little do they know ..."

"Know what?"

"What's really going on there, and what's going to happen there. Tomorrow night: Lucy versus Levi."

As though in some kind of trance state, he punched his fists out with so little effort he would've had trouble punching through paper. He accompanied his efforts with the appropriate sound effects, now looking as dangerous as a kitten. He scratched frantically behind his ear, then twitched.

"We got some dark times coming."

"Are you afraid?"

"Levi is worse than Lucy. She's been sitting in her tower untainted by the evil that men do. Levi has lived among it, swum in the fetid reality." He pulled a face of disgust. "He's learned the worst behaviors, the vilest actions, all from the ordinary people that inhabit this little planet. He is far, far worse. So yes, I am afraid. Everyone should be."

"Where is he?"

Phoenix laughed. "You think you can beat him? He's unstoppable. He will battle, he will win, and then he will challenge Him. And if Him falls, if Levi wins—*when* Levi wins—it ends badly for anyone not on the winning side. The gates of the night will be opened and he'll reign supreme over the universe for all eternity. When the night comes, you'd better pick which side you're on."

"That's easy. I'm on mine."

A crack of lightning, loud enough to deafen a fanatic, seared down from above, smashing through the wall of the tank. Bricks flew everywhere and steel twisted. I was thrown back against the rear wall, bricks raining down on me. I clawed my way free just in time to see lightning course down into the cell, illuminating and irradiating the room with fierce intensity.

Phoenix screamed in pain and collapsed to his knees. He stared up at me. His skin started to char. "You can't win," he said through clenched teeth.

His yellow eyes glared at me as his skin blackened. The growl of a demented demon rolled out across the darkening sky. The heavens opened and torrential rain fell. There was a crack of thunder so loud it shattered the remaining windows.

The wall collapsed, revealing a sinister form on the road. The figure stood there in his faded set of ex-army pants and old lumberjack shirt hanging open. He had his hair tied back and a large set of cheaters in some failed attempt at disguise. He stared in at me, still as a statue.

"We should stop meeting like this," I shouted through the howling wind and rain.

I clambered awkwardly over the rubble and came face to face with the big man. Well, more like face to chin. His height was still intimidating. But he had a ponytail, so you can only give a man so much credence before he shoots his own foot away if unguided by a decent female. The wind whipped across my face, blowing my hair into my eyes. Maybe his ponytail had a use, after all.

"Maybe we will," he said. "It's all coming to an end, so maybe we meet just once more, tomorrow night."

"You could end it now."

He laughed and shook his head. "No. *You* could end it now. The choice has always been yours."

"Do you have the rood?"

He nodded in a noncommittal fashion. I didn't know what he was afraid of admitting. It was what he'd wanted all along, and now he seemed hesitant to bask in the glory it afforded him. It had cost a lot of people a lot of things, including their lives. But he didn't seem to care. Maybe it was all just a bunch of bull and he'd found out the hard way.

But when I looked at the evidence around me—controlled lightning strikes, buildings destroyed—I had to ask myself how often I had to see something before I'd believe it. I could deny the madness that lay outside my head, but I would lose. What if we all moved our tents down the insane line? We either embraced it, or got taken down fighting it. Either way we lost. So how does anyone win?

To beat the demons in our heads we had to fight them on common ground, even if it was their territory. Sometimes we had to visit crazy town, with all its happy villagers, and burn it to the ground.

I went back into the tank, clumsily stepping over the pile of bricks. Phoenix had been replaced by a blackened pile of cinders. The cell had been unlocked. I flicked the opened padlock and sighed. When I kicked the heap of charred remains, it contained nothing living. In the air hung the scent of perfume, one that I knew well. Desire. Subtitle: Damnation.

On the edge of earshot I heard a buzzing. I grabbed a sheet off the cot and wrapped it around me, just as a swarm of insects flew straight at me. I pulled the sheet closer around me. I felt them bounce off the fabric. They were concentrating on my head. I swept the sheet up, capturing them, then flung it onto the floor and stamped on it until the buzzing stopped.

"It's time," I said. But it wasn't my voice. "The change is coming."

The remains of Phoenix had gone.

CHAPTER 36 ...

I went back upstairs to the tank. The lights were out. I'd never been in the building without its illumination. It was a lot like being unconscious. The place was deserted and deathly silent. Without windows it was pitch black.

Within a few steps I'd crashed into a desk. I fumbled around the edge of it and took it step by step, slowly, feeling my way in the dark. I heard a scuffling sound to my right. I paused, trying to establish its identity. Too big for a rat; too scratchy for a person. I inched forward, sliding my feet along the floor. Something brushed against my trouser leg. I spun around, but couldn't see anything. I waited until my eyes could make out the dim shape in the darkness.

There was a growl behind me. I wheeled around again and came face to face with a dog. Its red eyes glared at me, a deep glow coming from within. It was standing on a desk, hunched forward. Its jaws were at eye level.

I stepped back and knocked against another desk. I ran my hands along the wooden top, feeling for anything sharp, not taking my eyes off the mad beast in front of me.

"Good boy," I muttered. The dog deepened its growl and bared

www.BataviaPublicLibrary.org
Phone: 630-879-1393

Title: Sucker
Author: Lingane, Mark,
Item ID: 36173004311240
Date due: 5/10/2016,23:59

Title: Steam.
Author: Perry, Fred, 1969-
Item ID: 361 300 375757
Date due: 5/ /2016,23:59

Title: Jack Cloudie
Author: Hunt, Stephen, 1967-

Item ID: 36173003936799
Date due: 5/10/2016,23:59

Total checkouts for session:3

Total checkouts:3

its fangs. "Or would you prefer I called you bad dog?"

It stared at me. I could see drool dripping from its teeth. My hand landed on something long and thin. I whipped it around in front of me and thrust it at the dog. It was a pen. As a weapon it wasn't great. It occurred to me that the only time the pen is mightier than the sword is when you don't have a sword. Or when it's wielded by a bank manager. Most of the time a sword would be my preference.

In the dark you face your fears, and it defines who you are. Sometimes the most personal dark is the one you see when you close your eyes. All those things you've done wrong unroll in your mind, and that's when you have to face your darkest fear: the truth about you and the person you are. But coming a close second is a great big black dog with very sharp teeth.

You face your fears, and it defines who you are.

"Good boy. Look, a squirrel!"

And sometimes you're disappointed with the results.

The dog leaned out from the desk, its muzzle snuffling over my shoulder and face. Its drool trickled down, the smell a mixture of rotting meat and poor dental hygiene. It occurred to me that I might not be smart enough to outwit a dog. We were deep in the quicksand of primal confrontation, and the dog was the dominant player.

I flicked something heavy off the desk and it crashed to the floor, but the dog's eyes remained fixed on me. There was only one option left, the one any weaker opponent has in a confrontation: the element of the stupid surprise attack.

I lunged at the dog. It shrank back momentarily as I roared toward it. Then it recovered and launched forward again. I held up my arm against the attack and felt razor sharp teeth sink into my flesh. The dog had leaped off the desk. I caught it in midair, twisted around, and swung the beast in a wide arc. Its teeth tore from my arm as it sailed across the dark room.

I turned and ran, crashing into desks and throwing chairs to the floor behind me. I tripped up the steps to the entrance and scrambled on all fours toward the front door. I fumbled with the door handle, pushed through, and slammed the door closed behind me.

I was out in the night air. I slumped with my back to the door, with ferocious barking and scratching coming from the other side. And then the pain in my arm introduced itself to my consciousness, which quickly let me know it was not impressed by my foolhardy actions.

Angelina had come to my aid and done some pretty excellent bandaging of teeth marks. Thankfully she had changed her clothing.

"We don't have an angel," I said.

She'd pulled the bandages tight and I winced with the pain and pressure.

"I've been thinking about what you told me," she said. "It's only important to have an angel when you don't know when or where a fallen angel's going to appear. Levi said tomorrow night. We know when, so all we need is to find the place. Phoenix's church."

When she'd finished the nursing stuff I pulled my sleeve down over the bandages and buttoned up the cuff. I looked at her. It amazed me how much she'd changed. She'd faced her fears and come up with something better than *Look, a squirrel!*

I stood up from the chair and offered her my hand. She smiled and took it, rising up next to me.

"I've got some ideas," I'd said.

Now we had a map from the state library pinned up on the wall of my office. It covered the city and surrounding areas, including the wastelands. Angelina produced an oversized magnifying glass and searched inch by inch over the wasteland areas. She made a note of any building of significance, and the list grew.

The minutes ticked past and we were getting nowhere. My stomach was in knots, and I could feel the frustration boring into me.

"I'm getting nothing," I said, standing back from the wall and rubbing my eyes. I was seeing double. The nights without sleep were beginning to weigh on me.

"Sorry, what was that?" Angelina said, and then ignored me. "But where's the church? There are dozens of them out on the wastelands."

I glanced at my watch and out the window at the setting sun. We were running out of time.

Angelina stood up and wandered over to the window, examining her list.

I stood in front of the map and drew lines, trying to find some direction from the buildings within the city. But there were no clues.

"They're all well-known deities and sanctuaries," Angelina said. "But they all sound so innocuous. Why can't one of them be called Temple of Absolute Evil and Death?"

"It would only attract heavy-metal fans and elementary-school teachers? What sanctuaries?"

"The Animal Liberation Movement, Global and Fauna Spirituality, the Temple of Animal Claim, and the Academy of Biospirituality."

She continued listing other ridiculous names, and her voice disappeared into the background of my thought processes. My subconscious ran over the titles as I stared at the maps.

"Wait." I held up a finger.

"What?"

"Read out those animal sanctuaries again."

She recounted the titles. I closed my eyes and listened. When she came to the temple I held up my hand.

"That's where we're going."

"Where?"

"The Temple of Animal whatever." I grabbed my keys, and indicated for Angelina to get her weapons.

"Animal Claim."

"Animal Claim is an anagram."

"Of what?"

I didn't bother to lock the door. I doubted we'd be back.

"Let's get the others," I said. "This is going to be difficult. It's a temple to Mina Camilla."

(HAPTER 37 ...

We were halfway down the corridor when the phone rang. I hesitated. Would it be some feckless deadbeat wanting me to chase down his wandering wife, or was it Derek? I couldn't risk it. I turned back and picked up the receiver.

Derek's voice came down the line. He sounded shaken. The news was bad. Laura was fading fast.

I grabbed Angelina, against her protests, and dragged her along with me. Within fifteen minutes, after hijacking another diesel dimbox and pushing it to near destruction, we ran inside Laura's apartment. As we entered, a fierce, intense cold fell over me, chilling me to the bone. Angelina didn't seem to notice. I had one thought: Mina was still missing.

I looked at Laura's face. Her eyes seemed dead. She lay in a pool of sweat that spread out from her shoulders. It looked like she had wings. Her face was clammy, and her hair was stuck to it in uneven clumps.

"Please look at me," I whispered, sitting down on the bed. There was a tiny spark but it faded in an instant. I looked up at Angelina. "Are you sure it'll work?"

She sighed. Her eyes were compassionate. "I won't lie. It's never been done before. We're relying on myth and legend, which are even less substantial than old wives' tales and tax laws. But it's all we can do, and your guess is as good as mine."

"I'll pray for you," Derek said.

Normally I would mock a man for saying such a thing to me, but not today. I nodded a thank-you to him. We all bundled out of the bedroom into the apartment's living room. I held Laura close in my arms. I didn't want to let her go yet.

We all talked over the final aspects of the plan. At least, I tried to talk but images of a fast-fading Laura kept derailing me. In the end, Angelina took over.

Laura began to rouse, and Derek came over to her and took her hand.

"I need a drink before I go," he said. "My nerves are all over the place. Anyone else need to fortify their spirits?"

I looked at my hands. They were shaking. I'd been hiding it, but Derek's declaration was good timing.

Derek gently helped Laura to her feet, and led her into the living room with a supporting arm around her waist. He poured us both a drink. He knocked his back. Angelina kicked up a fuss and he poured one for her. I knocked mine back. The burning hit me straightaway, and my nerves calmed down.

I turned to leave, but the room swung violently. I caught my bearings and focused. The door seemed simultaneously a long way off and extremely close.

Angelina was speaking. Words were coming out of her mouth and falling on the floor in a jumbled mess. She reached forward, and then swung away in an arc. I reached out, but my tiny hand couldn't cover the four miles between us. She zoomed in and we crashed together with the speed of glaciers.

Derek was laughing, manic and disturbed.

Everywhere was dark. My head pounded with the ferocity of a chain-gang worker slamming in a thousand spikes. I opened my eyes a crack. It was still dark. My eyes weighed the same as a small elephant. I took a couple of breaths and tried again. I could feel them open this time as my facial muscles went into overdrive. Something was wrong; it was still dark.

I was resting against a wood-paneled wall. I could feel the texture on my fingertips. My head still spun around, the universe twisting in dangerous directions. I tried to step forward. My foot slammed into something and I stayed riveted to the spot. I moved my foot forward slowly, questing for the floor, but there was a dark barrier immediately in front of me. I tried to move my hands, but they wouldn't budge. The swirling started to die down. My body floated down from the heavens, and landed like a leaf after being tossed in a tornado, crumpled and frayed.

It sunk in; I was lying down. My hands were tied behind my back. I shuffled my foot around, feeling for my surroundings. There were walls to my immediate left and right, and one in front. That didn't bode well. I was in a box. There weren't too many wooden boxes specifically designed for the shape of a person.

It began to get warm.

There weren't too many places you could put a person in a box in a warm place.

I kicked the front panel, but it was so close I couldn't put any real force into it. The heat took a big jump, and smoke started to fill the box. I wriggled and squirmed, trying to get some leverage, but the box was too cramped. I slammed my knee into the wood, but it sent stinging jabs of pain down my leg. I levered myself into one corner and pushed into the other with my feet. The diagonal pressure made the wood creak, but that was all.

Smoke was pouring into the box now and the heat on my back was intense. The smoke started to burn my lungs, and I coughed, crashing my head against the wood. I slammed my legs down into the foot of the box. Stars spun in front of my eyes.

It suddenly dawned on me that I had slammed my feet down.

I twisted my legs and drew my knees up. I slammed my feet down again. I had enough room to get some decent power going. I smiled, nearly giddy with the possibility. I smashed down again, a solid thud into the wood. The exertion made me breathe in heavily. The smoke was filling my lungs.

I continued to hammer away with my feet. The board began to weaken. I could hear it cracking. The base finally gave way.

I saw a roaring fire approaching between my feet. The furnace spat out brimstone and heat, and the box began to blacken. I was trapped. There was no way back through the wooden end above me, and a slowly approaching death through the exit between my feet beckoned. A spark flew out of the furnace and landed on my pants. They started to smolder. A small flame flickered into life. The flames started to grow, engulfing my clothes. The box erupted into flames.

My vision started to fade as I fought for air.

There was a loud crack, but distant, in my ears, then an open space to my right. The smoke rolled away and fresh air filled my lungs. I coughed violently. Then I saw the face of an angel. Or an Angelina, which is pretty close.

She grabbed me and heaved her body against the conveyor. The headboard of the coffin closed in and approached the furnace. She was too late. I was inside the furnace. Heat and fire were everywhere and my lungs were burning.

Angelina disappeared and I closed my eyes. My body screamed in pain.

The coffin stopped. There was a loud crack from the headboard and the wood above my head vanished. A long hook descended from the flames and caught under my arm. My body slipped against the slow traction of the conveyor belt as each roller slipped beneath me. The hook slowly pulled me out.

As I emerged from the furnace I saw Angelina bracing herself against the end of the conveyor belt and heaving on the hook. She grabbed me, an arm under each of mine, and rolled me off. We collapsed onto the floor. We lay next to each other, gasping in the clear air. The furnace howled away as it made quick work of the disappearing coffin.

"Do you want the good news or the bad?"

"Tell me." I coughed violently and felt something shift in my throat.

"Well, you were about to die, and I—"

I was sitting by the pond. The man was stroking a baby fawn. I had watched him help the small creature stand, and then it staggered off. The beautiful lady stroked my head, brushing back my hair.

"He's so dull," she said. "All he does is look after the plants and animals. He has no sense of adventure."

"This is paradise," I said. "You don't need anything else."

The lady rolled over in the long grass, her naked body leaving an indentation in the soft vegetation. She rested her chin in her hands and stared at the dark wall that surrounded the parklands.

"What lies outside the wall?" she asked.

"Nothing but pestilence and death. The world is still forming."

"It sounds exciting. Something's actually happening. Why don't we both go and look at it?"

She rolled over and kissed me, and I swallowed.

"—saved you, so that's pretty good news," Angelina said. "Although my body aches like—"

"What happened?" I croaked.

"Where?"

"Here. Just now."

The roof swirled around. It was made from imitation wood. Out of one box and into another.

"I was speaking," Angelina said, "and you, unlike many men I've met, were listening."

"Nothing weird happened?"

"Other than what I just said about you listening? No. You want the bad news? Brace yourself. Derek believes that if he can sacrifice Laura at the right time, he can bring back his daughter."

"From the dead?" The concept was insane and I couldn't believe I was even asking the question.

"Yes, from the dead."

"He's mad."

"You noticed."

Then, in light of recent events, a worrying thought crossed my mind. "Can he actually do it?"

"Of course not, his daughter's dead. No one can come back from the dead. What would she come back to, a half-rotted body?"

"Then why's he doing it?"

"Simple. Like you said, he's mad."

"We gotta go."

She looked sideways at me. "You're a tough man, Mr. Avram."

CHAPTER 38 ...

I tried out my legs. Many people had used legs before, so I thought, given the occasion, I'd give mine a go. They shook violently as I stood and rested against the wall. "What happened to us?" I said.

"Nice Mr. Derek had an ulterior motive, it would seem. He drugged us, brought us here, and dumped you in the furnace and me in the icebox."

"Heaven and hell," I muttered.

"I have to admit it's a pretty lousy date."

I held out my hand and helped Angelina up. We leaned against each other and took in our surroundings.

We were in a funeral parlor. There was the distant sound of an organ being played inexpertly. Around us lay several deceased, some with tags around their toes.

"We're in a police morgue," I said. "With him being a cop, he probably has friends on the inside."

"But why is there an organ?"

"Could be private. Subcontractor, maybe."

We made our way toward the strained strains of an uplifting religious mainstay, unknown to me but Angelina hummed along to its pentatonic melody, probably stolen from the Christmas album of a delta blues legend.

We came to a T-junction. The organ ground away to the right, and to the left was a short corridor. Several wooden boxes were stacked against one wall. At the end of the corridor was the exit sign. I beckoned for Angelina to follow, a task not too difficult as she was clinging to me tightly.

We eased open the door into a graveyard. The golden glow of the setting sun reflected off the various forms of marble. I could hear the efforts of manual labor as a shovel hefted into the ground and was followed by a thud. Something Derek said clicked in the back of my mind.

"Quick detour," I said. I dragged Angelina in the direction of the digging while filling her in on the information Derek had been only too eager to impart.

In the heart of the yard, among the browning grass and wilting lilies, we found a gravedigger toiling away in the warm evening air. I called to him. He paused mid-dig and looked up at us. He frowned at me, but smiled when he saw Angelina. He looked at my charred clothes and bandaged arm, and Angelina's bruises.

"Either you're having the best or the worst date ever."

Angelina waved his comment aside. "Worst. No sex yet. Do you know the grave man up at Berkeley?"

"There are many serious and severe people up at Berkeley," he replied. He tilted his cloth hat forward, concealing his eyes.

"The lady means a cemetery worker," I said.

"I know what she means. There's not a whole lot of fun in this job." He removed his hat and extracted an old checkered handkerchief. He dabbed his brow before replacing the damp cloth back in the hat.

"Sorry," I said. "We're having a bad day."

"Not as bad as this one." He indicated the box beside him, ready to be lowered into the pit. The man's face went vacant for a moment. He nodded glumly. "It was disturbing, what happened up there."

"What's his name? Can we talk to him?"

"That would be a thing. Unless you have special powers then no. He's six feet under, and not for professional reasons."

"What happened?" I said.

He drove the end of the shovel into the soil and leaned on it, staring at us. "The police said Gerald found someone digging up a young lady, not that I'm making any judgments about reasons. Looks like Gerald surprised the desecrator, who killed him dead. One hit, precise and clean, like someone from the forces does."

"Like the army or police?" I said.

He nodded.

Angelina and I looked at each other.

"We've got to stop him," she hissed. "He could destroy the world."

We ran towards the main street to catch a ride. The sun had set and clouds were beginning to roll in. The night was turning sultry.

"How could he destroy the world?" I asked Angelina.

"Okay, this is a little, well, a lot, creepy. You've got the whole angel bit, standing above the two people in union, right?"

I nodded.

"That scenario assumes they're both living." She paused and screwed up her eyes. "If one happens to be dead, then all the dead will be brought back to life, and they'll be under control of the angel who stands above, and if that's Levi …"

"Union?"

She nodded.

"With the dead?"

She nodded again.

"But it's his daughter."

"Weeeell, I think the whole incest–taboo issue might go out the window once they're deceased, which, by the way, is the worst part. The Bible's full of incest stories. All of Europe is ruled by inbred offspring. It's gross, but not uncommon. Dead, on the other hand, is uncommon and gross."

"It can't work."

She shrugged. "Many of the old religions thought it was a way of communing with the dead. If you, er, do it while you've got the whole angel thing going on, well, the legends say it brings back all the dead."

"Why does he need Laura?"

"His daughter has been dead—no blood. You need the blood of the innocent, and as we're surmising, he's a long way from innocent. An army of zombies."

"We'd better hurry."

Out on the street, Angelina stuck out her leg to attract the passing attention of a wayward motorist, although she really didn't need to. Her outfit was enough to stop all the traffic.

I wrenched open the door of the first car that pulled up and hauled the driver out. We were lucky enough to grab a Diesel Sport 110, and within minutes we were speeding out of the city limits over into the desolate wastelands beyond. The reflections from the cats' eyes defining the road ahead, like seeds of truth, were mirrored in the windscreen as they rolled up the glass, one by one.

"You know," Angelina said, as she stared ahead, "it wouldn't have been that hard to find the place." She pointed ahead.

Clouds were swirling above an ancient church, with sheet lightning lining the clouds like fine linen. The night was crawling in. The headlights didn't provide much warning of the dangers that appeared before us. Metallic debris that was strewn across the barren lands continually tumbled in front of us, crashing off the vehicle. By the time we rolled up to the iron gates of the church the 110 was so battered and dented it could barely move.

There was no other vehicle present.

"How could we have beaten him here?" Angelina said.

"Maybe he's getting his daughter," I guessed. She had to be stored somewhere.

Derek could only be a handful of minutes behind us so we had to move quickly. Lighting stabbed down and destroyed a tree next to us.

"You think that was for us?" Angelina said.

I nodded. "Everything's going to be for us."

"Wait. We need to hide the car. He won't be expecting anyone to be here. If he sees it he'll know something's up."

She was right. Our only advantage was surprise.

We limped the car around the rear of the church and crashed it into a ditch. It was the best we could do. More lightning flashed down. One hit the car. It fizzled, and the electrics went wild for a few seconds. The wipers swished, the headlights flashed, and the horn blasted until it ended in a forlorn *blarp*. The car wasn't going anywhere.

We were marooned out here, in the heart of mechland with no way out. We could see them stalking around in the distance, the occasional blast of fire expunging the evil from the world.

We made our way through the gates and into the old graveyard. Angelina stopped at various headstones. She gasped. A tear trickled down her face.

"I always wondered where they were buried."

"Who?"

"My parents, grandparents, all the slayers. If I'd only known." She sighed. "What I said about them before wasn't true."

I nodded. "I saw your file."

"They were killed when I was young, then buried by a relative. I was never told who it was. Then I was adopted out."

"Would it change things to know who it was, or where they were buried?"

"Who knows? We grow up to be who we are. Life takes us down a path, and we live the best we can, taking each day as it comes. We can't change it so we might as well make the best of it."

I could hear the doubt in her voice. She didn't believe it. It hurt her and there was no making the best of it. I put my arm around her. She turned into me but looked out to the mechwarriors drifting around the horizon.

"Loss makes you stronger," I said.

"Loss breaks pieces off you every day until you crumble into a broken pile. Loss takes your spirit. Loss drains the color out of your life."

"It comes back."

"But it never replaces the loss. Tell me, Van, you look like a man who's seen a lot. Do you *really* think it comes back? Because when I look at you and the darkness that floats above your head, it sure doesn't feel like it."

"Come on. Enough with the merrymaking."

I led her through the withering trees, with barren branches that clawed at our skin as we passed by. The main doors were ajar and we squeezed through the opening into the vaulted main room. The solid doors looked untouched by time. The roof was three stories high, but there was a narrow balcony hugging the walls one story up. Moonlight radiated through the high windows and a large hole in the center of the roof, reflecting off armor and weapons scattered around the room's perimeter.

A large cross hung from a side wall. An old man was nailed to it.

The preacher wasn't long dead. Blood was dripping down the cross and wall in a thin stream, pooling in a red bubble. At the base was a five-pointed star, also sprayed in blood.

We made our way through the chamber, the giant pews spreading out like the ribcage of a Behemoth. Several creepy statues had been placed around the altar, all with evil intent scratched into the stonework.

Angelina ran her hand over one, and then quickly withdrew it. "It's warm."

I felt the stonework. It was smooth like marble, but it hummed with an unknown heat source.

Angelina looked at me. "Maybe there's a furnace below. Surely they can't be here all the time. They'd freak out all the parishioners."

"Depends on who they worship."

There was a scraping sound from the front gate and a distant boom from above.

"And so it begins," Van said.

"Or ends."

"Let's get some height."

We found a set of stairs leading up to the balcony. Several gargoyle-like statues stared down into the pews below. We took refuge behind them. We watched through the window as Derek approached. He was dragging a body bag behind him.

He lumbered slowly into the church, dragging the body down the aisle, apparently unfazed by the sight of the sacrificed priest. He was unaware of us watching him from the balcony.

The sight of the stone statues staring in at the altar was too confrontational. He steered around the strange effigies and approached the altar from the rear. He lifted up the body bag and placed it on the altar. The opening of the zipper echoed through the silence. It sounded like Derek was weeping. He rolled open the sides of the bag, revealing the pale face of a young lady about Laura's age. Her skin had a green tinge and was showing signs of decay. Derek ran his hand over the girl's face and kissed her forehead. He sagged to his knees and sobbed.

The minutes crawled by. Eventually he stood up, continued removing his daughter from the body bag, and laid her out on the altar. She was dressed in a short white nightdress. It was obvious she was wearing no secrets.

Derek stepped back and bowed his head. He stood looking down for a minute before leaving the church.

We moved to the window and watched him approach his car, walking as though in a trance, bumping into things as his path wandered from side to side. The car door squeaked open.

"I don't think he can do it," Angelina whispered. "Look at the way he treated her. When it comes to the act ..." She shook her head. She glanced at me, looking thoughtful.

Derek staggered forward into the headlights, struggling to guide a barely conscious Laura. As they crept forward toward the great gates, I could see a set of cuffs clipped around Laura's wrists.

Her head lolled around as she stumbled forward, tripping over the smallest obstacles. Clouds floated over the moon, and the churchyard went dark. The wind picked up and slammed the gates closed. They creaked loudly as Derek pushed them open. The sudden wind was making it a challenge for him.

There was a fluttering overhead as several crows flew in low before landing on a few of the gravestones. One crow watched Derek and Laura, uttering an occasional caw.

The two made their way through the wide doors of the church. Derek did a double take as he noticed the priest for the first time. The priest, crucified against the wall, was sagging from his wrists, his clothes dripping blood. Derek crossed himself.

"A bit misguided," whispered Angelina, "considering what he's planning on doing."

"I got to do something," I said, and started to stand up.

Angelina pulled me back down. "You can't go," she said. I gave her a dark look. "If you go down, well, in Derek's eyes you're another male who can do the deed with his daughter. If something goes wrong, we're one step closer to the situation we're trying to avoid. What if he has a weapon? Have you got one?"

She was right. She nodded and slowly made her way down from the balcony.

(HAPTER 39 ...

Derek and Laura made their way down the aisle to the rear of the church, stepping over pieces of debris and scattered Bible pages. Derek lowered Laura down to the floor and leaned her against the altar. She had no strength to hold herself upright and slipped down onto the stone floor. The clouds cleared and moonlight shone through a hole in the ceiling directly onto the altar. Sweat was pouring from her and her skin gleamed in the dim light. She was barely conscious.

I heard him mutter, "It's time."

There was the *tip-tap-tip* of the confident strut of high heels across the stone. Derek looked out from behind the statues.

Mina stood at the entrance to the church, her curves highlighted by the moonlight. She had a cigarette poised in her lips in a long silver holder.

Derek glanced around the walls. To his left was a medieval suit of armor, which held a large sword, and a more manageable axe. With his face full of rage, he lunged over to the suit and pulled down the axe. The armor topped over and crashed to the floor.

"You," he screamed to Mina. "You did this to my daughter."

With the axe in his hand, he charged at Mina. He swung it

wildly, emotions overriding judgment. Mina easily dodged his mad swipes and reeled back from his screams. His strength soon weakened, age getting the better of him, and his lunges with the axe became more sporadic. In the end he sagged to his knees, head bowed.

Mina laughed and walked up to him, strutting her Miami blues. She placed a shoe on his body and pushed him backward. "You stupid man. Why did you have to get so caught up?"

He knelt before her, mesmerized by her.

"You men are so dull and depressingly predictable. Once they get your scent, they'll track you until they die. I can see it in your eyes. It's hard to dodge the affairs of the heart."

"Dodge this." Angelina stepped out from the shadows and fired.

There was a loud crack, followed by the sound of the air being ripped apart. Angelina lowered her gun, stepped back and glared at Mina. Mina looked down. There was a stake sticking out of her stomach. She fell to her knees, clutching at herself. Her head fell forward.

Phoenix fell screaming from the sky, his great wings unfolded. His skin glowed red; black pupils stood out in his yellow eyes. He bared his oversized teeth and stopped between the two women. He spat at Angelina and brought around one of his massive claws, knocking her sideways across the church. He strode toward her, his heavy feet thumping across the stone floor. He reached down, wrapped his great hand around her throat, and lifted her up to the level of his face. She struggled ineffectually against his strength.

"I've been waiting to get even with you," he growled. "I might take your body as my reward."

She thrashed her legs, managing to get in several kicks, but achieved nothing. The sound of distant barking echoed from beyond the graveyard. Two bright lights shone in through the church doors. Phoenix raised his hands to shield his eyes against the fierce beams.

Out of the blur of light bounced a hound, initially a thin-sticked object in the light that expanded to become a huge dog. The black dog leaped, red eyes focused on Phoenix, baring its enormous fangs, which it sank into the arm holding Angelina. Phoenix shrieked. The dog dug its fangs in deeper.

Phoenix released Angelina. She fell to the floor and rolled away. Smoke rose from his arm. He tried to shake the dog free, but the fangs were embedded too deeply.

Derek ran up behind Phoenix and smashed him over the head with the shovel. Phoenix fell forward. Within the blink of an eye, the dog had its fangs digging into Phoenix's throat. Phoenix lay as still as a portrait. Every twitch or excessive breath was met by a deep growl.

Angelina leaped to her feet and ran to Derek. She grabbed him by the collar. "Where is Van? I couldn't save him from the furnace you left him in. Derek, you can't bring your daughter back like this."

"Your accent, it's different," Derek said to Angelina. "You were lying to me."

"Well, you put me in a freezer expecting me to die, so we have some degree of equilibrium, although I owe you a lot more pain. Give up this foolish endeavor."

"You can't tell me what to do. I've read the books. We can bring back the dead." Derek tried to push her away, but her grip was unbreakable.

"My family *wrote* the books. What comes back isn't the person, just a piece of reanimated meat. They took my parents. You don't think I haven't thought long and hard about this? You can't do it. It's wrong. You've got to let it go."

"I can't let it go, she was my daughter. I failed at everything with her. You can't stop me."

Angelina withdrew her second gun, stepped back, and aimed it at him. "Yes I can, and don't think I won't."

"Aren't you the plucky one?" Mina said. She was sitting with her back against one of the statues, watching them closely.

Angelina glanced over. "I'm surprised I managed to hit you.

You move too slowly to be one of them."

"I am the ultimate one." Mina smiled. "Their queen. I don't need to move fast." She placed her hand against her stomach. Blood was dripping out. She examined her hand, at the blood smeared over her palm. It was a deep, dark red.

"You're a royal pain in the ass," Angelina said.

Mina smiled again.

"Why is this a temple to you?" Angelina asked.

"Shouldn't every girl have one? God knows men put us up on enough pedestals. This is only one step up from that, taking it to the max." She stood up, wincing as the stake ripped her insides.

Derek tried to move quickly, but Angelina turned and waved the end of her gun at him. He slowed and raised his hands. She returned her attention to Mina.

"This has been built for you," Angelina said, "and it's very old. I think you are old. Very old."

"That's not a nice thing to say to a lady. But I have a good skin regime if you'd like to know."

"How long have you been their queen?"

Mina laughed. "How long does memory last?"

"It lasts as long as there's someone to remember. If I stop you, the memory will die. You'll no longer be a queen."

Mina laughed. "You can't stop what's destined to happen. You're dead. Your time is over and there's nothing you can do about it."

"I think you'll find I'm holding the cards. I have your angel, and although we have a male here in Derek, I can easily shoot him. What's so important about tonight?"

Derek's face dropped at the casual mention of his name linked with imminent death.

"Look up," Mina said.

Keeping the gun solidly in her grip, Angelina glanced up. She gasped.

"Not many humans have seen that vision. You'll be the last."

"What is it?"

"Creation. Enough power to change everything, to jumpstart a universe, or wipe out an entire race and start a new one. Power beyond dreams. And all wielded by whoever holds the rood."

"Where is it?"

She smiled back. "You'll find out soon enough."

"No. This ends now. Van isn't here. You have no mate."

"I don't need him. I wanted him, who wouldn't? But any male will do. Why do you think we dress them up so they all look the same? One lets you down, or bores you, or gets too needy, you move onto the next."

"No, Van was too important. He tested green. I've worked out what that means."

"Have you now? My, you are a clever little girl." Mina stepped forward. And again she looked at her blood-soaked hand. She licked it. Her eyes changed from deep blue to dark red. "But I'm telling you now that the only end is for you." She smiled, revealing a set of fangs, and leaped forward.

Angelina kicked upward, spearing Mina with her stiletto boot, spun and fired her gun. The stake shot out and buried itself deep in Mina's chest, in the center of her heart. Mina collapsed to the ground. Her eyes closed.

"Okay," whispered Angelina. She looked around nervously, looking at the bodies around her. "Demon trapped by crazed demon dog. Evil vampire queen dead. Disturbed psycho father immobilized through shock. I think it's all under control." She let out a sigh.

A lightning bolt ten feet wide struck down out of the turbulent sky above. The light hung mystically in the air for several moments before the air was ripped apart by the soundwave that followed. The impact knocked everyone to the floor and slammed the church doors closed. The lightning ceased. Everyone's eyes saw nothing but red.

Levi strode out of the lightning bolt, carrying the rood. He stood in the center of the church and slammed the rood down onto the stone tiles, which cracked under the force.

The dog cowered before him, but didn't let go of Phoenix's throat. Levi strode over to the dog, picked it up by the scruff of its neck—ripping out Phoenix's throat in the process—and threw it across the church. It yelped as it crashed into the far wall, falling into a silent heap. The dog shivered and dissolved into human form. Inspector Watcher lay unconscious.

Levi cast the rood aside, and it floated beside him wrapped in a pale green glow. Another sweep of his arm, and Levi knocked Derek into the pews. He fell heavily to the floor and lay there, unmoving.

Levi glanced at Mina. "Are you okay?"

"You're late. I'll survive. My clothes are ruined and I don't want to know the state of my hair." She stood up and ripped the spear from her chest. She concentrated, and the wound disappeared, leaving bloodied holes in her dress. "Can't you ever follow simple instructions? What is hard to understand about lying low, and turning up at a certain time?"

"It's their fault." Levi strode over to Angelina and grabbed her. "Always distracting us." He glared into Angelina's terrified eyes. "I've known you and your kind for centuries. You're always hunting us, always a thorn, always ruining our plans. The pain you've caused us all has been immeasurable. Now it's time to destroy your kind."

"Good," Mina said. "She's the last hunter. Well, she says she's the last, but the records were never good. There might be others."

"No, I'd be able to sense them." Levi sniffed the air noisily. "There are no others."

"You can't sense a hunter. You couldn't sense a bloodburger if it was directly under your nose."

"Don't tell me what I can and can't do. I don't care if there are others. I'll kill her anyway, and then there'll be one less."

Levi gripped Angelina around the neck. She fought against his strength, but it was futile.

"The battle with them has been raging for so long," Mina said. "The sickness that is humanity has left a deep mark on us. It will be strange having an era end."

"Why do you care?" Levi said. "They're nothing but vermin that seek to destroy us."

"Care? I don't care. But before you kill her you need to know one thing. She carries the blood from the countess."

Levi hesitated. His eyes shifted uneasily.

"I can't wait to see how you react to this," Mina said. "She's your great-granddaughter."

CHAPTER 40 ...

I watched the procession of unbelievable revelations below as they tumbled behind one another like a continental train wreck. I noticed a rear stairwell that would allow me to descend while keeping me hidden from view, not that they were focusing on anything except their own little melodrama.

Levi loosened his grip and stared at the curvaceous bombshell locked in his grasp. He lowered his arms and Angelina's feet touched the ground. She fought for a few breaths, filling her gasping lungs.

"That's a lie," he said to Mina.

"Oh, trust me, I've checked. I've been speaking with many old gravediggers who know real history. I've followed the family line all over the world, to here."

"It's impossible. The countess died."

"Do you know why they hunt us?" Mina sauntered over to Levi and ran her hand over his muscled torso. "It's because of you."

"Me?"

"Yes, you. They only started hunting us after your countess died. Look at her. She hates you. She doesn't know why, but I do.

You do too, deep in that big, black heart of yours. You have the truth inside you. Let me remind you of Mircalla Karnstein."

Levi hesitated. An emotion washed over him, something foreign, something painful. He lowered his head. "The countess. No, there would be some clue."

He still held Angelina by the throat. He twisted her head back and forth slowly, examining her features. "It's impossible. She died."

Angelina, still fighting for air, managed to squeeze out one sentence. "How can I be related?"

"Levi was once in love," Mina said in a singsong voice, dancing between the statues, "and like all men became a fool because of it. He met the countess one night. She was meant to be particularly pure and untouched by man, but she was sick. When Levi sucked the life from her, he sucked the sickness and she became half-human half-other. He granted the bitch equal status amongst us. That was his first act of betrayal."

Mina stopped dancing and looked at Levi. "Of course I never knew what you saw in her. She was so skinny and useless, just a pretty plaything, a distraction. Even her hair was the wrong color. It was black like those diseased gypsies."

Levi bared his fangs and growled at her.

She laughed. "Anyway, he took pity. How does that happen, Levi? A demon feeling sorry for a human."

"You didn't fall. You'll never know what it's like being cast out. You don't know the eternal loneliness and pain."

"Don't talk to me about eternal," she spat. "I've been waiting millennia after millennia for this." She pointed to the altar. "You should've been helping. I'm your queen, but you couldn't leave her alone."

"She was dying, and I couldn't save her. I couldn't watch it happen without doing something." He cast Angelina aside and strode toward Mina. "I went to Him, on my knees, to ask for assistance, but He said no."

"And He said no." She looked at him with a self-satisfied smirk.

She laughed again and waved a finger at him. "You're a fool. I watched this sorry state of affairs unfold. I knew what you were planning. I told Him you'd be coming and what would happen if He agreed to your request."

"You betrayed me. She was everything to me," Levi roared.

"I betrayed no one! You're the one who complicated matters. I am the queen. You were planning to put her in my place."

"That's a lie."

"Is it? Look into my eyes and tell me that again. I command you."

Levi's head twisted from side to side, filled with pain. "You think of no one but yourself. She understood. She could have fixed everything. We could have gone home."

"Home? That was never going to happen."

"You don't know that."

Mina sighed. "I would've thought the words 'you are banished forever' were self-explanatory. You were so angry and obsessed you never knew what happened afterward. You never knew her condition. She gave birth to triplet girls. Those girls grew and saw the pain of loss and love gone wrong, and they vowed revenge on all of us. They became the slayers and that's what they've been doing for centuries—running around and killing my beautiful people."

Fury rose in Mina's face. She stormed over to Angelina and pointed at her. "You think it was about right and wrong, good and evil, keeping the world safe. Well, I'm here to tell you it was always about revenge," she hissed.

And it's at a point like that when all logic seems to have disappeared and the inmates have taken over the asylum that you need to go where the current is taking you.

"Van! You made it," Mina cried as she wheeled around. "I knew you'd come."

Her transition from madwoman to temptress was so smooth I almost questioned my own memory that she could ever have been anything else.

"Let them all go," I said.

"I will free them of their pitiful lives. Just like I'll do with you," Levi replied.

"No!" Mina cried. She reached toward me.

Levi clapped his hands together and time froze. They were all riveted to the spot, their faces a combination of fear and shock.

"You and me," Levi snarled at me.

His blow came in like a thunderbolt, and I felt the force crack all the way down my back as it threw me into the air. I crashed into a pew and slid across the floor, finally crashing into the far wall. The dust billowed over me. I coughed—

Lilith wrapped her hand around the back of Samael's neck and pulled him close. The beautiful garden stretched out in all directions. Samael looked in the direction of the studious young man examining the plants that lined the pond leading up to the great tree.

"This is wrong," he said.

"Oh, and how," Lilith said.

She sank her desires into him as he did to her. They pulled each other close, and embraced in a moment of exquisite passion.

—and swallowed. The spinning roof of the church came into focus. My cars were roaring from the pain.

Levi's fists swung in from both sides in an unrelenting barrage of pain. For the eternity of damnation the unrelenting, ferocious pounding from the madman continued against my arms, held up in the only defense I could muster.

Then he relented, breathing heavily. I lowered my numb arms and staggered to my feet.

"This is your fault," he said. "If you hadn't run off with her …"

I stood against the wall with my head spinning and my senses on fire, feeling like every muscle had been ripped from my body. I coughed. Blood flew out of my mouth, splattered on the flagstones—

Lilith ran her hand over Samael's body, feeling the curve of his muscles. His wings were wrapped around them both as they lay by the pond under the shade of the tree.

"We can do whatever we want," she said. "It's just the two of us. It's a brand new world."

"What about … him?" Samael nodded in the direction of a man laughing with joy as he chased a small creature through the bushes.

"Hah. He barely knows I'm alive. He just sits and counts and names things all day."

"Okay."

—and I swallowed. The world swirled. An enraged Levi charged at me again. His punch caught me on the chin and sent me back against the altar, leaving a crack through the center.

I coughed again, this time with more conviction. I felt an intense irritation at the back of my throat. I tried to clear it. A wave of coughing rolled over me, like I was being punched in the sternum, and forced me to the ground on all fours. I gasped for air. Images flashed in front of my eyes, flickering between the reality in front of me and some forgotten fantasy—

Great gates were slammed shut. Levi took the sword. The pain came down from above. The laugh of love came from the most beautiful woman on the planet. The running. The playing. The love. The regret. The understanding. The choice.

—and I coughed violently. The cough turned into an intense retching, until I was bringing up blood and mucus. In one final, violent heave, my muscles thrust me forward and I brought forth a tiny seed. It shot out of my mouth and sailed across the altar. My vision turned red. And then everything came back.

"Finally," Levi said as he stalked toward me. "This will make victory sweeter."

My back ripped open and my wings unfolded for the first time since they'd been clipped. I felt the stretch as the compression of the millennia eased away. The white wings unfurled, ruffling in the wind, with a few feathers falling free and floating away. My clothes ripped apart as my muscles filled out, and I felt for the first time in a long while the vitality of refreshed blood flowing through my veins. The power of the earth seeped up through the ground, flowing into my limbs. My hair fell around my shoulders in white strands.

I felt burning in my hand and looked down. I raised the whip of flame and cracked it over my head. The ground shook.

"Forget your mace?" Levi said.

"I don't need it for you." I closed my eyes. I could feel the vitality and the drain of eternity, both exhilarating and debilitating. Memories lost for so long filtered down. "I'll give you a choice: surrender or die."

"You can't kill me," he said. "We have the agreement. We are the same."

I shook my head. "I am fallen, but I am not evil. I'll never be forgiven, but it doesn't mean I cannot do good."

"Heaven will not kneel to take your hand and raise you from the fire," he spat. "There's no purpose in doing good."

"When you walk among humans, you learn one of two things. Both revolve around love, and how it leaves you. Just like you, I fell for love. For an angel, it was the prize and the punishment when He bestowed freewill. We all did, especially Lucy, who put us in this predicament in the first place. But we can choose how it affects us; it can lift or drown."

"Lucy could never see past the first commandment," Levi said. "She refused to love anyone else but Him, so when He said she had to worship humans, she flipped out. How dare He make us, born of fire, bow to those of clay."

"But we did bow before them," I said. "She mocked, as you do, their perfection, yet we all fell for it."

"You remember His last words, when He cast us out? 'Repentance is not possible and sins are irreversible.' How can you not be brimming with anger?"

I shrugged. "Time heals all."

"No, it doesn't," Levi cried. "I've carried this pain for hundreds of years. And I've never forgotten the countess. Every day hurts as much as its predecessor. He tricked us, He lied to us, and He punished us."

"We did it to ourselves. When he gave us free will, he also gave us consequence. The fault was, we weren't prepared for it. Humans were. That's why they're better."

"No!" Levi blinked, and in his hands appeared the flaming sword and the mace of death.

"Those aren't yours," I said.

"I take what I want."

He roared and charged forward, swinging the mace wildly above his head.

(HAPTER 41 ...

I cracked the whip. It wrapped around the chain on the mace and I pulled. The force pulled Levi forward, toppling him onto one knee. I twisted around and heaved on the whip, snatching it over my shoulder. The mace was ripped free of Levi's clutches and flew over my head. I lashed out at him with the whip again.

The burning rope wrapped around his wrist. He screamed in pain as the long threads seared into his flesh. He slashed at it with the sword, but the blade merely glanced along the strands. I breathed in and sent a burst of energy down the whip. Flames erupted with an explosion that ripped into Levi. The ball of flames spun around him, ripping at his flesh, draining the color away and leaving only blackened, charred remains.

The flames receded, leaving Levi standing as still as a black statue. He bared his teeth and the flesh cracked around his face, leaving glowing fissures of red and yellow across his head. Flames continued to crack, spreading over his body, and with a roar of hatred he shook free of the burnt remains, stepping forward in his true form.

The black, horned beast stalked forward, growling, flexing, and twisting the sword toward me. He towered several feet above me, but we had met before. The sword came crashing down, but became tangled in the whip's thongs. With a flick of my wrist, the sword went wide and I moved in close to him. I smashed the handle knot into his throat.

He gasped for air and his eyes bulged. I slammed my fist into his stomach and lifted him off the ground. He sailed back against the altar. He crashed against the great stone carving, cracking it in two. His arms were thrown wide and he roared in frustration. He lumbered back onto his feet and came forward. He brought the sword around wide. I stepped in, catching his hand. I swung my elbow into his throat, twisted, kicked out his knee, and brought down a left hook that drove him to the ground.

The sword fell from his hand. He swung wildly, knocking me down, then snapped out, grabbing me by the throat and lifting me up. The force made me drop the whip and I struggled against his strength. He fumbled for the sword and brought it around slowly. I clutched at his hand, trying to break free. His grip was too tight. I switched muscle groups and my arms went limp.

Levi smiled.

My wings bent around and speared down into his face. He screamed and dropped me. My wings curled around, softening my fall to the ground. I felt the muscles switch back, and feeling returned to my hands.

Levi charged. I dived for the whip and snapped it at him. It caught his arm and jarred the sword outward, flipping it into the air. It flew upward, tangled in the coils of the whip. Then it stopped, seeming to float in the air as it reached its zenith.

I wrenched down on the whip handle, the thong tightened, and the sword speared down, driving straight between Levi's eyes and into his head. He dropped to his knees, his arms hanging by his side, his wings wilting.

Time froze. The earth started to shake, and the stone walls vibrated. The fissures in Levi's face and body glowed white. He started to vibrate, and parts of him fell away, leaving a blinding white light. The vibrations intensified.

I ran toward the others, quickly wrapped my wings around them, and looked back over my shoulder.

There was an intake of air as reality was sucked into Levi. It was a moment of healing, and possibly there was a faint smile on his lips. A tear rolled down his face and the intake exploded. The ball of energy smashed outward, taking with it the walls of the church. The roof went skyward as the power roared past us, burning the air around my wings. The others cowered inside the little cocoon, waiting for the blast to end. The sound of a million screams thundered around us and a final beam of light shot up into the black sky.

Then there was silence. Then there was stillness. Most of the church had been destroyed, with only parts of the walls remaining. Everything inside except for the altar had been flattened. A few errant pieces of paper, pages from the Bible, fluttered down and settled back on the floor of their home. I curled my wings back behind me and stepped away from the group. They stirred, coming out of their trance.

"He is truly beautiful," Angelina said, looking at me.

"I think the word you're after is angelic," Mina said. She stepped forward tentatively. The rood clattered to the ground, startling everyone. "All in all, that rood has been a disappointment," she said.

"The rood channels power," I said, "but it's limited by your own worth. It takes you up or brings you down. It was only ever meant to be a conduit between the earth and the heavens. Some people got the wrong idea and saw it as a weapon, and the power as a destructive force, when it was simply an elevator. It was a foil for good. It sent Jesus skywards, that's all, and it meant to bring him down on his reunion tour."

The sword lay on the charred flagstones, flames licking up and down the blade eternally. I picked it up and twisted it in my wrist. Muscle memory flexed, and the certainty of my grip brought a smile to my face.

"But this, on the other hand, is the real deal." I turned the point down and rested it on the charred flagstones, with my hands resting on the pommel.

"You look like a king standing in that position." Mina sidled up to me, and scuffed her foot over Levi's remains. "You killed him. Pity, he would've been handy."

"He killed himself. His greed and hatred led him into a whirlpool of his own demise," I said.

"In a way. But you actually steered the sharp bit of the sword of death into him."

The sword glowed menacingly in front of us. The other red daggers paled into insignificance against the onslaught of raw power from a true divine relic.

Mina reached out for me. "Come join me by my side. You are my king."

I turned to face her and drew her in close. It was time to go home. I smiled at her. "It's now about you and me."

"It always was, honey." She raised her eyes and looked up into my face, placing her hand on my chest. "Let's do what we were destined to do."

I raised the sword into the air and held it above us.

She looked at it uncertainly. "Are you going to do something with that?"

"It's not a sword. It's a key."

I twisted it and the world dimmed. Everything drifted away and the two of us were left standing isolated in our own little piece of heaven. Levi had been using the sword at Eden Lane. He'd worked out that much, but no more. He'd stood at the gates of Eden, but had never been in and never even knew why.

Mina ran her finger down my stomach. Around us, the dimness of the world was replaced by a garden of immense beauty. A small lake lay to the north. On the far side was a great tree. A perfect one.

Mina eventually noticed her surroundings had changed. She looked around cautiously. "I ... know this place."

"Yes."

"Where have you taken us? This isn't where we're meant to be. We're supposed to be in union upon the altar. I was really looking forward to that part."

"Then what?"

"What?"

"Then what would happen? After the union?"

"We will have the power. The old will be wiped away and it will be our turn to rule. And I will reign supreme over the new world. I will birth the vampires as we did once before."

"And that's what you think you are?"

"Yes. I am their queen. I've ruled over them for millennia, waiting for this moment. You and I will create a whole new race."

"We made a choice once before."

"No, we didn't."

"We realized then that what we did was wrong, and everything suffered because of it. We made a choice. I chose this and you chose something else. You're not a vampire. You're not what you think."

"I have no idea what you're talking about. I know exactly who I am. And who you are."

"So much of your mind is a deluded mess. None of this is what you think it is."

"I'm not the deluded one who's blocked out the past. I know exactly what I've done, and I wouldn't change any of it. But let's not fight, not now."

I waited until she'd calmed down. She started to fidget, with uncertainty wrapping around her.

"Where do you think you are?" I asked her.

I twisted the sword once again and we went all the way home. Not into the limbo where Levi lived, but our real home. The birthplace. Mina gasped as the illusions around her faded away. Paradise was lost. The clouds of unreality began to clear, leaving the truth stripped bare in front of us.

I reached out to her and pulled her close before she could see too much. We kissed passionately until I felt her defenses melt away. She closed her eyes and drifted into her fantasies.

"I'll give you anything," she whispered, her voice low and seductive. "What do you want?"

"The same as you. Redemption."

I let her go and she collapsed to the ground. She convulsed violently, her stomach heaving. Something inside her twisted and started to make its way up her throat. Her skin bulged and warped with the entity inside of her that was bending her out of shape.

"What's happening to me?" she gasped. Then she gagged.

A black, twisted root, closer to a snake than a plant, writhed out of her mouth. She vomited the thing up onto the ground. It thrashed around, flailing, searching for something. Tiny shoots started to appear from the surface of the root.

"Samael?" she said.

"You return, Lilith …"

I stepped away and allowed her to watch the landscape unfold. The vista continued to strip away, paradise melting into the background to be replaced by a sickened forest, overgrown and dying.

"… to the garden of Eden."

She looked around. A black snake with glowing red eyes coiled out along a nearby branch. She held out her hand. It glided onto her palm and wrapped around her arm.

"This is you," I said.

Her feet sank into the stinking mire.

"Every evil thought."

Deformed baby creatures staggered around on mutilated legs, biting each other as well as themselves. Desperate, beady red eyes that knew nothing more than pain pleaded for early extinction.

"Every despicable deed."

The loud clicking of insect life mixed with the fetid eruptions of putrid swamp gas. A low growl echoed through the twisted vegetation.

"Every innocence betrayed."

"No," she cried. "It was *never* like this. It was beautiful."

"It only ever reflected the beauty and innocence within the walls. You stayed beautiful, while the garden died. Eden is your mirror. You are *of* Eden, and you betrayed it."

"Don't lay this at my feet," she hissed. "You were happy to go along with it."

"I know. It's my betrayal. It's why I fell, and I've paid dearly for it. We did this, together."

"We can fix it now."

"No. It's broken forever for me, but you can save yourself. There is redemption for you. It's your home and you can fix it."

"Why are you doing this?"

"Because I loved you once." I paused. "I'm sorry I tricked you into swallowing one of the seeds. It was meant to make you forget me. Forget the love and the pain. Do you remember Adam?"

"Yes." She was hesitant. "He was dull. With a brand new world, I couldn't tolerate being stuck with him. I loved you."

"No. I loved *you*. Adam loved you. You loved the idea of me. When you abandoned him, you drove a seed of loneliness into his heart and everyone's been suffering for that ever since. I couldn't see it. I was too immature. We left and it all fell apart, and Eve had to pick up the pieces."

"It's what she was good at, goody two-shoes that she was. Except she wasn't, was she?"

"I guess it runs in your blood, but it was unfair on her."

"She deserved everything she got."

"She was your sister."

"She made her own choices, just as I made mine, and I don't regret them for a minute."

"That's because you haven't had to pay for them. Now is the time. Come with me."

I took her by the hand and led her deep within the garden, through the dead marshes and darkened trees that tore at us. I stopped on top of a hill in the center of the garden. We could see the whole of existence from here, and it wasn't pretty.

"I remember this tree." I ran my hand down the ancient wood, now more stone than living material. "God knows how old it is. Still, it's older than us. Where it all went wrong."

"It was a stupid tree. It wasn't even evil. It was a showpiece, Him showing us His perfection. He overreacted like He does with everything."

"It was the Tree of Knowledge of Good and Evil, His masterwork, where He finally got something perfect. Then you came along and kicked it all down, like a sandcastle. No wonder He was angry. Then, after Adam healed the tree, you got him and Eve kicked out. He was just a guy trying to make her happy so she wouldn't run off with the next angel that came along."

"All right. Sorry. There, I've said it. Happy?"

"I'm not your judgment, or repentance, your salvation or damnation. I'm your deliverance."

She looked around. "What are you planning on doing?"

"Me? Nothing. I've delivered you here." I lowered my hands and indicated the garden. "The tree would like to discuss things with you. I made my peace, and accepted my punishment. Now it's your turn."

"No, it's the past. We can leave it behind. It's our time. This stupid experiment with the apes is over. Just like the snakes. How dumb an idea was that, making snakes into dinosaurs. Nearly as stupid as monkeys into people. This whole human being thing was only a test. That's the problem with Him: everything is a test. We are the pure creatures. It can be our planet."

I shook my head. "You forget your origins. I condemn you to stay here until the garden is fixed, until the tree is healed." I twisted the sword.

CHAPTER 42 ...

Eden faded away and I was left with screams and wails ringing in my ears.

"Where did she go?" Angelina said.

I stared at her. She seemed so slender and frail to me now. Her eyes flicked over my body. She gulped; leaving the clothes behind was probably a bad idea.

"She's up there."

Angelina struggled to wrest her eyes away from me, glancing for the shortest possible time into the skies. "Is there a heaven?" she asked.

"Not as such," I replied.

"But you said "up there.'"

"Symbolically. It's like a dimension shift. She's living another life. Think of the universe, and time and space, as a book that's been opened. It's now on your page. But if you press hard enough, sometimes you send your words through to another page."

Her face screwed up. She was having a lot of trouble following me. "Who wrote the book?"

"You all wrote it. Or are writing it."

"Can we flip to the last page to see how it ends?" She gave me a mischievous smile.

"No one knows the ending until they get there. And once it's all over, their page will be closed and the next will open. But their page will always be there. It's history. They will be remembered."

"But a book only has value when someone's reading it."

"Who says no one's reading it?" I shrugged. "Part of the process, part of the reward, is the creation. Everyone has to get their ideas out."

She stumbled over her words, trying to deal with the casual existentialism. In the end she shook her head and changed topic. "If you want to get her back," she said, indicating Laura, "then you need to, er, you know ..."

"But we won't be at the feet of an angel."

She looked up at my wings towering above us. "Well, it could be argued that an angel involved in any part of the process would count, but I'm not an expert."

"Fine. It seems wrong. I should be holding her."

"You will be. It's meant to be an act of love."

She couldn't stop her eyes roaming over my body. Her face was flushed. "Afterwards, could you see to, um ..." She slowly raised her hand as though she was asking permission.

"No. She's the only one for me."

"Fine, you'll need this," she said hurriedly, handing over a small knife. She let her eyes wander over me again, momentarily reaching out then stopping herself. "I'd thought I'd ask." She let out a long sigh, and gave me one final glance before walking away.

I stepped over to Laura. I could feel her heartbeat, and it was weak. Her skin was gray, and her breath almost gone. I lifted her up and cradled her in my arms. She wore nothing other than a sheer nightdress. I laid her upon the altar.

In the dance of the stars that rolled above us, while a bleak infinite looked down uncaringly, the moment of unification arose and we made our own little universe of forever. She arched her back and her head rolled. I could feel her heart stop as she exhaled one last time. I took her wrist and cut across the veins. Blood trickled out and fell onto the altar. There was an intense glow between us. The light grew stronger until it engulfed us completely, and then winked out.

I was left in human form. Laura's legs were wrapped around me and her body was draped over the stone. Her eyes were blank. Her mouth was open, and she lay still, not breathing.

"No, please. This was how it was supposed to happen. You were meant to come back." I stroked her face and felt the tears roll down my face. They fell onto her skin and sizzled as they touched. I held her lifeless body close, clutching her head against my chest.

"I've had the strangest dream," she murmured.

I released her, and a flood of joy swept through me. I kissed her on the forehead.

She looked around the church. "Where on earth are we?" She looked down at me, and her legs straddling my waist. "And what exactly do you think you're doing to me?" She half smiled. It was wrong, but her inclination to complain had diminished.

"I feel so … alive," she said. A feather floated down and landed between us. "I did have a dream, didn't I?"

I smiled at her.

Could I stay? There was no choice; there was nowhere else I could go. But sometimes things just don't work out. Laura will die one day, and I will live on. That was the punishment of Eden. This time it'll be worse because I'll never forget her. But for now, I'll be by her side day-by-day, unchanging as the mountains. Then she will be gone. And what will greet me, what will I have left?

It will be an eternity of staring into the face of contemptible people doing depraved deeds as long as Eden is diseased. Secretly they're looking for the same thing, but in their own ways, that flash of light shining between them. But it's where I belong until the page is turned.

I have done wrong. I have done right.
But I am not good, neither am I evil.
I am not defined by my labels because I am me.
And I am free.

Don't miss Mark Lingane's earlier novels.
Available in both paperback and ebook format.

Partly comedic, partly sc-fi/fantasy, entirely detective, film-noir, genre busting debut novel. In *Beyond Belief*, Joshua Richards takes on reality in a fight to the death.

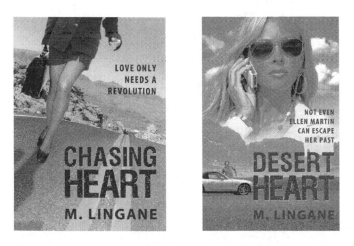

The Ellen Martin Distasters. Fun and pacey reads full of adventure, danger and laughs. *Chasing Heart* is where it all started to go wrong for Ellen Martin. *Desert Heart* is where things get worse.

The Tesla Evolution.

The multi award-winning teen/YA dystopian series following the journey of Sebastian and his friends.

For more information on past and future publications, visit: Mark-mywords.co